east fifth bliss

by
douglas light

Behler
PUBLICATIONS
California
USA

**Behler Publications
California**

east fifth bliss
A Behler Publications Book

Library of Congress Cataloging-in-Publication Data is available
Control Number 2006922344

FIRST PRINTING

ISBN 1-933016-40-X
Published by Behler Publications, LLC
Lake Forest, California
www.behlerpublications.com

Manufactured in the United States of America

For Evdokia

Acknowledgments

In gratitude of their support, I would like to thank the Jentel Arts Residency Program and the Writers Room in New York City.

For their critiques of this novel, my deepest gratitude goes to John McCaffrey, Chris "CR" Ross, Heidi Durrow, and Stefan Marti.

There are two theories.

The first:

After brothing up a world with water and soil and fish and plants and beasts that stand on two feet and talk and would eventually want credit cards and cell phones and satellite TV, God dipped his finger in the wetness between New Jersey and Long Island and summoned forth the rock called Manhattan. By doing so, He set in motion His austere plan: one day, there'd be an island replete with towering steel buildings and shabby brick tenements, dying trees, and co-ops with monthly maintenances more than most Americans' mortgage payments. It'd be a paradise filled with hundreds of concrete parks littered with losing lotto tickets and fried chicken bones. Rats would frolic on doorsteps. Dogs would defecate on the sidewalks. Squirrels would charge at the passing people, having no fear.

His plan called for a place where bulimic make-up salesclerks, who hide their cold sores with dark lipstick, would fit in. Myopic Midwesterners, who swear they've read *Ulysses* when they haven't, would have a home. The Hasidim would feel comfortable hanging their beaver fur hats there. It'd be a place for all, even Italian restaurateurs who claim that stale toast with a little tomato and a spot of olive oil is bruschetta and charge twelve dollars a plate. Even obese Hispanics in tight stretch pants who wave their nation's flag while screaming that they're being stereotyped. All would be welcomed with open arms. All would be embraced. His plan called for an island of everything. An island the world turned to.

The second theory has to do with strange gray and green and purple gases, tiny jumping particles, a spark, and then a Big Bang. *Presto*! Earth's formed. Manhattan's made. Then some slimy being flopped from the waters onto the land, gasped for air, and has since raged for millions of years to become mankind today.

Following either school of thought, this fact stands: Morris Bliss is thirty-five years old. He's lived his entire life in Apartment 8 in a weathered, red brick tenement on East Fifth Street near the corner of First Avenue. Has lived his entire life with his father.

But Morris has plans, big plans. Life altering plans. He's starting them today, or this week. This month. He's starting them very soon.

Morris Bliss has never left home.

One

Morris stares at Stefani jumping on his bed, unable to break himself from watching. She's like a movie star or a brutal car wreck or a fireworks display on a clear, dark winter's night, something he can't take his eyes from.

A tepid, damp breeze laps in the apartment's propped window. Early April, and the late afternoon's light is clear and unsettling. It cuts the island and the streets, bright, blemishing, blinding.

New York City. Manhattan. East Village. Fifth Street.

"You know," Stefani says to him, bouncing naked, "I know you." Freshly turned eighteen-years-old—a fact she doesn't tire of stating, repeatedly opening her sentences with "Now that I'm eighteen..."—she attends the St. Benedict's Ukrainian Catholic High School on East Seventh Street. She's only a junior, though, held back her fifth grade year.

Thirty-five years old, Morris could be her father, a thought that isn't lost on him. A thought he works to reconcile, or at least suppress. "Yeah, I feel I know you, too," he tells her, the lightness of his three beers all but over. "Like we're connected," he says, and, feeling he sounds stupid, adds, "Or something." Naked himself and slightly slouched, Morris's body is the body of a swimmer who hasn't swum in years—thin and long limbed, but no longer fit. His looks are the calm, intelligent looks of an elementary school principal on summer break and his fingers are the fingers of someone who takes care of what he touches—fingers of a concert pianist or bomb defuser or a painter who executes detailed portraits on grains of rice. They are fingers that poorly serve Morris. They're too precise for him; he's clumsy, often drops things. Yet they'd held Stefani, run over her skin, touched her.

His best friend N.J. once theorized that there are seven defining moments in a person's life. We're born with them, like a tongue or toes. "Seven, man," N.J. said, holding up an open hand and two fingers.

Morris asked him to identify the seven, to explain what they signified. "For me to tell you that, man," N.J. replied, "would be like explaining a poem by playing the bagpipes. It doesn't work."

"What's that supposed to mean?" Morris asked.

"It means what it means, man." N.J. was fabricating his theory on the spot, Morris was certain. It was something N.J. did, fabricate.

Morris asked, "So what happens after I experience all seven?"

"You won't make the seven, man," N.J. informed him. "Only people like Jesus Christ or Evel Knievel make it to seven. Only people filled with wonder, man."

Initially, Morris felt he'd burnt through two moments this afternoon with Stefani. Now, he can't claim certainty.

Stefani says, "That's not what I mean by knowing you." The bedsprings twang and groan under her weight. He wishes she'd stop moving, wishes she'd remain still so he can compose the image of her in his mind. Hold her fast. He wants something to remember, wants something of importance. "I know I know you, but I mean not from here," she says. "Not from now and all this." She's large for her age, large for any age, nearly five foot eleven, almost as tall as Morris, and she wears too much foundation, too much makeup to cover the acne high on her cheeks. The birthmark on her inner thigh is shaped like Italy or a wilting zucchini or snubbed out cigar. "Not from our doing what we are doing," she says, and stops bouncing a moment to study herself in the streaked mirror across the small room. Her hair's long. It's nice hair, runs to the small of her back and is conditioned and glossy and shines darkly like ground mussel shells. It's her prize, something she cultivates, prides herself on.

Smiling an open-mouthed smile, she examines her teeth in the mirror. Already, she has six cavities from lack of care.

Her hair is her prize.

"I know you from before," she says, turning her attention to her belly. She pinches a soft fold of skin and holds it tight. She pouts at her reflection. "Buy me some cigarettes later?" she asks Morris, resuming her bed bouncing. "I don't have any money."

"No. No cigarettes," Morris tells her, rubbing the small, blue-black scar on his left bicep, a scar he's had since age fifteen. He got it playing The Chow Mein Masters Match, a game he and N.J. made up. The game involved baseball mitts, shaving cream, and Chinese throwing stars. There were no rules. The entire East Village was the playing field and the action didn't stop until someone got hurt.

Morris got hurt, came home with a bleeding arm and tight face. His total focus was on not crying. He was determined not to cry.

Had his mother met him at the door, she'd have rushed him to the hospital for a tetanus shot and stitches. Had his mother been alive, she'd have hounded him until he revealed how it'd happened, then grounded him for a week.

But it was his father he came home to. After a quick examination of the two-inch cut, his father got a bottle of hydrogen peroxide and his tool kit. "Ain't much of nothing," he told Morris, pouring the disinfectant on the cut. It foamed and bubbled, the wound washed clean. Morris's eyes glossed with tears. "Had worse cuts from opening mail. Hold tight," he told his son, then taking two small metal butterfly clamps, he pulled the skin tight and pinched the cut together. "In a couple of days," his father said, "you won't even notice it."

Blood welled from the wound. "It's not working, Daddy," Morris told him, studying the make-shift dressing like it was a failed science project. "It's not holding. It needs something more to hold it together."

Seymour dug about his tool kit, pulled out a glue gun.

Morris stared at his father, not believing he was serious. His father plugged the gun's cord in, letting it heat. He was serious.

"You're not glue gunning me together. I'm going to need stitches," Morris said. "Maybe we should go to—"

"Maybe we shouldn't be gabbing so much," Seymour said. "Maybe someone should let me do the fixing here," he said. "What's a doctor know that I don't know?"

"How to stitch a cut," Morris answered.

"I can stitch," Seymour said. "I can fix this," he said, ending the discussion.

Morris sat patient, quiet, as his father rifled through Morris's mother's old embroidery kit. The only needle he could find was a three-inch curved tapestry needle used to detail throw pillows. Morris turned his head and bit the inside of his cheek as the needle dipped through his skin and the thread tugged tight. His father sewed five lopsided stitches with black needlepoint thread. And while the experience was painful, Morris was pleased; he was spending time with his father. His father was paying attention to him, a rare occurrence.

Over the week, as the cut mended, dye from the stitching seeped into the wound, causing the scar to take on a dark, burnt hue, a stain that remains today, tattooed in his skin. "It's a badge," his father told him of the colored scar, but a badge of what, he never said.

Stefani yells at Morris, "Come on," and jumps higher on the bed, nearly hitting the ceiling. "Now that I'm eighteen, you should buy me a pack of cigarettes," she tells him. "As a birthday gift. Come on, come on, come on," Stefani calls to Morris, peaking off the mattress. "One pack. Camels. Camel Lights. Kools. Please." She lands on her butt, springs back up onto her feet like a trampoline artist. The mattress shifts on the box springs after each strike. "Just one pack."

"No," Morris tells her again, his fingers fidgeting over his scar. "No cigarettes," he says, then asks, "What do you mean you know me from before?"

They met today at Norman's Sound & Vision on Third Avenue. Morris's father's birthday is in a few days, on Tuesday. He wanted to buy a present, stopped in to look for an album of *Rembetika*, Greek folk songs. It was something his mother used to listen to, something he recalled his father enjoying.

Stefani was in the store, too, staring at him as she absently thumbed through the R section of rock CDs. Her look was one of rapt interest. She seemed to be challenging him from across the aisle of music, her eyes hard on him, waiting to see if he'd speak to her.

Feeling awkward, like he was forced to perform, Morris milled about, occasionally glancing up to meet her gaze. His face flushed each time his eyes caught hers. Normally, he'd be too embarrassed, too uncomfortable, to follow through. But he was held fast. Something in her appearance resonated with him, like hearing the faint notes of a favorite song long forgotten. Something about her made him want to be near her. He couldn't leave.

The three beers he'd had didn't hurt, either. His inhibition was replaced by daring.

Finally, after five minutes of fumbling his fingers along the dusty bins and stealing peeks at her, he gathered courage. Holding up a used album he'd grabbed at random—Meatloaf's *Back Into Hell*—he asked her, "Excuse me, is this—do you know if this is any good?"

"You've got something on your face," she answered, her eyes not breaking from him. "Something weird and kinda nasty, like cheese sauce or bird shit or something." She touched her cheek, indicating where. Morris took a paper napkin from his pocket, wiped his face, and looked at the napkin. He saw nothing. "No, here," she said, pointing to the other side. He wiped. "Got it," she said, then pointing to the album he was holding, added, "Meatloaf sucks. That album sucks. My dad used to listen to him, like, I don't know, twenty-five or forty years ago. But this," she said, holding up a CD by a band named Forty Ounces and a Mule, "this is great."

Coming to his side of the aisle, Stefani explained her likes in music, and then told him about her school, and the girls she calls friends that were the kind of friends that borrow lip-gloss or money or an occasional boyfriend and then not return them. The kind that fade over summer break. Friends that truly aren't.

After talking a half hour straight, she said, "Let me show you something," and motioned him to follow her to the record store's basement, with its stacks and stacks of used CDs for sale for a dollar. Once downstairs, Stefani said, "Get over here." Taking Morris's hands, she wrapped them about her hips, and forced a hard, wet kiss to his lips, her tongue frantically working past his teeth and into his mouth. She tasted of lemon drops and Pine Sol, a taste that lingered and pleasantly stung. "I want to see your place," she told him.

"I don't even know you," he told her, feeling choked and confused, like he'd just stumbled out of a house on fire. It wasn't right.

It was so right.

"Stefani," she said. "My name's Stefani."

"I know your name; I just don't know who you are."

"You don't like me?" Stefani's eyes brimmed as her fingernails sharply held Morris by the waist. "Why don't you like me?"

"I like you," he said, "but I don't know you."

"But I know *you*. I know you and know you and know you," she told him, her breath spicing his skin. She kissed him again, and as she kissed him, he felt himself being peeled away, like a mountain climber coming off the face of a cliff. He felt himself fall.

The afternoon unfolded in a consuming heat.

Daylight savings time ends on Sunday, the clocks moving forward an hour under the cover of dark. Morris pulls on his brown socks. He feels like a freshly molted crab, his hard casing cast off. He's tender, senses everything, is free and susceptible.

The world continues. Spring's arrived. Easter is soon. Morris slips on his underwear. They sag in the butt.

"You look *just* like a Calvin Klein model," Stefani says, her voice jarring with each bounce. "My granddaddy used to dress like that," she says, "socks before pants. You always put your socks on before your pants?"

"Stefani," he tells her, feeling the desire to take her in his arms.

"Auggh," she says, and drops on her back like she's been shot dead. She lies rigid, taut, her bare arms flat to her side and her eyes tightly closed. She giggles. "You're going to have to speak up," she shouts. "I can't hear you. My eyes are shut."

Morris sits on the edge of the bed, touches her leg, her smooth calf, and experiences a clean comfort.

"You're already starting with the words?" she asks, her eyes still closed. "The horse race has just finished and your mind's already on glue. But I know, I know," she sings, holding up her hands, "I know it *all* by now." Then, standing up, she resumes her bed bouncing. "And I know you. We've met before."

"Before today?" Morris asks, still sitting on the bed.

She nods. "Five times."

"Impossible," Morris says, though he's not a hundred percent certain. Her jumping forces him to stand. "I'd remember."

"Okay," she admits, "I've *kinda* met you."

"Five times?"

"Just once. But I've seen you bunches, around the neighborhood," she says, then shouts, "Steven Jouseski."

Morris stares at her like she's slipped into a foreign language. "Who?"

"Steven Jouseski," she shouts again, rising and falling. "My father. That's how I know you."

Morris shakes his head.

"Jouseski! You went to high school together."

The name registers, hits Morris sooty and hard, like debris blown from a building's roof. Steven Jouseski.

Stevie Jetski.

Jetski.

That's what he was known as in high school.

"Jetski's your father?" Morris asks.

"Jetski?" Stefani asks, still bouncing. "Jouseski. That his last name. Mine too," she says. "It's also my mom's last name." Then, pointing to Morris's jeans on the floor, asks, "You use those to wash the windows or something? They look all, I don't know, all gross."

Morris glances at his jeans. He needs new clothing. Needs money, needs to find a fulltime job.

Work-wise, it's not been a stellar year for Morris. He was forced to quit his job of nine years at St. Mark's Used Books after his allergies overwhelmed him. He loved the job; his days were spent cloistered and reading. Occasionally, he'd ring up a sale or offer advice on which book was good, which was not. But mostly he read and read and read. And sneezed and coughed. And increasingly had trouble breathing when in the store. For nine years, it went like this, a gaining, crippling flu from the moment he walked into the store, a rapid healing the moment he left. The books were to blame, and not just the old, dusty ones with their damp smell, either. New ones gave him problems, too. The trace fumes from the bind's glue or the chemicals used to bleach the paper or the inks for book jackets reacted poorly with Morris's system, made his eyes swell shut and his ears turn a bright red. He could handle a book or three, but sitting around stacks and stacks of hundreds of books caused him grief.

Still, for nine years, he mustered through his day, tearing into boxes of Kleenex and antihistamines. The attacks progressively got worse. It was only after the second hospitalization, his face puffy and pale blue, his hands stiff to the point he couldn't form a fist, and his lungs feeling filled with sand, that he quit his job.

"I'll miss seeing you," the owner of the bookstore told Morris. Morris knew this wasn't true. The moment he left, the bookstore owner wouldn't remember what Morris looked like. It wasn't that he disliked Morris; Morris was certain the owner liked him very much, thought him his best employee. But the owner had prosopagnoisa — face blindness. Morris knew that the memory of his face — of anyone's face — was stripped the instant he left the owner's sight.

Morris's next job lasted only a month. Working as a salesman at a leather and fur store on Orchard Street, Morris was fired after spilling coffee on a three thousand dollar fox stole. The following gig, manning the counter at Russ & Daughter's Appetizers on Houston Street, ended when he knocked over a fifty gallon barrel of pickles, the brine and garlic and turned cucumbers flowing over the customers' shoes.

Out of work for eight months, he's been actively looking.

Just this morning he had a job interview. It was for a position he knew he'd hate; telemarketing seven-hundred-dollar self-help business CDs to harried banking executives. It was a commissions-based job, no benefits. "Get the product out," the manager who interviewed him kept saying. "That's what we say around here." It was the office mantra; it was written on the dry erase board in purple marker. The manager claimed the company had been in business over two decades, but the whole operation seemed a sham. Morris felt certain they could close up and abandon the space they operated out of in less than an hour. "My question to you is," the manager said to Morris, pointing at him with his forefinger and pinky of his left hand, "are you ready to make some money? Are you ready to be the man you want to be, fulfill your potential?"

A bald black woman wearing huge orange earrings interrupted the interview to tell the manager she quit. "I'm a member of the Nation of Islam," she said, "and this bullshit flies against the grain of my beliefs, against everything that makes me strong. I don't give no fuck about no 'team spirit,' because I don't like ripping people off, even if they *are* white. Especially not for the cracker change you pay me. So I asked myself, 'What would Louis Farrahkan do?' And you know what I realized? Farrahkan wouldn't telemarket for no white bitch chump."

The manager had her escorted out of the building by security, but not before she'd sprinkled a handful of powdered sugar and pine ash around the edge of the room and loudly conjured a hex on the entire place.

"So," the manager said to Morris, smiling broadly as he sat back down, "when can you start?"

Morris said he'd check his schedule, let him know.

The interview had so disheartened Morris that he'd decided on a beer at the Old Homeplate, which turned to three beers, which depressed him more; he was spending money he didn't have.

Flopping down on the mattress again, Stefani says, "I met you once when my dad said 'hi' to you. I was with him and my mom." She lies on her stomach, her knees bent and her heels to her butt. "We were on Thirteenth Street and you were going into that comic book store. Forbidden something. Planet or Asteroid, I think. My dad saw you and said, 'Hey, Twisted Bliss.' You looked at him funny, nodded, then headed into the store. I asked my dad who you were and he told me you were friends in high school."

"He said we were friends?" Morris never liked Jetski, never liked the crowd he hung around with. In high school, Jetski was always angling something, working a grift. Once, Morris overheard him brag that he'd figured a way to pocket twenty bucks a night at the movie theater he worked at. "They can't count each kernel of popcorn they sell," he explained to a girl he was hitting on. "So they count the bags. Same with the soda cups. But check this out," Jetski said. "I get the used bags and cups from the trash after each showing, use them again, and bank the cash."

"Yeah. Said you were good friends," Stefani tells Morris, kicking her legs. "What's with the map?" She motions to the large, sun-bleached world map on his wall. It's flagged with nearly a hundred colored pins.

"I'm going to all those places," Morris says, not looking at it. The map's been on his wall since he was fifteen, since he first read George Orwell's *Homage to Catalonia*. He had to see Madrid and Barcelona.

He rarely leaves the city, has never left the country. Every season he says, "I'm going," but never goes. It's always something— money, work, his father—always a reason not to go. "Resistance, man," his friend N.J. said each time Morris's planned trip fell through. "Break through the resistance and go. Lee Strausberg taught me that when I was studying acting with him, man. Pulled me aside and said, 'N.J., son, break through the resistance.' "

Morris knew he was right about resistance. Morris also knew N.J. never studied acting with Strausberg, or anyone else.

Picking up an unframed photo of his mother, Stavroula, off the top of the pressed wood bureau, Morris closely studies the picture. She'd traveled, been around the world before the age of five. Born in Greece, on the small island of Kos, she and her family had lived in South Africa, Spain, and Scotland before settling on Long Island. In the photo, Morris's mother's in her mid-thirties, the age Morris is now. It was taken during the three-month period she'd left Morris and his father. Slightly turned, she looks directly at the camera, like someone called to her. Her hair's pulled back and she smiles a small, mischievous smile, like she's done something she doesn't want to be reminded of, doesn't want to later be held accountable for. The afternoon light casts in from her left, cleanly striking her face, her body. It's early morning, or late afternoon, deep in the wilds of Oregon. A shadowed mountain looms behind her.

"Anyway, I thought you were cute so I looked you up in my dad's yearbook," Stefani tells Morris, scratching her thigh. "Then I saw you today and I thought, 'He's a friend of dad's.' That's why I talked to you," Stefani says, then, "We studied this guy in school today. A guy from Britain or England or somewhere. Joe or Jack Rustyskin or Ruffian or something like that. Wrote about architecture and art and stuff. I like art."

"John Ruskin?" Morris ventures, putting the photo down. The thought of his mother sends a pang of loneliness through him. She died soon after she returned home. Morris was thirteen.

"Yeah," Stefani says, chewing on her hair, "him."

"You study Ruskin in school?" he asks, surprised. *The Stones of Venice*. He'd found a copy of it on the street years ago. It was in a pile of books and magazines someone had thrown out, the hard green cover faded and worn. After reading it, he stuck a blue-headed pin in Venice.

"Well, yeah," Stefani says of Ruskin. "We study a lot of different stuff. Why not this guy? He's famous, I guess," Stefani says. Pausing a moment, she adds, "He loved little girls. I mean, really little girls. That's what the teacher said. Girls younger than me. But he stopped loving them when they started to grow and get breasts and their hair."

"He died a virgin," Morris informs her.

Stefani rolls onto her back, rubs her belly. "I didn't say he loved them the way you just did me," Stefani says. She runs her fingers through her pubic hair. "Some girls in my class shave. You think I should shave?" she asks.

From the apartment above, Morris hears Mr. Sofar's footfalls as he starts his evening pacing. From the north end of his apartment to the south, a pause, then back again. 5:45 p.m. every evening, for fifteen minutes. The man's frighteningly habitual. Morris can set a clock by him. When he hears Sofar start to pace, he knows it's quarter to six. Soon, Morris's father will be home.

"We need to get going," Morris says. He doesn't want the tangle of explaining Stefani to his father.

He picks up Stefani's school uniform skirt, a green and blue plaid, and hands it to her. She looks good in her uniform.

"Go?" she asks, tossing her skirt to the floor. "What do you mean? I'm starving," she says, hopping off the bed. She wanders past Morris, out toward the tiny kitchen. Her body has an instant rhythm when she walks, almost a dance. "It's not even four o'clock," she says. "I don't have to go."

"Quarter to six," he says, following her. "If you want, we can go out for a snack."

"I have to eat something now," she says. "I'm weak." She opens the refrigerator, bends to gaze in, her smooth, full butt jutting out. "What is all this stuff?" she asks. Everything's wrapped in crinkled tin foil, from a ham down to a half eaten boiled egg. They're ordered on the shelves by size. Even the condiments have foil twisted over their spouts. The entire interior glints and winks in the weak light, like it's a collection of fallen asteroids or an orthodontist's stockroom.

"I'm afraid of what's going on in there," Stefani says, kicking the door closed. "Got anything to eat, cookies or sausage or something? Something that isn't wrapped in foil?"

"Let's get going."

"No," she tells him, folding her arms and sulking. "Where's your TV?" she asks, then, "Why do I have to go?"

"Because Daddy's—"

" 'Daddy'?" Stefani's face beams. She lightly bites into the meat of her thumb. She laughs. "You still live with your 'Daddy'?"

"Da-nny," Morris lies, surprised he publicly called his father "Daddy." "My father's name is Danny." It's Seymour. "And yes, I still live with him," he says, irritated with himself. "He lives with me."

"You said Daddy," Stefani says, laughing harder. Then, speaking in baby talk, she says, "Does he tuck you in at night, shake your pee-pee after you're done tinkling, or does your mommy do it?"

The afternoon's euphoria flakes away. "Stefani," Morris says, his voice firm. "Time to go."

"Ah, come on," she says, her laughter dying. "Don't be like that." She looks pained, her feelings hurt. She wipes her nose with the palm of her hand. "I was just funning with you, you know." She opens a kitchen cabinet, looking for something to eat. "Couples do that, you know. They fun with each other."

"Please," he says, his tone softer, "get dressed."

"Where's your mom?" Stefani asks, pulling down a box of shrimp-flavored crackers from the shelf.

"She's dead," he says. "Died when I was young."

"People do that, I guess," she absently says, shaking the cracker box. "Die and all, I mean. My grandmother did. It ended up making the *Post*, you know, the way she died. Accidentally hung herself opening her front door."

Morris recalls the story. The elderly woman was found hanging from her front doorknob, a key-laden shoestring twisted about her neck and her key in the lock. It was written up as an accident; somehow, she'd fallen. No matter how many times Morris read the article, he couldn't make sense of it.

"You know what I don't like?" Stefani says. "The fact you're so old. It's gonna be kinda weird, you know, having a boyfriend so old. When I finally turn twenty-one and we can go to bars together, you'll be, like, I don't know — you'll still be a lot older."

"Boyfriend?"

She nods and digs into the cracker box, pulls out a handful of small squares. "Yeah, boyfriend," she says, stuffing her mouth. She chews twice, then, her face tightening with disgust, spits the chewed cracker back into the box. "Eeegh, God, that's gross," she says. She leans over the sink filled with dirty dishes, puts her lips to the faucet to rinse her mouth. She gargles, spits, then wipes her tongue on a dishtowel to remove the last of the lingering taste. "Christ, I've never tasted anything so gross. Where did you get these?" she asks, holding up the box and looking at the label. "Chinatown? They always have disgusting stuff like this in Chinatown. Crackers made of fish blood or seaweed or ground up things you wouldn't feed a dog. You know, they sell frogs down there, like to eat. Frogs and turtles and other things, things that are usually pets and not dinner. Have you ever seen those restaurants," she asks, "that have the pig faces hanging on a hook in the window, snout and all? It looks like a barbequed Halloween mask. Totally foul. I mean, who would eat that, a pig face? *How* do you eat a pig face? I mean, how's that served, like whole on a plate with a serving of beans or something? Think about it looking up at you as you go to stab it with a—"

"Let's get going," he interrupts.

"Jesus," she says, "all right. Relax. Don't get so snippy." She puts the crackers back on the shelf, ambles back to the bedroom, her flesh rippling with each step.

Morris follows. "I'm not being snippy," he tells her. "It's just time to go."

"You're afraid Daddy won't be happy to see me," Stefani says, sitting on the bed. She draws her knees up, holding them.

"Danny. And no," he says. "Or yes. I just don't think right now would be the best time to introduce you. He's old and—"

"Older than you?" she asks. She picks at her toenails, chipping off the powder blue polish. "Is he like one of those two-hundred-year-old guys you have to carry around and feed and bathe and stuff? Does he wear one of those big diapers?"

"He's not old like that," he says, thinking of his father, their relationship. He can think of nothing to say. They don't share a strong bond, a closeness. His father won't have it.

Stefani picks up her bra, fiddles with the small metal clasp. The air in the room is fusty and thick. Morris opens the other window. Watching her closely in profile, Morris is struck by her look of unawareness, innocence.

"Do you mind not staring at me?" Stefani asks, not turning her head. "I feel like you're eating me with your eyes. Can I have a little privacy here without you getting all creepy?"

Morris leaves his bedroom, closing the door. He waits in the hall.

Upstairs, Sofar continues to pace, the noise dropping through the ceiling.

"One of the pictures of you in the yearbook," Stefani calls to Morris as she dresses, speaking through the door, "is really funny. I cut it out and put it in my album. You're at a basketball game or dance or something and your hair is all poofy and real big, and you're wearing a—what band was it?—*Men at Work* muscle T-shirt and you've got no muscles, just these scrawny arms. At first," she says, "I thought you were pretending, you know? Like it was a costume party or something. Like you dressed like that as a joke. But then I realized you hadn't. You dressed like that on purpose."

The door opens. She's dressed, her bag over her shoulder. She studies her face in a compact. "You got a rubber band?" she asks, and applies root beer-flavored lip-gloss to her lips.

Morris goes to the kitchen, opens a drawer filled with jumbled silverware, wads of tinfoil, and old bread bag ties. He sifts through the items and finds a thick, blue rubber band that once held a bunch of California asparagus.

He hands it to her.

She pulls her hair back into a horse's tail, ties it off with the rubber band. "How do I look?" she asks. She's added a fresh layer of foundation, flattened out her features. She looks washed out, like her face has been sanded smooth.

Morris nods. "Great," he says, reaching for her hand.

She takes his and turns it over, drags her fingernails along his palm. "Feels good, huh? I love it when my dad used to do this to me. He won't do it anymore, but he used to. A lot. You like that? You like me doing that to you?"

A chill runs across his chest and down his sides. "I like that," he tells her.

She leans in to kiss him then licks his nose. "Buy me some cigarettes?" she sweetly asks. "I'll give you a kiss if you do."

Before Morris can answer, the front door's buzzer rings. His father's home; he's standing out front of the apartment building waiting to be let in. "Time to go," Morris tells her, heading to the apartment's door.

Stefani slides her bag off her shoulder, drops it on the floor. She folds her arms across her chest. She isn't going. She's holding her ground. "Cigarettes," she demands.

"Stefani," he·says. "I said no. Come on."

"You promised to buy me cigarettes."

"No, I didn't."

"Yes. You. Did."

She has him, he knows. She won't leave until she gets what she wants. "I don't like you smoking," he says, feeling through his pockets for money.

"Now that I'm eighteen—"

"Hold up," he says, and quickly goes to his bedroom. He returns with a large, brown leather two-fold wallet shiny from years of sliding in and out of his back pocket. The wallet's bordered with a looped, burnt red stitching. The letters MORRIS are deeply tooled in the leather. He's had it for years. It was a present from his mother when she returned home from her three-month absence. "Here," Morris says, handing Stefani a twenty dollar bill, one of his last.

The buzzer rings again, this time longer, louder, his father impatient.

"That's pretty faggy," Stefani says of his wallet, then, "You're not coming with me?"

"Can't," he says. He picks up her bag, guides her to the door.

"How am I going to get cigarettes?" she asks.

Morris is struck with the notion that Stefani's lied, that she's not eighteen, that she's younger. Her physical maturity says one thing while her emotional says another. His stomach knots like he swallowed a tray of ice cubes. "You told me you're eighteen."

"I *am* eighteen," she says, then recites her birthday. She opens her purse, digs around. "I just don't have ID, and these deli guys are assholes about carding."

Morris holds up a hand, silencing her, then presses the talk button on the intercom. "Yeah?" he asks, hitting the listen button.

"Me," a voice, his father's, crackles back. "Let me in."

Morris opens the apartment door, ushers Stefani out into the hall. "Go to the bodega around the corner, right here on First Avenue," he tells her. "Mr. Charlies is the name of the place. It's the name of the guy at the counter."

"He'll sell them to me, this Mr. Charlie?"

"Charlies," Morris says. "Plural, with an 's.' "

"What kind of name is that?"

The buzzer rings again, three short, grinding blurts.

"He'll sell you cigarettes. Just tell him that Mr. Charlies sent you."

A look of bewilderment clouds her face. "Tell Mr. Charlies," she says, "that Mr. Charlies sent me?"

"Yes," Morris says, pressing the door button to let his father in. "Just tell him that and he'll sell you whatever you want."

"Beer?"

Downstairs, his father pushes into the building, the hinges on the front door screeching like a wounded hawk.

"Go," Morris tells Stefani.

"First," she says, stepping back across the apartment's threshold, "tell me you like me."

Morris presses against her, not allowing her any farther. The warmth of her body makes him think of letting her back in, of taking her to his room and staying with her for days and days on end, of never leaving. "I like you," Morris says.

"Tell me you love me," she says, rubbing up against him.

From down the stairwell, he can hear his father mounting the first flight, his worn boots scraping each step. Morris feels sick, like he drank tequila all night and now has heavy lifting to do. "Stefani," he says, his voice low. He looks her in the eyes and knows it's the only way to make her leave. He relents. "Okay, yes," he tells her. "I love you." The words sound awkward, tender but hollow. False.

"And that you're sorry for being so crabby with me," Stefani says, smiling. But before he can answer, she says, "Oh, I left you a present. A surprise." She kisses him.

"What is it?"

He can hear his father reach the second landing, hear him pause a moment.

"This weekend I'm busy," she quietly says, stepping back. "Monday, Ray's pizza. After school. Be there. Don't play with me. And call me, call me often."

"What's the surprise?"

"You'll see." She waves bye with her index finger, moves to the stair, then stops. Holding up the twenty he'd given her, she asks, "I can keep the change from this?"

"Yes. Keep the change," he says, quietly closing the door.

There's never change with Mr. Charlies.

Two

The door clicks softly shut. Leaning to the peephole, Morris eyes Stefani, her image rounded and distorted, like she's fallen into a fishbowl. Through the fireproof door, he feels her presence, her heat.

She pauses and glances back, knowing Morris is watching. The hallway light casts from her left, cleanly striking her face. Tightening the rubber band on her hair, she smiles a small smile.

Seeing this, Morris is filled with reassurance, a well-being. He knows this moment, has witnessed it before; Stefani standing as she stands, smiling as she smiles, the light brushing her face as it is now. He's experienced it a million times, morning after morning, year after year.

But it's never happened. Not with Stefani, not as now.

It's his mother he's seeing, the photograph of her on his dresser.

She and Stefani look nothing alike, and still, there's something similar about the two. It's Stefani's hair, or her unguarded mannerisms, or how she smiles. Or even just the fact that she's female.

It's none of these. There's no resemblance at all. But somehow, in a skewed, distant way, seeing Stefani standing as she's standing summons the memory of his mother. It's like certain colors reminding one of a moment long past. Or when a whiff of an odor sparks an incongruous memory. Certain smells do that to Morris. Woodchips, for one, remind him of his first wet dream, more a nightmare than an erotic experience; the hot, clinging stench of a packed subway station after a heavy summer rain evokes the afternoon Mr. Sofar tried to make Morris put on a dress; and the dark, moldy odor of freshly turned earth brings to mind his fourth grade teacher, Ms. Wagner, and her hairy arms that she used to constantly scratch.

And something about Stefani makes him think of his mother.

She wiggles her index finger at Morris, and then heads down the stairs.

Morris rests his forehead to the door, closes his eyes. He's held the memories of his mother tight, held them near his heart, yet the weathering of some twenty years has turned them to tumbled seaglass; all the sharp, poignant recollections have been worn smooth, the details ground away with the passing of time. What he now recalls best is not his actual, physical mother, but the things associated with her: the lemony, stewing smell of the *dolmades* she made every Saturday; the trail of coffee cups she left about the apartment; her quiet voice from a farther room; the *slip-slap* of her sandals as she walked.

The pounding on the door jars Morris.

His father's home.

"Open this bastard door," his father calls from the hall.

Slowly, Morris opens the door. "Hey, Daddy," he says.

"What were you doing in here?" Seymour asks, his breath already malty and stale from drinking.

Sofar's pacing in the apartment above abruptly stops. It's six p.m. Exactly.

Seymour glances around the apartment, sniffs the air like an animal sensing danger. He carries a bag with two lightning blue king-sized bottles of Bud Iced Turbo Load beers, one of which he's already opened, partially drank. Packed with caffeine, ginseng, and alcohol, it's Budweiser's answer to the energy drink craze. "Gets You Up When You Want to Get Down" is the tagline. Seymour had wanted plain Budweiser, but Mr. Charlies was out. Mr. Charlies is always out of the product desired. "I buzzed you," Seymour says, his thick, damp moustache making him look like an agitated beaver.

"I was in the bathroom," Morris answers, moving to the kitchen. Act normal, he tells himself, though he's not sure how he acts when acting normal. That's why it's normal. "I'm heading over to N.J.'s," he tells his father, needing out of the apartment. "Need anything while I'm out?"

Seymour tosses his keys on the kitchen table. The kitchen needs cleaning. Coffee grinds speck the warped, gray countertop like ants rolling across a dry creek bed. The windowsills are grimy, the tabletop dusty and stained with tomato sauce. The floor needs sweeping, a detailed mopping. The entire apartment, overcrowded with belongings, needs a clearing out. "You get that job talking on telephones?" Seymour asks of Morris's job interview.

"Looks like it," Morris tells him. He could have it. He needs the money and will probably have to take it. He doesn't want it. "The interview went well. Should know by next week," he says, hoping his father will forget the whole thing by then. Hoping he'll have something else lined up by then. He plans on putting in an application with The Sock Man on St. Marks Place, a small, street-side stall that sells only socks. People often stop him when he passes the place, thinking he works there. He answers their questions as best as possible.

"Should've seen what I just seen," Seymour says.

"Yeah? What's this?" Morris answers, already knowing. Stefani. On her way out. He pats his pockets, feeling for his keys, then looks on top of the refrigerator for them.

"Should've seen it," Seymour says, opening the refrigerator. He grabs three foil-wrapped items, items only he could identify without unwrapping them, then, with his beers in hand, heads to the back room, the room that serves as the dining room, the living room, and Seymour's sleeping quarters. Turning on the TV, voices, cheers, and canned laughter rattle through of the apartment. The small screen's image is a moving Monet painting, vivid and blurry. They have no cable, no satellite dish to pull the program waves from the air, just a bound bundle of wire hangers covered in foil attached to the top of the set. Seymour doesn't believe in spending money that way, wasting it on things that should be free, things that once were. "Some fifteen-year-old girl," he calls to Morris.

Eighteen, Morris wants to tell him. He finds his keys tucked under some travel brochures on Croatia; he ordered them right after he finished reading Rebecca West's *Black Lamb and Gray Falcon*. It's on his schedule of places to visit, right after Paris, which is after he visits

Turkey, which is on his agenda following Thailand, which comes after Finland, Australia, Mexico, Beirut, and the North Africa tour. He keeps an ordered file with all his plans, all the information he's gathered on the places he's going. "I'm heading out," he says, thinking he might be able to catch Stefani at Mr. Charlies.

"This girl was on the stairs," Seymour calls to Morris, working on his beer. Fifty-seven years old, Seymour's a shop steward for the carpenters' union. It's his responsibility to watch out for his men, make certain they show up for work, not get too drunk at lunch, and fill out the proper paper work when they're injured. He calls the ambulance when one twists his knee or bruises his ribs. He's seen men crack their heads open, seen them take a two-story fall and hit the hard pavement or rubble littered ground or bounce off an I-beam then, laughingly, stand-up and brush themselves off, and say, "That was dumb" or "Hard head" or "Who's buying drinks?" He's seen worse.

"Sure you don't need anything?" Morris asks, opening the front door.

"Mors," his father calls from the back room. It's a nickname his mother first came up with, wanting more of her Morris, of her boy. More of his hugs, his kisses, more of his cheerful voice calling to her through the narrow rooms of the snug apartment.

"Yeah?" Morris answers, half out the door.

"Bring me some crackers 'fore you go," his father says over the noise of the TV.

Closing the front door, Morris steps into the kitchen, grabs the box of crackers from the cabinet and takes them to Seymour.

Near the back room, hung on the wall, is a small, tarnished brass plaque, one noting Morris as the most valuable swimmer of the 1979 summer season. When young, Morris aspired to be an Olympic swimmer, to train and compete in places with names like Paolo Alto or Zurich or Fort Lauderdale, places far away and foreign to him, places with deep pools with twelve lanes and fifty meters in length. He dreamt of winning races, of touching the wall a moment, a microsecond, before the swimmer in the lane next to him, dreamt of lifting his head from the wetness to find he'd broken his personal best record, broken the pool record, the world record.

His mother first introduced him to swimming, took him to classes at Asser Levy at the age of nine. The pool was a three lane, twenty-two yard pit on Twenty-Third Street and FDR Drive. It'd been built in 1921 as a way to encourage public hygiene, built in hopes of stopping the spread of cholera and typhoid fever through the promotion of showers and disinfectants. A city pool, it was owned and run by the New York Parks Department, and had a foul and murky locker room with communal showers where the gays would go to soap each other. Morris's mother never allowed him to wander into the locker room, kept a watchful eye over him when he went swimming. He'd put on his suit at home, wear it under his pants, change there on the pool deck. After class, his mother made him wear his jeans over his wet suit, which made him look like he'd pissed his pants. When he complained of this, said he wanted to change in the locker room like the others, his mother countered, "There are worse things than wet pants, and they're all in that locker room."

He had no idea what she meant, but her stern tone, her concerned voice was enough to terrify him. He didn't want to see what the locker room held.

During the summer months, he'd swim at the Hamilton Fish pool, a fifty-meter, Olympic sized outdoor pool on Houston and Pitt Street. It was beautiful, the distance from one end to the other stretching and straight and marked by a black line on the pool's floor. Morris's first laps of the summer were always a struggle, not being used to such continuous swimming. At Asser Levy, a handful of strokes took him to the other end, where he could grab the wall and rest a moment before turning around. At Hamilton Fish, there was no rest. No stopping. But he built his strength, improved his stroke, competed in meets.

At the end of his second summer of swimming, he took first place in the twelve and under 100-meter breaststroke in the All City Swim Meet. His mother was manic with delight. Her boy had won, had taken the blue ribbon. His father wasn't around.

The coach saw promise. Not Olympic promise, but promise still. He named Morris most valuable swimmer that summer, gave him a small plaque with etched lettering. "Keep him swimming, keep him practicing," his coach would tell Morris's mother.

But then his mother left, and all Morris's desire to swim left with her. He felt no reason to continue, felt no joy in winning. He had no one to win for.

He hasn't been in a pool in years. Still, he has his swim ribbons in his bureau's top drawer.

Pausing beside his father's chair, Morris holds the box of crackers out for him.

"How much the phone job going to pay?" Seymour asks.

"It's commissions," Morris says. "You get a percent of what you sell."

Seymour nods. He says, "Should've seen it. A clear shot." A half empty beer bottle is balanced on his knee. He lifts his hand like he's sighting something on the wall above the TV, pointing it out.

"A clear shot?"

"This girl," he says. "Right in front of me, top of the stairs. Standing all sexy," he says. "Sexy and smart-assish. Had a clear shot of her womanhoodliness. No panties. And she called me Daddy," Seymour says, in near reverie. He takes a sip of beer, balances it on his knee again. " 'Hello, *Daddy*.' That's what she said to me."

"Wow," Morris answers, his voice flat.

"Wow's right," Seymour says, taking the crackers from his son. Opening the box, he shakes them, then dips his fingers in for a handful. "I got a good smell of her when she passed. She smelled — "

He breaks off. Looking up at Morris, his face is a knot of disgust.

"What?" Morris asks, but he knows. His father's made the connection. Knows about Stefani, about him, the whole afternoon. He can smell it in the air, throughout the apartment.

"I hope I'm not thinking what I think I'm thinking," his father says, repulsed. His nostrils open wide, air rushing in.

Morris's on the spot; he has to explain, like someone caught cheating on the driver's license exam. "Daddy, it's what you're thinking," Morris admits, trying for the best spin. "But it's not the *way* you're thinking. If you let me explain—"

"I ain't a fancy man," his father says, his voice hard. "But I ain't an animal, either." He pulls his hand from the cracker box, holds it out. In it is a mass of damp, pale, partially chewed crackers. The ones Stefani spat back into the box. "What's wrong with you?" Seymour asks. He scrapes the glob back into the box, wipes his hand on his pant leg. "This ain't a zoo. When we eat, we eat."

Morris stands silent, waiting for more, waiting for his father to say, "And that girl I saw on the stairs…" But he doesn't. He doesn't say anything, focuses his attention to the TV and acts like Morris isn't even in the room.

"I'll buy you some more crackers. I'll get them right now," Morris says.

Seymour doesn't answer, doesn't acknowledge him. He stares at the TV, takes a sip of beer. The speaker blares with guffaws and chuckles. The show isn't funny.

Studying his father in profile, Morris is hit with the fear that once he exits the room, exits the apartment, his father will cease to exist. That it'll just be Morris, alone. "Daddy," he says. He wants to tell his father something important. He has an urgent need to hug him. "Daddy," he says, but his father doesn't answer him.

Morris picks up the cracker box. "Okay, then," he says, and leaves the room, leaves the apartment. Leaves his father in a crowd of false laughter.

Three

"I'll tell Morris," Stefani shouts, stomping out of Mr. Charlies with a pack of Basic filterless cigarettes and no change from the twenty Morris gave her. Evening's settled in swift and softly. "I'll tell Morris and he'll…" She can think of nothing he could do. "I'll tell all my friends," she yells, "and they'll tell their friends, until no one in New York shops here."

Striding north on First Avenue, she furiously tears the package's wrapper, pulls out a cigarette. "That asshole will pay," she says, then calls to the couple ahead of her, "Hey. Hey listen." She sidles up to them, touches the man on the arm. "Listen to me. That Mr. Charlies place, don't shop there. Don't shop at that place back there."

"No, none thanks," the man says. In his hand is a *Slumming through Manhattan* guidebook. The couple pick up their pace, trying to move ahead of Stefani.

"Serious, you know," Stefani says, "don't buy anything from that guy." She struggles to keep up with them, her large purse banging her side. "I'm telling you," Stefani says, "listen, this Charlies guy, he steals, and the place reeks, like he's got some health code violation going on, you know? And," she says, unable to think of anything else, "he steals."

"None, none, none," the man says, tightly holding the hand of his girlfriend, "none, thanks." They escape by crossing against the light, hopping through the traffic.

Pausing for breath, Stefani wedges a cigarette in her lips. "What's wrong with you?" Stefani yells at them, then turns to an approaching woman and says, "Hey, you know that Indian or Mexican store down there, Mr. Charlies?"

The woman has a ferret on her shoulder. Dressed in a tiny pink and blue knit sweater, the ferret tentatively sniffs the air, its head bobbing like a Styrofoam cup in the East River. "Jesus," Stefani says, seeing the animal, "like, what is that, an opossum? And why's it wearing that stupid little cape? Can I touch it?"

"Ariel's a ferret," the woman answers. She has the worn, life-weary look of an ex-drug addict or born-again Christian, and smells of nervous sweat masked by Right Guard. Around her neck hangs a large crystal on a chain, a cracked geode the size of a racket ball. "That's a sweater she's wearing, to keep warm. She's very susceptible to chills. And no," she says, "you can't touch Ariel. I've just had her chakras aligned." The woman walks off, the ferret clawed to her shoulder.

"Just remember, don't shop at Mr. Charlies'," Stefani calls after the woman, then gives up the venture. Pulling the rubber band from her hair, she redoes her horse's tail, pushes a few stray strands of hair behind her ear. "Well," she says, "I won't shop there, and Morris won't shop there. I'll make certain of that."

Setting her purse to the pavement, she opens it and digs around for matches or a lighter. "I won't shop there because I know better," she says, rifling through the contents of her bag. The size of a small suitcase, the purse is packed: hair barrettes; a bottle of Sweet-on-Him perfume; a Tower record receipt with some boy's phone number written on the back; Kleenex in floral prints; a half eaten donut from this morning; a letter from her school counselor, asking to meet with Stefani's parents; root beer and choco-berry and cherry favored lip glosses; a small Pearson Mason English boar bristle hair brush that she stole from Anderson's Drugstore; a large plastic brush with missing bristles; aspirin; a broken purple Swatch; a grape Blow Pop; a lucky rabbit's foot her father gave her for her tenth birthday; two make-up compacts, the mirror cracked in both; a small, leather bound photo album; and, at the bottom, a scattering of Skittles and pennies and pennies and pennies.

Pulling out the photo album, she looks at a four-year-old picture of her and her parents at South Street Seaport, their faces shining with forced smiles like they're out to prove they're having fun. She's an only child, lives on East Thirteenth Street above a Laundromat that belches out a warm, chemical fragrance of flowers and baby powder fourteen hours a day, seven days a week. It's a ten-minute walk from Morris's place and a world away.

She touches the picture, her fingers resting on the image of her father. Ever since her puberty set in at age fifteen—she was a late bloomer—her father, Jetski, has acted strange around her. He can't adjust to this new creature, this different being. Stefani's asked her mother what's wrong with him, why he acts so weird. "Stress of his career," her mother replied, referring to his job as a construction foreman.

But it's more than that. Stefani knows it's more, can sense it. Something has change between her and her father. The household balance has shifted. She's no longer her daddy's little girl, no longer the daughter he actively seeks out. Now she's a woman he actively avoids.

The life she once had has been breached by something corrupt and awful. Their home has been infiltrated, tainted. Stefani's a stranger to her father. She can tell he's disquieted by her; he won't tuck her in at night anymore, won't even enter her bedroom. The two of them no longer watch TV together like they use to, no longer playfully wrestle around like they once had. Jetski now locks the bathroom door and when Stefani enters a room, he finds a reason to leave.

More than once, she's caught her father staring at her the way boys at school sometimes stare at her. I'm your daughter, she wants to remind him, feeling sick about what he's probably thinking. I'm your little girl.

Stefani flips the album to the picture of Morris that she cut from her father's yearbook and laughs. Morris stands tall and thin, all bone and gristle in his Men at Work muscle T-shirt. "Morris, Morris," she says to the photo, then quietly sings, "If my father only *knew* about me and you. Oh, Morris, oh Morris, how he'd be *stewing* knowing what his best-friend was doing."

She turns back a few pages to Tom Ginkins, her first boyfriend. He's standing by the black square sculpture at Astor Place, his eyes near closed as he squints in the bright sun. Tom had been the first boy she'd been intimate with—or near intimate. He was tall with a thick neck and overlapping teeth and had the habit of making everything he said sound like a question. Two years ago, Stefani's freshman year, he'd asked her to a school dance and afterward, in a third floor classroom that was to have been locked but wasn't locked, she had let him touch her in places she'd only touched herself. He'd been terrified but determined and wouldn't stop repeating the Lord's Prayer the entire time.

After, he asked if she'd be his girlfriend. She said sure, why not?

He brought her to meet his parents the following week. They dated, or what he termed dating—a movie followed by a few minutes of quiet groping then a goodnight kiss—for over three months.

But it ended when Tom's mother walked in on him masturbating in the kitchen, Stefani's class photo propped against a pig-shaped ceramic cookie jar.

His mother, stunned and revolted, made a sharp sound like a parrot being shot. "This is where we eat," she said, thinking of how her son had helped her with dinner the night prior, had tossed the salad and handled the food. "Food's served here."

The entire house was thrown into chaos by the event. His mother wept for two days straight, yelled at her husband that it was his fault that their son was mentally tainted. "Come on, mom," Tom repeatedly pled, embarrassed and angry. "It's not like I killed someone."

"No," his mother tearfully answered, "it's not. It's worse." She demanded he get professional help, see a doctor, which ended up being a dermatologist who was related to the family in some distant, difficult-to-trace manner—Tom's mother feared the stigma of having her son go to a shrink. She forbade Tom from seeing Stefani anymore.

Tom explained to Stefani that he could no longer see her. He loved her, he said, but "outside forces, forces larger than you and me" made it impossible for him to keep seeing her. Having grown bored with Tom, Stefani was hardly hurt by the break-up, but still she acted the role of the jilted lover. In the school, when they passed, she turned her head down and ignored him. For nearly two weeks, the girls Stefani sometimes hung out with harassed Tom, calling him "Asshole!" or "Dicklick!" in the halls between classes, slipping nasty notes into his locker. They started rumors he had Ebola or E. coli or some frightening disease you get from doing something you shouldn't do. Loyalty and friendship to Stefani were not the wellspring of their actions. The girls taunted and berated Tom out of sheer adolescent cruelty, because there was the opportunity.

Then there was Gary and Greg Black. The Black brothers. She'd met Gary, the younger brother, at a Methodist youth group gathering her sophomore year. Being a Catholic, she'd gone not for the religious aspect, the community of Christ, but for the free snacks and screening of the movie *Halloween*. "You like Mountain Dew?" Gary asked her, seeing she'd poured a cupful. She wore tight, elastic, purple flare-bottom pants and a zippered Rocawear hoodie. "Yeah," she answered, "and Cherry Coke. I like Cherry Coke a lot," she told him. "And regular Coke. But not Pepsi. Tastes like sugared tree bark, you know?"

"Word," he said, nodding in agreement. He asked if she wanted to sit next to him during the movie. She did, and grabbed his hand twice during the scary scenes.

His confidence was what Stefani liked. He said what he felt, wasn't shy or goofy like most the boys she knew.

She handed up her virginity that night in the choir robe closet and on Monday, told Susan, a girl in her gym class, all about it. "You had sex with a black Methodist?" Susan said, crossing herself. "That's definitely a sin."

"His name's Black," Stefani corrected. "Gary Black. I met him at a Methodist youth ministry thingy," Stefani said, but it was too late. She'd lost the rights to her own story; the tale quickly spread, getting distorted and embellished with each telling. By end of the day, word was that Stefani was fucking a black minister addicted to Methadone.

She dated Gary for seven and a half weeks, then started going out with his older brother Greg, because he had a battered, old Nissan Z28. He was cool, had all the confidence of his younger brother and half the acne. He drove her into Brooklyn to go drinking at a Polish bar that never carded, or up into Washington Heights to a Dominican bar that never carded, or out to Queens to an Albanian bar that never carded. Or he'd buy a twelve pack of beer with his fake ID and drive out to Staten Island where, parked on a quiet cul-de-sac with aluminum-sided houses, they explored each other's bodies.

When she'd come home at midnight or one or three a.m. on a school night, her mother would explode, demand to know where she'd been. "Bowling" or "Youth group" or "Getting my nails done" she'd answer, her clothing wrinkled. She'd list about the apartment, like the floor was uneven or warped. "What have you been drinking?" her mother would demand. "Milk and milk and more milk," Stefani would reply. "Does the body good." She'd smell salty and fetid like she'd sprinted five miles then napped on a mound of fish sticks and mangos. Her mother would yell, all empty threats. "Okay, okay, okay," Stefani'd say, staggering to her room to collapse on her bed.

The next night she'd be out again.

Her father did nothing, stayed clear of the fray and let the women work it out.

Stefani and Greg's relationship stalled when Greg graduated and joined the Coast Guard. "I'll write," he promised her, "and visit when I'm back." She knew he probably wouldn't.

He didn't.

Since then, Stefani spends most nights at home flipping through *Seventeen* and *Elle* and other magazines she finds on the street for recycling, drawing flowering doodles with Magic Marker on the faces of the models.

Taking one last look at Morris's picture, she tosses the photo album back in her bag, then shifts about the purse's contents, looking for matches or a lighter. Junior prom's approaching, and thinking of Morris in a rented tuxedo and a cummerbund, she laughs to herself. "Yeah," she says, thinking of the surprise everyone will have when she shows up at prom with Morris. Her father will flip when he sees Morris at the door, a corsage in hand. Maybe she can get Morris to spring for a limo and dinner out at a nice place with a tablecloth and two forks at the setting.

And liquor, she thinks, lots of liquor.

She finds a battered pack of matches, strikes one. It hisses to life. The cigarette catches. Stefani, coughing violently from the smoke, grabs her bag and heads west on Ninth Street, planning which pages in her photo album she'll put the prom pictures. Planning which pages will be dedicated to Morris.

Four

Heading out his building's front door, Morris runs directly into a flabby, homeless black woman.

"Excuse me," Morris says, startled.

The woman eyes him suspiciously as she gnaws on a crab leg she found in the garbage. Dressed in an oversized pink skirt and a tight, faded red *Make-Out Bandit* T-shirt, her rolls of fat give her the appearance of three sets of breasts, one stacked on top of the other. The sidewalk's littered with the trash she's pulled from the can, littered with damp coupon fliers from Rite Aid, ripped, cancelled checks from someone named R. P. P. LeRoy Lee III, and orange take-out menus from Ali Bayou, the new Turkish-Louisianan fusion restaurant that specializes in deep-fried Snickers and Doner kebabs.

"Naw, naw, sweetmeat," she tells Morris, then shakes her hips. "It's me that needs excusing." Hiking up her skirt, she urinates on the sidewalk.

"Ah Christ, come on," Morris says, scooting to the side. The urine puddles then runs toward the street. "You have to do that here, in front of me? In front of my building?"

She laughs a laugh of ripping velvet. "When the muse is ringing, sweetmeats, *the muse is ringing*," she says, the crab leg protruding from her mouth.

Sickened by the scene, Morris stalks off to Mr. Charlies.

Mr. Charlies is the owner of Mr. Charlies Deli and Beer, a twenty-four hour bodega around the corner from Morris's place. A small man, Mr. Charlies has thick, black hair and an overbite that makes him look like he's constantly smiling. "Hey, buddy, hi buddy" is how he greets everyone who enters the store. He's originally from India, or Argentina, or from a country with a royal family and a large heroin production. It's hard to say. His story varies, depending on who asks, and his accent's strange and shifting, like he's trying to emulate some actor he's seen on TV. If pressed as to where he's from, he'll answer "The Island" and leave it at that, never saying what island he's speaking of.

His store—once a Laundromat whose dryers often caught fire, then the fabric store TWEEDS U NEED that sold only Sudanese tweeds, then the home of a Lebanese family who hung a neon sign in the window claiming to read Tarot cards but really only stole credit card numbers and identities—is narrow and long and excessively lit. It has linoleum flooring that was once white but is now a scarred, ghostly gray. There's a faint smell of incense, cinnamon, and bleach, and a crudely painted gold and black sign in the window announces: MR. CHARLIES SERVE COLD BEAR SNACK & MANY SPICE. Passersby pop in and ask Mr. Charlies the ingredients in his "cold bear snack." Is it, they ask, a snack made *for* bears as a between meal tide-over that won't ruin their dinner? Or is it made *of* bears and nibbled on by humans while, say, watching a movie, or waiting for the bus, or coming off a three day bender with vicious DTs? Mr. Charlies, never grasping the question, tries to sell them batteries with fast approaching expiration dates or foul smelling liver-wrapped-with-bacon appetizers held together by toothpicks that he claims his wife—the "Mrs." he calls her—has brought *just now*.

No one has ever seen his wife, not even his two employees, a somber pair of Colombian twins who stock shelves and stop shoplifters by tackling them the moment they exit the door. Mr. Charlies doesn't even have a picture of his wife, or of the one or two or five children he occasionally mentions.

Toward the front of the store, next to the cash register, is a compact display case with a cracked glass front filled with dry-looking meats, wilting lettuce, and darkening cheeses. On the counter sits a gleaming metal meat-slicer that is always broken, a bottle of Witch Hazel, and a five-liter container of orange Mayonnaise that never seems to empty. A Plexiglas container that rests on top of the counter is filled with stale hoagies, blueberry bagels, and Nan bread as stiff as Frisbees.

Lining the walls of the store are standing coolers packed with beers from around the world, soda, souring milk, and strangely colored sport drinks. The shelved aisles at the front of the store hold canned goods, potato chips, curry powder, tamarind, nutmeg, toilet paper, almonds, hair oil, marshmallows, and candles shaped like men or women that, when lit and prayed over, bring happiness and improved sex to a relationship.

Farther back, in the rear of the store, the shelves are lined with items that one searches for less often: multi-hued pipe cleaners; 40 watt light bulbs and Christmas light replacements; dusty jars of Vegemite; brown shoe laces for ten, twelve, and sixteen eye shoes; cod-liver oil; mustache wax and beard anti-dandruff creams; bunion ointment; men's sock garters; and Ma Rose's Miracle Metal Cleaner for silverware, brass, and copper.

It's a store that has everything, everything that is not exactly what one wants. Need a pint of half-and-half? Mr. Charlies has only heavy cream, and only in the rare gallon size. Want a specific brand of cigarettes? He has them only in menthol. Unless menthol is what is desired, then he only has the non-filter version of that brand. Want a roast beef sandwich? He has salami, which he awkwardly cuts— rather, hacks—by hand with a cleaver that could take down a small tree. An ounce of spice called for in a recipe requires buying a sixteen-ounce bag. Hostess Snack Cakes? No, Drake. Frito-Lay? No, Wise potato and corn chips. Unless one wants Wise, then he's out. Or that last bag is opened, has a hole in the side, like a rat got to it. "On order," he says when asked if there are more. "Tomorrow." For a can of black beans, he'll hand you pinto and tell you they taste the same. Coffee, decaf. Diet Coke when Coke is wanted, Fanta when Sprite is desired. Mr. Pibb instead of Dr. Pepper.

And he is always in his shop. Twenty-four/seven he seems to be at the counter, greeting each customer that enters with a "Hey, buddy," and a "Yes, buddy, what else can I get you?" No matter if they are male or female, old or young, they all get the same salutation. With one exception: Morris.

Morris remembers the day Mr. Charlies opened, in the fall of 1985. It was two months after the police closed the Lebanese Tarot card shop, arresting the entire family, including the thirteen-year-old girl, who had, with her parents' help, filed seven different personal injury lawsuits against the City, each one for breaking her leg in a pothole on Avenue D and Second Street, a nonexistent intersection. Mr. Charlies opened with no fanfare, no announcement. One day it was there, like it had been the block's anchor store for over a century. There was dust on the items before they even went on sale.

Morris, a sophomore in high school at the time, was trying to grow a moustache in hopes of looking older, in hopes of being able to buy beer, get into clubs and bars and impress the girls. But after three months' growth, his moustache was still frail and patchy, making him look more like he'd kissed a piece of charcoal or sniffed a melting chocolate bar than reached manhood.

It was a rainy Wednesday. Damp and uncomfortable, Morris was on his way home from school when he saw the already tattered MR. CHARLIES sign for the first time. The store wasn't there that morning, he'd swear. Pausing in front of the deli, he touched his sparse, rabbit fur-soft moustache and looked in. For the last year he'd been trying to buy beer, but the delis and stores in the neighborhood knew him, had known him for years. Each time he tried, he was turned down. "Stick with the soda, Morrie," the deli owners would say, or "Try milk—it'll help that 'stache of yours grow." Morris never protested, always put the beer back in the large standing cooler, and walked out.

But with the opening of the new deli, a place that Morris had no history with, he saw a chance to score.

Morris pulled out the ten-dollar bill Mr. Sofar had mailed him for his birthday. Morris used to walk his dog, Hambone, for him, before Hambone was dognapped. Sofar had lived in the building longer than the Blisses, longer than anyone. He'd witnessed Morris grow from a baby to an adolescent. Stavroula, Morris's mother, and he were close friends, and Sofar was especially kind to Morris. During the three months Stavroula was gone, Sofar would rip open a package of Nutter Butters, warm them in the oven for five minutes, then carry a tray down one flight to Morris's apartment every few days. "Made from scratch," Sofar would say, handing them over. "And I made too many. Take them, please."

Morris, in turn, stopped by Sofar's apartment after school to take Hambone, a graying dachshund with patchy fur and the distemper of a child with a stomach achingly full of candy, for a walk. Morris didn't like the dog, didn't enjoy taking it out and having to drag it by the leash. Hambone hobbled and whimpered and paused every five feet to try to defecate, unsuccessfully. But he walked the dog as a favor to Sofar, a favor he was well paid for.

Then Morris's mother died. Hambone was stolen. Sofar cracked, got strange and creepy.

Morris stopped visiting Sofar.

Standing out in the misting rain, the ten-dollar bill damp in his hand, Morris was determined. He strode forward, walked right into the glass door, thinking it swung in, not out. Stepping back, he prayed no one saw, then pulled the door open. Standing tall, he walked in. "New place," Morris said as he passed Mr. Charlies and the front counter.

"Yes, buddy, yes," Mr. Charlies answered, excitedly. A customer. He gazed at Morris like he was pure platinum. "Yes, welcome."

Morris went straight to the standing beer cooler, where he grabbed a forty-ounce Ballantine Ale. He placed the bottle on the counter, took out the ten-dollar bill.

Seeing the beer, seeing how young Morris was, Mr. Charlies' exuberance wilted.

"So," Morris said, holding his bravado. "You the owner, you Mr. Charlie?"

"*Charlies*," he replied. "Mr. Charlies." He studied Morris closely, like he was searching for defects. Morris held still, fearing movement would somehow provoke the man.

Mr. Charlies shook his head.

The gig's up, Morris thought. He'd ask for I.D. or laugh at him or chase him from the store, yelling, "No, buddy, no, no, no."

But he didn't. His face knotted like he'd heard the reputation of his only daughter had been soiled. Still, Mr. Charlies bagged the beer and rang the cash register. "One twenty-five," he said.

"All right, fair price," Morris said, looking at the register. He wanted to stay silent, to get his beer and leave, but he couldn't help talking, his nervousness overwhelming. "Fair price," he said again, handing him the ten-dollar bill. "You know, Mr. Charlies, some of these other places—"

"You Mr. Charlies," Mr. Charlies said, snatching the money from him. "*You* the Mr. Charlies here."

"I—" Morris said, but broke off, confused.

Mr. Charlies held the bill up to the light, licked his forefinger and thumb, felt the bill's texture and gauge, then, determining that it was real, opened the till drawer.

Morris sensed the exit ten feet from him, felt the draw of the door.

"Oh, no, no. Mr. Charlies, I'm so sorry," Mr. Charlies said to Morris, looking into his till. "Problems, problems."

"You know, why don't we just—"

"So sorry, Mr. Charlies, but I've no change."

"No change?" Morris asked, baffled. "How can you not—"

"Here, Mr. Charlies," Mr. Charlies said, taking a bent, crusty flyswatter from under the counter, "take this, buy more."

"I don't want more," Morris said, watching Mr. Charlies stick the flyswatter in his bag. He ran the till for another dollar.

"And how about this?" Mr. Charlies said, grabbing a handful of Lipton's tea bags.

"How about some cigarettes?" Morris asked. "Or another beer?"

He headed back to the standing cooler.

"Okay, okay, Mr. Charlies," Mr. Charlies said, dropping the tea bags in the sack then ringing up another dollar. He excitedly searched for items. "And these, Mr. Charlies," he called to Morris, packing up a plateful of bacon-liver snacks, "you'll like these. Mrs. Charlies made them."

Morris returned with another beer.

"Ten dollars even," Mr. Charlies said, and patted the stuffed bag. "Oh, oh," he said, seeing the other beer. "You want to buy more, another beer?" He hit the cash register again, ringing up the extra beer. "Eleven twenty-five."

By the time Morris left the store—after a solid five minutes of arguing, each calling the other Mr. Charlies—he had a bagful of useless items and rancid snacks. He also had no change. But he felt elated, like he'd just exited a Middle-Eastern bazaar, penniless but thankful for his life.

And he had a beer. One beer.

"I'm never going there again," Morris told himself, tossing all the items except his beer. "Never, never again."

But he went back. It was the only place he could buy beer or cigarettes. And whenever Morris entered the store, he was Mr. Charlies; whenever he exited, he had no change.

~~~

Stepping through the door, Morris scans Mr. Charlies' store, looking for Stefani.

"Ah, Mr. Charlies, hello, hello," Mr. Charlies says to Morris.

"Hey," Morris replies. His nose starts itching from the acrid smell of spices and dust. He doesn't see Stefani. "Has a woman—"

"No." Mr. Charlies smiles.

Morris stares at him, a sneeze building from deep within. "I haven't even asked you the—"

"Ah, yes, I know. And no."

"Well, did she say—"

"No."

The Colombian twins stand at the back of the store, studying him. He's never heard them say a word. Morris says, "When did she—"

"No, Mr. Charlies," Mr. Charlies says. He lifts his hands, palms down. "The girl, no problem. I tell her, come anytime, all the time. A friend of Mr. Charlies is a friend of Mr. Charlies," he says, then, "She's your daughter, yes?"

"Daughter?" Morris says. "She's a..." He sneezes once, then again. "No," he tells Mr. Charlies. "She's not my daughter."

Mr. Charlies expression shifts. "Oh. Understand, understand."

"I'm certain you do," Morris says, heading down the tight aisle for a box of crackers. He grabs a bright orange box of Cajun curry barbequed beef crackers—the only kind of crackers Mr. Charlies has—and sets it on the counter. "You don't have any other kinds?" he asks, though he knows the answer. "Cheez Its or Triscuits, something ordinary?"

"On order," Mr. Charlies says, ringing up the three-dollar purchase. "Tomorrow."

Morris takes out a five-dollar bill to pay. "You got some new spices in here?" He struggles not to break into a sneezing fit.

"Yes, yes, Mr. Charlies, many spices. What do you need?"

Morris shakes his head and sneezes. "Nothing." He hands over the money.

Taking the money, Mr. Charlies flicks the bill with his fingers, then opens the till. "Oh, no, no. Mr. Charlies," he tells Morris. "So sorry."

"Don't tell me," Morris says, sniffing.

But Mr. Charlies tells him. "Problems, problems," he says. "I have no change."

Five

With the box of crackers in hand and his nose running, Morris wanders the East Village. The avenues are crowded with graffiti tagged newspaper boxes, people returning from work, and Chinese food deliver boys on bikes. Bicycle delivery boys terrify Morris, the way they zip, cut, and race through traffic. He witnessed a woman plowed down and killed by a bicycle delivery boy from the Sun No. 1 Chinese restaurant. It was a direct hit, the front wheel and handlebars of the bike catching the woman and slapping her to the ground. Her head cracked the concrete; she was dead on the scene.

The delivery boy tumbled over the bike, executed a somersault that landed him on his butt. He nimbly jumped to his feet, yelled an apology that sounded like "Scurvy" then picked up his bike, and swiftly rode away, oblivious to the extent of the injury he'd inflicted. Morris chased after him, yelling for him to stop. "Scurvy, scurvy," he repeated, peddling off.

Morris's account of the accident and a Sun No. 1 menu dropped at the scene gave the police the lead they needed. They found the delivery boy calmly sitting in the restaurant's kitchen smoking a hand rolled cigarette, waiting for his next dispatch.

Arrested, the delivery boy was assigned a state lawyer and a Chinese interpreter with the habit of fondling her left breast. Morris testified, and after a two-hour trial, in which the accused showed no remorse and said only that accidents were the cost of living in the city, the delivery boy was sentenced for manslaughter. He served two years, then was deported for being in the country illegally.

Turning onto East Fifth Street, Morris heads past his building and walks on toward N.J.'s, just off of Second Avenue. It's the time of evening Morris dislikes the most, when the day's light stops being light to start being something else. His mind sets to churning; he worries about money, his father, where his life is heading. And now there's Stefani.

He stops by N.J.'s place, hoping to talk. Buzzing his apartment, there's no answer. He hasn't seen N.J. in five days, since Sunday. Last he spoke with him was Monday, on the phone. "Can't talk, man," N.J. told him, out of breath like he'd run up six flights of stairs. He lives on the ground floor, in a studio apartment. "I'm blowing up here, man," he said, overwhelmed with something. "Fucking. Blowing. Up." He promised to call Morris later, tell him all about it. He's yet to call.

Settling on a bench in the small strip of park across the street from the ninth precinct police station, Morris rests. The park is littered with hamburger wrappers and credit card applications. A plastic I ♥ NY grocery bag skips by on a breeze while three teenage white boys in oversized Spurs basketball jerseys amble past. Smoking peach-flavored Philly Blunts, they shout at each other, call one another whacked niggas and bitch ho's. During the week, they wear Catholic school uniforms, say their rosary.

In the flickering street light, Morris studies the detail work chiseled on the precinct façade. The building's over a hundred-and-twenty-years old, built of thick limestone quarried from Indiana. To the right and left of the main entrance are huge double doors that once led to the horse stables. It's beautiful, a Hollywood set; it was Kojak's headquarters and the precinct where the officers of NYPD Blues battle through their days. A half a block from his home, it's been a mainstay of Morris's life.

Now the building's slated to come down.

Someone from the City said, "We got a budget. Demolish the ninth precinct house on East Fifth Street." An exact replica of the building, only with two more stories and an elevator and better office décor, is to be built in its place. Tens of millions of dollars will be spent and no one will be able to tell the difference from the outside. The project's to take three or five or seven years, depending on who's talking. In the interim, while the building's brought down then put back up, the entire ninth precinct, all the men, the cars, the scooters, the guns, the copiers, handcuffs, pencils, pens, computers, records, and radios have been packed up and moved in to the new Police Service Area building, the permanent headquarters for the Lower East Side's meter maids and school crossing guards. The building, on Eighth Street and Avenue C, is designed to please everyone.

No one likes it.

Brand new, it already looks old—like it was built in the late fifties by a committee of community college graduates with too much vision and not enough skill.

The demolition of the ninth precinct was to begin the week after the police had vacated six months ago. But due to delays, false starts, petty arguments, and failed agreements, it's still not begun.

Morris opens the box of Cajun curry barbequed beef crackers, tastes one. The crackers are awful, like smoked cardboard soaked in Tabasco sauce. Forcefully, he swallows it down.

The Stones of Venice. Ruskin. Stefani mentioned the book. Morris has read it, read many books on architecture. He knows the difference between stones, what part of the world they are quarried in, though he's never seen a quarry or traveled the world. All his information he's gotten from books.

Morris recalls the basics of construction. To build a building, he knows, one must dig down, have a firm foundation that runs deep, roots the structure. Without this, all is in danger of collapse.

~~~

One of the two light bulbs in his building's foyer is burnt out, giving the small space a jaundiced yellow hue. Night's arrived in earnest. Bent down, Morris struggles to coax his mailbox open with his slightly bent key. There's a tap at the door, and looking up, he sees her through the cloudy Plexiglas window: Andrea Goldman Angel. Her hair is shiny and stiff. In her mid-twenties, she lives in Apartment 5 with her husband, George. Morris knows her the way he knows the counter help at the café down the street; brief and fleeting. He has difficulty placing her when he sees her on the street, outside the safe environment of the apartment building's hallway.

She taps on the window again with a manicured nail, wanting in. Morris lets her in.

"Right, thanks. This bag, you know, the things. I can't find my keys," she says, holding up her juice-box sized purse. "Thank you, right?" She's attractive in a vague, tabloid way, all gloss and gossip. Morris guesses she spends an eternity each morning to achieve her stylish just-thrown-together look. "This day," she says, moving past Morris, "is a terrible day. The mail's come?" Her head rocks while her hair stays formed, unmoving.

"I think so," he tells her, jiggling his bent mailbox key in the lock, hoping to pop the mailbox. "Can't seem to get my box open." Morris rarely converses with the neighbors. A greeting, good morning, or "Hey, how are you" at most. Rarely more. A crowded city is often isolating.

"What happened there?" Andrea asks, now having no problem finding her keys in her purse. She opens her mailbox, pulls a stack of mail from her box, multicolored bill envelopes, two glossy catalogues for overpriced clothing, Condé Nast's *Traveller*, and *Snap*, a fashion magazine that focuses on how to please your boyfriend in one article and how to exact revenge in the next. "Your mailbox, right? It's broken?"

"My key." Morris had used it to try to retrieve a quarter stuck in the slot of a soda machine. The key bent. He didn't get the quarter. "There was a fight," he says, jokingly.

"A fight?" she asks. "Did you take your shirt off?"

"Why would I take off my shirt?"

She moves forward, places her hand to his arm like she's comforting a disaster victim. Kosher restaurant menus litter the floor. A tattered Ellsworth Kelly poster is taped to the wall, placed there for no reason. "Right," she says, "to fight." Her eyes are a spill of green and brown, like crayon shards melted on glass. There's a ghostly stain on the left breast of her blouse and her lower lip is substantially thicker than her upper. The intimacy throws Morris off; it arouses him. A flush of warmth runs to his groin. "I was actually just jok—"

"You weren't hurt, right?" she says, her hand tightening on his arm.

"My key was hurt," Morris says, holding it up. "It got bent."

"Oh," she says. To Morris's disappointment, she lets go. "Right." She turns her attention to her mail. "It's been such a bad day," she tells him. She quickly flips through the mail, pausing momentarily to read a postcard advertising a 60 percent off sale at APC. "What a bad day. Had to come home early."

"Early? How late do you work?" Morris asks. It is after nine. He sees her *Traveller* magazine, the cover shot of Prague. "Is that a good magazine?" he asks.

"The make-up tips and sex advice are wrong, right?" she says, opening up *Snap*, the fashion magazine. "But hairstyles, how-to-lose weight, and tidbit articles are usually pretty good. Like this, right," she says, pausing on a page. " 'Banana's are a great way to battle PMS and chronic split ends,' " she reads. "I didn't know that. Did you know that, right?"

"No, I didn't," Morris says, adding, "I was actually talking about the travel magazine."

"Oh. Right." She hands him the magazine. "Well, here, have it. I never read it, right? Don't even know why we get it," she says, then, "You travel much?"

Morris takes the magazine, thanks her. "I travel a lot," Morris says, studying the cover. "Or, I mean, I plan to travel a lot. I haven't been anywhere yet. But soon," he says.

"Right," she says, then holds out an envelope from the Bowery Mission and Homeless Shelter. "Look at this." It pictures a hunched, bearded man with a spoon raised to his month. The text reads: "We all want to eat this Easter."

"My God, can you believe this?" Andrea says, agitated. "As if my taxes aren't enough, right? I work and work, then come home and am guilted into helping people who don't pay a cent? This guy looks like my husband George's grandfather. How can I say no, right?" She forcefully shuts her mailbox. "We all can't have the *easy* life, the government covering our food and rent," she says, smiling a pinched, acidic smile. "We all can't be as *lucky* as *some* people in the building."

"No, I guess not," Morris says. He wonders if she's referring to him, but then realizes she's probably talking about the Dominicans in apartment 2. They're a mid-aged couple who've lived in New York for nearly ten years and still can't speak English beyond a few basic words. Morris has helped them with small tasks, like carrying heavy groceries, or changing a light bulb, setting up mousetraps. The woman's two sisters, her mother, and her mother's sister are permanently visiting. They're a gentle people who communicate by screaming. The government covers half their rent, provides public assistance.

Keep working hard. Millions on welfare are depending on you. Morris saw that on a bumper sticker the other day. He thinks of sharing this with Andrea but then decides not to. She wouldn't find it funny.

Turning to head up the stairs, she says, "Well, right. Take care, Troy." Her lavender thong peeks out above her black skirt. It's like a glowing ember in a pitch-dark cave.

"Morris," Morris corrects her, watching as she mounts the stairs. "My name is Morris." He gives up on his mailbox, on getting the mail.

"Morris, right," she says. At the first landing, Andrea turns and says, "Let me ask you, right? What are you doing Sunday at five p.m.?"

"Nothing I can think of," he says, heading up the stairs toward her.

"Great. Then let me ask you, right? Do you eat…" She pauses, searching for the word. "What's that stuff called?"

"What stuff?" He reaches the first landing and catches a whiff of her perfume, a spicy orange scent that charges through him.

"The Mexican stuff, right?" Again, she touches him, touches his chest, near his collarbone.

He nearly drops the magazine. "Tacos?" he asks, excited and confused. She's married, he reminds himself, hoping the cold realism will settle him. It doesn't.

"No, the stuff you put on tacos," she says. "It's all chopped up, right? Tomatoes and onions. Comes in a bottle."

"Salsa," Morris says.

"Right. Yes, salsa. Do you eat salsa?" Her fingers linger.

"Not often, but yes. I eat it."

"Right, great," she says, then heads up the next flight of stairs. Morris follows. "You want to make a hundred and twenty-five dollars?" she asks.

"What would I have to do?"

"Nothing," she says, stopping in front of her door. "Or next to nothing." She pulls out her cell phone. "I need you for a focus group on a new salsa, right? All you do is look at some print ads, make some comments." She dials a number. Overhead, the florescent halo bulb shines its cheap, thin blue-white light.

"Ronda? Andrea. Right. Listen," she says into her phone. "Sunday, the salsa focus group, right? One male. Morris." Then to Morris, she asks, "What's your last name?"

"Bliss."

"Bliss," she says into the phone. "Right, Bliss. Great." Hanging up, she gives Morris the details, where the office is, what time he needs to be there.

Keying her door, she asks, "You want to come in, right? Have a drink?"

Before Morris can answer, the door swings opens from the inside. There stands George, Andrea's husband. Tall, heavy-set, and in a pair of cut off sweat pants and a tattered banana-green T-shirt that reads *Where's the Beef?*, George glares at Morris. "This another stray you've picked up?" he asks his wife, Andrea.

"Oh, Georgie, come on, right?" Andrea says, speaking in a voice Morris hasn't heard before. It's forcefully bright, yet pleading and worried.

"I'm Morris," Morris says, holding out his hand. George doesn't take it. "I live upstairs."

"Keep it that way," George says, then says to Andrea, "You promised no more strays."

"It's for work, Georgie," she says. "He's our neighbor, right?" She steps past Morris, into her apartment. "Salsa, Sunday?" Andrea says to Morris. "See you then, right."

"Or not at all," George says to him, firmly shutting the door. The locks click, the noise echoing down the stairwell.

Two flights up is Morris's home. The city and the street are below. "Sunday," Morris says to himself, two days' time.

Everything can change so quickly.

Six

The apartment's a brown-black dark, a city dark, the outside sky caramelized by the street and building lights. Morris carefully opens the door to the back room, his father's room, and peeks in. The TV's still playing, dancing a bluish ghost against the walls. The sound's off. Seymour is in his lounge chair, asleep, his head rolled to one side. "Jesus, Daddy," Morris says, seeing the wads of tin foil resting in his lap, the *Post* next to two empty beer bottles on the floor. Morris picks them up, then drapes a ratty, blue blanket over his father.

Standing over him, Morris finds that Seymour seems small and old, a wizened child in the shifting stream of the TV's glimmer. The sight startles him, like he's come upon something broken and discarded, something that isn't meant to be seen. This man before him isn't the all-powerful father he knows. The man before him is exposed and frail, mortal. The man before him can easily be killed.

This isn't his father. His father can never die.

Studying him, Morris recognizes something even more disquieting; he sees himself, sees his lineage, his features, hands, and face. He's his father's son. Before him is himself in two decades' time. He's trapped by the fact.

I am a Bliss, he says to himself as he tucks the blanket around his father. He turns off the TV. "I'm a Bliss," he quietly says.

Seven

Asleep in the lounge chair, Seymour's dream plays out, vivid and thick.

Nineteen sixty-eight. The tellers' windows are open, nothing dividing the customer from the banker. Not like now, with the bullet-proof glass and slots and holes to speak into. Seymour's back from military service, from fighting in Vietnam. Atlantic Bank on Thirty-Eighth Street and Madison. The tellers' windows. Friday afternoon, four-thirty. And a teller is waiting. Stavroula is waiting, seems like she's always been waiting, always been there. He'd only had to look, to find her. She'd been waiting.

It's the first time he sees her. She's pretty, but pretty in an odd, disproportioned way; her eyes are too big for her face and her jaw line's too sharp, like sheared stone. When he sees her, something long viscous breaks and percolates a whiskey heat through him.

Check in hand—his pay for the week's work on the construction site—he smoothes his hair, licks the tips of his moustache, then approaches her window. "Stavroula," he says, reading her nameplate on the counter. Pronouncing her name fairly well, he smiles. "It means 'The Cross' in Greek."

Her large eyes are dark, like they swallow light. She's surprised. "Yes," she says, "it does. How did you know?"

"I know a few things," Seymour says. He likes this woman, her peculiar face, her voice, the way she holds herself. He likes her and can no more explain why he likes her than he can explain the workings of the sun. It is there; it offers warmth. This he understands.

She asks him if he speaks Greek. He admits he can't. "I work with a Greek," he tells her. "His wife's name is Stavroula. It's such a pretty name." He looks at her directly, looks into her oversized eyes. "It fits you."

Stavroula's face blossoms. She fumbles for a pen. "How…how would you like this, Mr. Bliss?" she asks, clumsily stamping his check. "Would you like this in tens?"

"Fives," he says, and watches her long, elegant fingers meticulously count out the bills.

After that, Seymour makes certain to always go to her window, waits an extra ten minutes just to have his transaction completed by her. She's glad to see him, her greeting different with him than with others. As she slowly lays out his money, they talk of the upcoming weekend's weather or a new movie coming out. He compliments her on her dress, or on how nice her hair looks. She looks away, flustered and appreciative of the attention.

He asks her out. "I'm thinking bowling, maybe, then dinner. Or the other way around."

"I…no, I can't," she says, then quickly adds, "Bank rules. Tellers aren't allowed to fraternize with clients."

"I don't want to fraternize you," he says. "Just take you to dinner."

Still, she says, she can't. "If you weren't a client here, if I'd met you elsewhere," she says, "then…" Her voice trails off.

"Stavroula," he says, then stops himself before saying anything more. He nods, then leaves without another word.

The following week, he arrives carrying a small bundle of tight budded yellow flowers. Tulips. "I can help you over here, sir," an open teller says to Seymour. He stands in Stavroula's line, waiting for an elderly woman to complete her transaction. She has a year's worth of collected coins spilled out on the counter, is counting them out.

"I'll wait," Seymour says to the free teller.

"But I can help you here, sir," the teller insists. "I'm open."

"No," he tells her, adding, "thank you." He motions toward Stavroula, the old woman counting coins. "I'll wait."

When it's finally his turn, he strides up to Stavroula and holds out the flowers. "I'm taking you to dinner, tomorrow night," he says.

"Mr. Bliss," she says, "I—"

"Seymour," he tells her. "I want you to call me Seymour. And I don't bank here anymore," he tells her. "I closed my account. So you can go to dinner with me and it wouldn't be fraternalizing."

Stavroula looks confused, uncertain what to say. "I don't know how to answer," she says.

"Answer yes," he says.

"It's just—" She breaks off.

"It's just what?"

"You can't come to my house," she says.

"Then meet me here, out front of the bank, six o'clock." Without waiting for an answer, he turns. "Tomorrow," he says, and walks out before she can answer.

Eight

Stavroula's always felt like an outsider, that she didn't belong. Having moved to the United States at the age of five, she's neither Greek nor American, but an odd amalgamation: A Greek who spoke flawless English, or an American with a long, funny name. She was everything and nothing, depending on the moment, the day. And being trapped in this vacuum of fluxing identity, she experienced the frictions of the two cultures clashing.

She wanted to be American, but her family didn't understand the importance of fitting in, going to slumber parties, or having the right tennis shoes. "I don't want you sleeping at someone else's house," her mother would say. "Why would you want to sleep elsewhere?" Or her father would say, "It's not the shoe; it's who's inside the shoe," and launch into a tale about how, growing up on his island, they'd get only one pair of shoes a year.

She wanted to stay Greek, even though the kids at school couldn't pronounce her name. To them, she was a weirdo who ate goat and squid. "Staffer...Starva-roll-A..." Her teachers would stumble with her name when they took roll on the first day of each school year. Giggles filled the room, the other kids laughing. There was no attempt at her last name. "You can call me Roula," Stavroula would say, hoping it was easier for everyone. But the name quickly morphed into "Ruler," then just "Roo," which led to her nickname "Kanga," a name that followed her through her senior year in high school.

She took it in stride, never showing that the barbs wounded. But she always longed to be accepted.

The dutiful daughter, she got a job as a teller in a bank managed by Greeks and contributed her paycheck to the family. Each week, she'd attend church with her family. Each week, she'd tactfully rebuff her mother's blunt efforts to set her up.

But now she has a suitor, Seymour, and the prospect terrifies her. Her folks will never approve of him. Bliss isn't a family name they know. He isn't a member of their church, or any church for that matter, she guesses. Her father has spoken of non-Greeks often: they are fine for everything but family. A Greek can never marry a non-Greek; they will infect all that's important, all that has been obtained through great effort and struggle.

Stavroula decides to stand Seymour up, not show for the date. Then she decides it'd be wrong of her. Just this once, she tells herself. One quick date, then it'll be over, she tells herself.

"I'm going out with a friend tonight after work," she tells her parents at breakfast. "A girl from the bank. We're going out for dinner and a movie." She feels soiled by the lie, feels certain her parents will see right through her.

"That sounds like fun," her mother says, and nothing more.

Seymour is waiting for her outside the bank at six p.m. One quick date, Stavroula keeps telling herself.

They go to dinner, then out for bowling, and while they don't talk much, Stavroula has a great time, enjoys herself thoroughly. Enjoys Seymour's company, his attention.

At the end of the evening, Seymour asks her out again. She hears herself say "Yes." There is no other word that comes to mind.

She lies to her parents, then lies again. One date, then another, then a third. She and Seymour go to Rockefeller Center, Coney Island, Central Park. Seymour doesn't talk much, doesn't like to talk much about himself or the things he's done, his past. Still, Stavroula grows accustomed to him, his stance, the way he walks with her, making certain he's between her and the curb. She grows to love his gruff affection.

Now, with Seymour, she's found acceptance. She's found the affection and appreciation that she so desperately longed for. She has something she's never had before, a feeling of comfort and freedom. With Seymour, she's found herself.

And while she knows what her parents' reaction will be, she has to let them know, has to tell them of her fortune.

"I can't keep this to myself anymore," she tells Seymour. Stavroula's told him of her situation, about her parents, that she's kept their dating a secret for all these months. Even her elder sister, Christina, who she's close with, doesn't know about Seymour.

"Let me talk to your parents," Seymour says.

"They won't understand."

"I'll talk to them and tell them—" He breaks off.

"Tell them what?" Stavroula asks.

"Ah, you know. I'll just tell them."

"What? What are you going to tell them?"

Seymour swallows hard, looks away. "I'll tell them that I love their daughter," he says, turning his attention to his feet, the ground. "That I'm going to marry her."

The strength is swept from her heart. Stavroula falls into Seymour's arms, weeping. "Seymour," she says, holding him tight, so tight that it hurts him. He loves her, loves her for who she is. "My Seymour," she cries, kissing and kissing him, her sharp, salty tears biting his lips.

It's the first time she truly feels loved.

"There's someone I'd like to bring to dinner tomorrow," she informs her family one evening. She and Seymour had been secretly dating for seven months. "A young man," she says. Her mother stops knitting, the needles held mid-stitch. Her father looks up from the TV, his eyes focusing directly at her. He doesn't say a word. He doesn't need to. All is spoken in his eyes. Already, she sees the outcome. Stavroula's heart falters. Seymour will sit at the table, she realizes, but he won't be welcomed.

The next night, Seymour arrives dressed in pressed pants and a suit jacket, flowers and a bottle of wine in hand. He's cordial, polite, and respectful. The evening passes in awkward starts and fits. The pasta is undercooked, the steaks burnt. Her father refuses to speak to Seymour in English, forcing Stavroula to translate everything he says. Seymour speaks of the food, of how much he enjoys Stavroula, her company. All his comments are met with stony silence.

After dinner, Seymour asks Stavroula's father if he might speak with him. Stavroula had coached him on what to say, to ask her father's permission for marriage. It is all useless. "Sir," Seymour says, "it is my intension to marry your daughter. I ask for your blessing."

In clear, sharp English, her father says, "No."

"I..." Seymour says, caught off guard by the curt response. "I have money saved, and I feel confident that—"

"No." Her father sits back in his chair, stares at Seymour with thick contempt. It isn't Seymour specifically. It's who he isn't: Greek.

Seymour says, "I believe Stavroula has some say in this matter."

"You believe wrong," her father tells him, rising from the chair. "Your friend is leaving," he calls to Stavroula in Greek, "for good."

That night, Stavroula's admitted to the hospital, the pain in her chest crippling. She's examined, tested, and examined more. The doctors can find nothing wrong. "We can find nothing wrong with you," the physician tells her, checking her blood pressure one last time. "Your blood work came out well; your pulse is a little high, but normal, and your blood pressure's on mark. Everything seems fine."

"You're not looking at the right things," she tells him, her face pale. "You are looking at things that don't matter."

The next night, she sneaks out her parents' house and heads to Seymour's apartment. Her face is swollen from crying. "Tell me to go," she yells at him, standing on the threshold. "Tell me to leave." She pled her case with her father, asking him to reconsider. "Seymour's my happiness," she told him.

"There are things more important than happiness," her father said.

"Name one."

"Family," he replied. "Your mother, your father. Our name."

"But Seymour's family," she said, wanting to explain that he's the only one who understands her, makes her feel whole. "He's family," she says, a bitterness rising in her throat and choking her. "I can't break from him."

Now, she stands before Seymour, her lungs burning with anguish. She will do as her father told her. She'll finish with Seymour.

"I can't marry you," she tells him. "I can't love you."

Seymour steps forward and slides his arms around her, pulls her to him and holds her. "But you do," he tells her. "Stavroula, you do."

Later, as she lies in Seymour's arms, her hair fanned across his chest, she knows she can't return to her parents' house, knows she had no home to return to. That life is behind her now, dead. She's made a choice.

Her home is in Seymour's arms.

Her home is Seymour.

Nine

Morris is not in bed but ten minutes when the phone rings. It's one a.m. It's after one. He fumbles for the receiver before the second ring. "Yes?" Morris asks, expecting a wrong number.

"We need to talk."

Morris sits up in bed, turns on a small lamp. He's fully dressed; jeans, a T-shirt, and tennis shoes. He's ready to go at moment's notice. It's a discomfort he's grown accustomed to; he's slept this way since age thirteen, when his father woke him at three in the morning, telling him to hurry and get ready. It was his mother. She was in the hospital, her illness racing its course. The doctor had called. They'd best come. Hurry.

Confused and half asleep, Morris flailed about his room, trying to dress. He couldn't find a shirt. His socks were mismatched. His shoes were missing. It took an eternity. "Come on. Come on," his father kept yelling, waiting for him in the hallway.

By the time they arrived, she'd passed. His mother was dead.

Morris now sleeps fully clothed, ready at a moment's notice.

"Stefani?" he asks, the phone to his ear. There's a silence on the line. "Stefani, is that you?"

"I'm outside. We need to talk," she says, then hangs up.

He finds her out front of his building, smoking a cigarette and straddling a motorcycle parked at the curb. It isn't hers. The night air's pleasant, cool, holds the fragrance of broken lemons and freshly turned earth. The buds on the trees ache to open. "You okay?" he asks. He studies her closely, looking for the traces of his mother he saw earlier. They're nowhere to be found.

Stefani hops off the motorcycle. "Don't worry, I'm not pregnant," she tells him, squinting from the cigarette smoke. She's wearing low-rider jeans, a pink baby T with the words *All City Princess* written in gold, and a blue St. Benedict's windbreaker jacket, the kind summer church camp counselors wear, the kind that invariably have cigarette burns in them. "But I realize things," she says, flicking the cigarette to the street. Her face is framed in the fragile light of the street lamp. "Now that I'm eighteen," she says, and kisses him on the chin, his nose, then on his lips. She kisses him deeply.

Like tumbling down a flight of stairs, the act is swift and bruising. Stefani stops before she's really begun, leaving Morris's face aflame. "Stefani," he tells her, fighting to form words.

"Now that I'm eighteen," she says again, tugging at his shirt, "I realize things. I realize that I like you, a lot. I like this Morris-and-Stefani thing we have, but I realize that this" — she taps his chest, then points to herself — "our 'you and me,' isn't going to work. I have plans, you know, dreams," she says. "You aren't a part of them."

"I'm not apart of them?" Morris says, slighted. Her words sting.

"No," she says. She smells of sugary strawberries and Elmer's glue, a smell that reminds Morris of elementary school art projects.

"What kind of plans are you talking about?" Morris says, now wanting to be a part of her plans. Shut a door and one wants in. It's a human condition: we desire what we're denied, even if we don't want it.

"Owning my own Subway sandwich shop, for one," she says.

He looks at her hard. "Come on, be serious."

"I *am* serious," she replies. "This boy from my class, Robby Robinovitz, his dad owns the Subway on Twenty-third and Seventh Avenue and makes a ton of money. And Robby can have any kind of sandwich he wants at any time. He has them delivered to the school for lunch. That's the way he makes friends, ordering them free sandwiches. It's the only thing people like about him 'cause Robby's kinda a sickening flab. Hands are always sticky, like he's just sneezed in them. Or worse. Oh, Christ." She jumps, like she's been hit with a jolt of electricity. "Mother may I!" she says, looking past Morris, toward the building.

"What?" He turns to see what she's looking at.

"Is that a rat?" she asks.

Near the trashcans, there's a scraping noise, then movement, dark and hurried. "Oh God, it's a rat," she says, leaping at Morris. She locks her legs around his waist, arms to his neck. It nearly brings him down. "Kill it," she says, her voice pitched. "Kill it."

Morris staggers a step, two. "Get off me," he tells her.

"Kill it!"

"Get off!"

Stefani lets go, slides off him. "It ran down that way," she says, motioning toward the precinct. "I saw it run." She shivers, holds herself. "God I hate rats. They're worse than horny cousins, the way you got to fight them off," she says. "This one time, we had a rat in our building. It used to hang outside our apartment's door, like he smelled the frozen pizzas my dad always heated up. You had to look through the peephole before opening the door, make sure it wasn't waiting. The Super wouldn't do anything, so my dad put out those sticky traps and the other kind, the kind that snap, put them all around our door. But rats are smart. Or this one was smart. Nothing worked.

"So this one morning," she continues, "my dad heard the rat scratching outside our door and got so angry that he grabbed a mop and went and killed it himself."

"He killed it with a mop?"

"Well," Stefani says, "he *tried* to kill it. He went out in the hall naked except for his underwear and the rat was sitting there with this 'What do you want?' look and my dad whacked it with the mop, but it's one of those sponge mops, you know, so it doesn't hurt the rat much."

Morris's skin prickles. Rats he can handle; it's the thought of Jetski in his underwear that gives him pause.

"After he hit it, the rat took off. Cut down the stairs. But my dad chased after it. He gave it another good wallop, really hard, you know, and somehow, the rat got hooked on the mop. Its tail or something wrapped around the handle, and as my dad yanked the mop, the rat came flying up, doing flips and twists like a gymnast or something. And for a split second," Stefani says, "for a tiny, split second, the rat came face level with my dad." She holds her hand horizontal to her nose. "Came up to right here," she says. "They looked each other in the eye." She claps her hands. "My dad said he's never seen so much evil as he saw in that rat's eyes. Then the rat fell down the middle of the stairwell, hitting the banisters as he went down, *bang, bang, bang*," she says. "When my dad went down to look, the rat was gone."

Stefani pulls her brush from her purse, rhythmically strokes her hair. Her tone shifts. "I don't mean much to you, do I? I'm just another girlfriend to you," she says. "One of probably three zillion you've had."

"Three zillion's on the high end," he says. One of three was closer to the truth.

Aside from the awkward school dance date and or the homely girl he was paired off with at a church function, Morris's first girlfriend was in eleventh grade. Mandi Haggisbottom. They dated for only two weeks, but it was an intense two weeks.

Raised in a military family—her father and both her brothers served in the Army—Mandi entered Morris's high school as a transfer student in the spring semester. She sat directly in front of Morris in German class. Her hair, a deep auburn, the color of dead leaves, was cut in a severe Dorothy Hamill-style that left her pale neck exposed. At the base of her skull was a mole that looked like a chewed licorice Ju-Ju Bee or a replica of a Hawaiian island, a mole that emerged each time she got a hair cut, like a rock at low tide, then would slowly, slowly disappear under a growth of hair with each passing day. Sitting behind her in class everyday, Morris got a terrible, urgent desire to poke her mole with a sharpened pencil, to see how it reacted, if it broke open. To see if she even felt the prick of the lead. He imagined what she'd look like naked, wondered if she had any more moles, if they glowed large and dark against her watery, white skin.

Mandi was always formal, terse, even addressed her teachers as "Sir," no matter their gender, a habit Ms. Strom, the German teacher, found irritating. For the mid-semester class project, Mandi, Morris and two other girls were assigned to perform *Little Red Riding Hood* in

German. Mandi took charge of the venture, arranging the practices at her house after school, where her mother would lay out after-school snacks of caramel popcorn and black pepper cookies and then disappear into the kitchen to nip on her vodka and ice tea.

That first practice, Mandi established the roles. "I'm the hunter," she informed the group. "I'm the one who kills the wolf."

"I guess that means I'm the wolf," Morris said, unhappy because the wolf had the second largest amount of lines. Only Red Riding Hood had more.

"Tammy'll play the wolf," Mandi said, and forcefully landed a hand on Tammy's shoulder like she needed to be reminded who she was. Tammy was born for the part. She looked like a wolf, with a long, pointed jaw and sharp eye-teeth that flashed when she smiled.

Morris said, "But that means—"

"We're relying on you," she answered. "You've the most important part. Odile will play the grandmother, and you, you'll play the title character, Red Riding Hood."

Morris protested. "No way am I playing a girl. You play Red Riding Hood, I'll be the hunter."

Mandi's body went taut and she instantly seemed taller, larger than Morris, bigger than anyone else in the room. "I play the hunter," she said, her voice clear and cutting. Her focus fell cutting on Morris, bore into him like a scorching, blue-tipped skewer hitting a brick of butter. "I kill the wolf," she told him. "Is that understood? Do we all have an understanding?"

"I'm not playing Red Riding Hood," Morris said, though not as firmly as before.

"This is not up for discussion," she said, and ended the rehearsal. "Same time tomorrow," Mandi told the group, then dismissed everyone. "Have your lines memorized. As of tomorrow, no looking at the script," she said, leading the two girls to the door.

Morris followed, determined to quit the group, to demand that Ms. Strom give him a different set of partners.

"You," Mandi said, stopping Morris before he left. She grabbed him by the wrist. "Follow me," she said, and directed him to her bedroom, which had a sterile feel. The walls were bare, the bed tightly made. Nothing was out of order, no shoes or bra or *Seventeen* magazines lying about. The entire room was in muted, earth colors, like a hotel room off an abandoned highway.

Closing the door behind her, she stepped up to Morris and said, "I want a good grade on this project, and to get a good grade, we need to present a single front here. We need to all be together."

"I'm not playing Riding Hood," Morris said again, unable to look her in the face. "I'm not playing a girl."

Mandi's breath, smelling of Basel and anise, warmly brushed Morris face. "I need you on my team," she said, still holding his wrist. Gently, she placed his hand to her small breast. "You will play Red Riding Hood. Do we have an understanding?" she asked. She pressed her lips to his.

They had an understanding.

For two weeks, they practiced the play, Morris taking the lead of Red Riding Hood. Mandi held sway over the group, commanding and ordering them about, telling them how the lines should be executed, how the scenes should be blocked.

After each practice, after the other girls had left, Mandi lead Morris by his wrist to her room and went through roles not described in the script.

"I've got a great idea," Mandi said on their final night of practice. They were to perform the play the next day, a Friday, in class. "When we go to cut you open with a knife," she said, pointing to Tammy the wolf, "Odile should be under the table and squirt ketchup like it's blood. Spray it all over the place." No one voiced their thoughts, not knowing what to think. No one wanted to contradict her. "And I'll bring a liver, take it out of you, like I'm operating."

"Should we make a knife out of cardboard?" Tammy asked, looking to Morris, then to Odile. "I mean, to be safe."

"Cardboard?" Mandi asked. "*Nein, meine Kinder.* I'm not about to trade a grade for 'safety.' We want realism. We want a good grade."

Morris wanted to object to the knife, the ketchup, the liver, but the look on the other two girls' faces, a look of resignation and exhaustion, told him he'd get the same wilted, non-support he had gotten when objecting to having to play the role of Riding Hood. What do I care? he thought, not being the wolf, the one under the blade. All he cared about was getting practice over with and going to Mandi's room.

The next morning, Mandi arrived at school dressed in her father's camouflage fatigues. In a large, brown duffle bag she had a cow's liver, a squeezable bottle of ketchup, and an eight-inch butcher's knife. Over her shoulder was slung a .22 rifle.

Stopping Mandi in the hall, Mr. Stanley, the assistant principal, asked, "Is that a real rifle?"

"Props, sir," she answered. "In acting, they're called props." She unzipped her bag and showed Mr. Stanley the contents. "All of this is for Ms. Strom's German class, sir. We're doing a play, 'Little Red Riding Hood,' in German."

"It's awful realistic," Mr. Stanley said, warily eyeing Mandi.

"Thank you, sir. That is my intention," she answered, then excused herself. "I don't want to be late for class."

Everyone had their costumes: Morris wore a red blanket tied around his neck like a cape and a red stocking cap; Odile wore a frayed, brown crocheted shawl her mother had made and put flour in her hair to turn it white; Tammy wore black and frantically smiled her wolfish smile. The play went flawlessly, the lines spoken in stilted, basic German.

The rifle was aimed, the wolf killed. The knife was flashed and the blood was sprayed. The liver was extracted then Grandma and Red Riding Hood were rescued from the wolf's stomach.

Ms. Strom was terrified. The rifle, the knife, and the liver were real.

By the time the principal arrived, the play was complete. The class was clapping and hooting as Mandi and her props where escorted from the class, from the school. Morris, Tammy, and Odile spent the rest of the day in the principal's office. But their two weeks of acting, their practicing at pretending, paid off: they convinced him that they had no idea Mandi would bring *real* weapons to school.

All three received a stern warning. Mandi received a transfer to a school for violent and troubled children. And for the rest of the semester, Morris received malicious taunts for having played Red Riding Hood.

After high school, he had a brief relationship with a girl named Cheryl he met at a City College information open house. A junior in the mathematics department, Cheryl wanted to eventually work for the government or for the WTO. Morris was contemplating pursuing a degree in French or Spanish or Russian, a degree that would help him in all his travels, all the places he planned to go. Cheryl showed him around the campus, talked about her trip to Mexico the spring break prior. She worked her way through college, bartended at Loopy Larry's, a sticky bar near Columbia University that had all-you-can-eat nacho night and Jell-O shots, a bar that catered to the college crowd. She was friendly, open, liked to talk and laugh. After the tour, Morris asked if she'd be interested in getting a coffee. She said yes. They got along. He asked her out for the night next. They started dating, being boyfriend and girlfriend, but after a few months, she developed a tongue lesion. Open sores sprung out on her hands and arms. Her body was sensitive; it hurt when Morris touched her. Morris was worried, told her she should go to the doctor. She was strange and evasive about the whole thing, like it didn't exist. "What are you talking about?" she kept saying, her arms folded to hide her hands.

Morris decided against college, worried that class responsibilities would keep him from his travels. He didn't date Cheryl anymore, worried he might catch what she had.

It wasn't until he was twenty-five that Morris found his next girlfriend. He was riding with the Department of Transportation pothole crew, his first real job, a job his father secured for him through his union connections, drinking buddies, and low-level blackmail. It paid well. Morris hated it. Day after day, he rode out with a crew to fill potholes, repair damaged streets, smooth pavements all over the city, in all the boroughs. The smell of heating asphalt, the smell of the other men, sweaty and ripe, the violent rattle of the jackhammer, and the exhausting labor made him light headed, ill. He dropped tools, couldn't properly operate machinery. He wasn't built for such work, didn't thrive in grueling conditions like his father did.

On the team was Lilly, a sturdy, twenty-year old Haitian woman whose job it was to wave an orange flag, stop traffic, direct it around the work crew, making certain none of the men got run over. All the guys on the crew playfully hit on, harangued, and harassed her. It was part of the game, what one had to endure when working on the team. She took it in stride, ignoring what she wanted to ignore, firing back a vicious verbal assault when provoked.

Morris greeted her as he greeted everyone on the crew each morning, told her to take care at the end of the shift, but said little else to her during the workday. And at the end of each day, she'd decline the men's offers to go for a beer and headed home to her apartment on West 122nd Street.

Into his fourth month on the job, Morris had an exceptionally arduous day. Seven calls for problem potholes, all which they fielded.

He didn't want to go home after work, didn't want to spend the evening alone. He wanted company, someone to talk with aside from this father or N.J., someone with something more interesting than what the guys on the crew talked about.

Clocking out, he said goodnight to Lilly, then, with the bolstered courage of a bank robber, asked Lilly if she wanted to see a movie or maybe grab some dinner.

To his surprise, she said yes.

"Great," Morris said. "How about—" He broke off, drawing no ideas as to what to do. Lilly suggested they go to Hooters on Fifty-Fifth Street. "They have a buffalo wing special until seven," she said, her English so heavily accented it was nearly indiscernible. While Hooters wasn't Morris's ideal, he agreed. He wanted company.

Working on their third plate of wings and their second pitcher of beer, Lilly said, "I always wanted to be a Hooters girl, to work here and wear the orange T-shirt." Celery, sauce, and wadded, sauce-smeared napkins littered the table. "Just think of the money, the tips."

"Why don't you?" Morris asked, his fingers stained a bright, spicy red. Lilly was pretty, but not in a Hooters-pretty way. She had rugged, healthy features, like a well-handled carving, the patina smooth, shiny, radiant.

"My English isn't good enough, and because," she said, taking a sip of beer, "my family would kill me if they knew I worked at such a place."

"They'd rather you do dangerous manual labor?" Morris said, somewhat joking. The flag job was the easiest of jobs. Women and the working injured were given that task. It was like being a majorette for a marching band, whipping the plastic flag about all day. Even the crew's foreman, a lazy, religious man who held work as a sin, did more on the job than Lilly.

"As long as I keep sending money home, they don't care about the danger. But something like this," she said, lifting her eyes to a waitress. She shook her head. "Working here would really be dangerous. If word got back to my family that I was doing this, waiting table dressed like that, my mother would personally swim from Haiti to murder me."

Morris laughed, then saw she was serious.

"Sometimes love is too much," Lilly said, finishing the last wing.

It was after seven when they left. Morris didn't want the evening to end. Neither did Lilly. She enjoyed having someone to talk to, someone who wasn't making crude jokes or being vulgar. Someone who wasn't a fellow countryman. "You'd think being in a different country, we'd all watch out for each other," she said of Haitians, of the community. "Help each other. But it's the fellow countryman who's the first to rob you, the first to kick you to the pavement, the first to kill you for nothing."

After an awkward moment of silence, Morris took her hand to say good-bye. It was rough, callused, the hand of someone used to work. "I had a good time," he said.

"Why's it ending?" she asked.

Morris had no answer.

She invited him back to her place, where she played her favorite albums and showed him pictures of her youth, growing up on the island.

They began spending time together after work and on the weekends, though they kept a cordial distance during work, not wanting the others to know. Not wanting to endure the hazing.

"Lilly's such a pretty name," Morris said one morning as they lay in bed together. He wore cargo pants, a tank top, and a pair of sneakers. "Why do you sleep with your shoes on?" she asked the first night he stayed over. After they'd had sex, Morris had showered, dressed. Lilly thought he was leaving, but he crawled into bed with her.

"Just in case," he told her.

"Just in case?" she asked, wrapping her arm around him.

"Yeah," he said.

"Of what?"

"Emergencies," he said.

"Emergencies?"

"Yeah."

She laid her face to his. There'd been many things she'd experienced; this was another. She didn't press the issue. Sleeping fully dressed was just something he did.

"My birth name is Anchorage," Lilly told him.

"Anchorage?"

"It was my father idea," she said. "He'd been there once, when he worked on a cargo ship, and thought Alaska the most beautiful place in the world, the whiteness, the cold." Pausing a moment, she said, "My father always said that Haiti would be beautiful if it weren't for the Haitians. It has everything, he'd tell us," she said, resting a dark arm against Morris's slim chest. "But they're things you don't want.

"My name, Lilly," she continued, "the name I go by now, is the name I picked when I first came here. I was fifteen when I first got here, and was very sick, to the point of dying. Some infection. I couldn't hold food. Even water made me ill. Someone brought Mrs.

Rethco to me. She was a nurse, worked at a clinic. She knew what was wrong with me, was able to get me drugs that helped. I would sleep for nearly the whole day, wake only for the medicine. Slowly, slowly, I got better." She paused. "I never liked the name Anchorage," she said. "So I took my new name from the red pills that saved me. On each one was written 'Eli Lilly.' "

"Did you think of taking the nurse's name? She saved you as much as the medicine did," Morris said.

"Her name was Bertha," Lilly said, making a face. "Anchorage is bad, but Bertha?"

It wasn't a raging love, but Morris's heart was with Lilly. She'd endured so much. He felt tethered to her. She made him happy, content. He could see a life together.

As they lay there, a long, pleasant silence building between them, Morris listened to the gaining morning, to the day turning. It was a security, a peace he hadn't felt in some time, in years. It was a security he hadn't felt since he was a child, since his mother's death. He didn't want to leave the bed, didn't want to get up and shower and pull on stiff clothing and go to work. He wanted to remain where he was, with Lilly's arm across his chest, barring him from leaving, barring the world from getting to him.

Then Lilly said, "My husband is coming back next week. He called from Florida and said he is coming back home."

Morris laughed.

"It's true," she quietly said.

Morris laughter hardened in his throat. "You're married?" he asked, a metallic taste coating his mouth.

She explained; she'd married for her citizenship, had to marry to stay in the country, and had lived with this man for six months before he left to Florida to work at a dog track. She hadn't heard from him in over two years.

Now he'd called. He was coming home.

"But this isn't his home," Morris said, glancing about the apartment. Everything had become so familiar, comforting. The home was his and Lilly's. He'd left his mark on the place, he felt.

"No?" Lilly asked. "Then whose home is it?"

Ours, Morris wanted to answer. It's ours.

But it wasn't. He knew it wasn't. It was hers, Lilly's, and whoever she decided to share it with.

Lilly made coffee, made breakfast as she always had before work. Nothing seemed changed for her. Morris gathered his things. They'd leave for work at different times, ten minutes apart, so as to not show up together. "See you at work," she called to him as he left. She wouldn't.

Morris skipped work that day, and the next, and the following, spending his time in bed. Lilly called but Morris didn't answer the phone. On the fourth day, his father came to his bedroom and said, "What are you doing? You sick or something?"

Morris told him the story. He concluded, "Lilly's married, Daddy."

"You talking about that black girl that waves the flag?" Seymour asked. "Hell yeah, she's married. Everyone knows she's married. I don't even know her and I know she's married."

After a week of not showing for work, Morris was fired.

"What's your plan now?" his father asked, angry that Morris gave up such a solid job. "What're you going to do now?"

Morris had money saved. He had no responsibilities. "Travel," he told his father. "I'm going to travel."

The farthest he went was to Mr. Charlies, for provisions. He went nowhere.

After ten months, his money dwindled. He got the job at Saint Mark's Used Books, a job that lasted him nine years until his allergies laid in.

Now, again unemployed, he asks Stefani, "What other plans do you have?" He can't envision Stefani running a business.

"I've a lot of plans," she says.

"But none that I fit in."

"You just don't seem..." She pauses, searching for the word.

"I don't seem what?"

A fire truck heaves past, its lights and siren cold. "You know," Stefani says, "you just don't *seem*."

"What's that mean, I don't *seem*?"

"Before I forget," she says, ignoring him, "I got you a gift." The purse opens. Out comes a twelve-inch wheel of Brie in Saran Wrap. She hands it to him.

"You got me Brie?" It's soft, like warm clay, and has a tangy odor.

"No," Stefani says. "It's cheese. French, I think," she says. "It's expensive stuff."

"Where'd you get it?"

"Mr. Charlies."

"You bought this at Mr. Charlies?" he asks, not surprised he'd carry Brie.

"I didn't exactly buy it," she says, smiling.

"You stole it?"

"That asshole owed me," she says. "He robbed me of that twenty you gave me, didn't give me any change. So I went back in there and, you know, did some shopping to make up for it. Those twins he has working there are all shout and no chase. They didn't even try to stop me."

"But he knows who you are, knows I know you," he says, guilty. Few things he holds as wrong—stealing is wrong.

She shrugs. "So? He stole from me first. And anyway, it's not like we're ever going back there."

A drunken couple mill by, the woman carping at the man. "You were staring at her breasts all night!" the woman keeps saying. The man says nothing, stumbles along. A taxi honks. Another follows suit.

Stefani pokes Morris in the stomach. "Okay," she says, standing close.

"Okay what?" He feels held in a fatal gravitation, trapped in a collapsing orbit. He wants Stefani to stay and go, wants his old life and wants to be cured of it.

"Just, you know, *okay*," she says, then, "Give me a kiss."

"Does that fit in your plans? I don't want to ruin your plans."

"It won't ruin them," she says, smiling. "I'll make it fit." She kisses him once, then turns and heads off toward First Avenue.

"Where you going?" he asks.

"Guess what I'm thinking," she calls to him, walking away backward.

A feral, orange cat hobbles down the street, a small piece of fried chicken in its jaws.

Morris's fingers sink into the Brie.

"Guess. What. I'm. Thinking!" She pauses at the corner.

"What are you thinking?" he answers, though not loud enough for her to hear.

Still, she answers. "I'm thinking my plans might have changed," she calls to him. "I'm thinking you might be in my plans." She wiggles her fingers at Morris. "Remember Monday, after school. Ray's Pizza."

Ten

Stefani rounds the corner, is gone. Friday night is now officially early Saturday morning. The bars and clubs are peopled with those who've passed over or under a river to enter the City. They frantically drink off the week's worries, crafting what's to blossom into a crippling hangover.

From behind him, Morris hears, "Who's the girl, man?"

"Jesus," Morris says, startled. He spins around. It's N.J., dressed in an ill-fitting tuxedo. "You scared me," Morris says. "Where've you been all week, and what's with the bad tux? You getting married?"

"No, man, and that's the blessing. A pure blessing. Buy me a beer?"

Morris pauses. N.J. should be the one buying him a beer. He still owes Morris the ten dollars he borrowed last week, still owes him the thirty from three weeks prior. He owes Morris a lifetime of drinks. Looking at his friend N.J., he's pleased to see him. "One beer," Morris says. "But just one. I'm nearly broke."

They go to a Polish tavern a block away, the Old Homeplate, a place whose name conjures an image of baseball, sports. It has nothing to do with activity or exercise. It's a dive with a checkerboard patterned linoleum floor, a tilted pool table, and the odor of old tuna. Open at eight a.m., it serves until four in the morning.

There are only three others in the bar; silent, pensive men who are worn past use. Their money's out before them, their thick, rough hands resting next to their drinks. The front door stands open; the air inside is still, stagnant.

"What's with the cheese?" N.J. asks of the Brie Morris places on the bar. "Smells like it's turning, like it should be eaten now."

"It's a gift," he says, ordering two two-dollar draft beers from Mrs. Cruxo, the Old Homeplate's matriarch and owner. She has a face like a baked apple, shiny and wrinkled. Smoking a brown Nat Sherman cigarette, she sets the beers in front of them. Morris pays.

"A gift from that girl I saw, man?" N.J. asks. "The girl that looks like your mom?" ·

The comment rocks Morris; he fights to breathe. "My mom? Do you even remember what my mom looks like?"

"Yeah, like that girl, man," he says, taking a sip of beer. "At least a little. In the face. Maybe."

Morris coughs, turns the shade of bleached bone. "My mother?"

"Or maybe not," N.J. says, backing off. "Thinking about it, no. No, man. Not at all," he says, then, putting his hand on Morris shoulder, changes the subject. "All week, man," he says, "I've been risking my life. Mors, man, I swear, I'm lucky to just be sitting here. Mawmaw's, man, it saved me this afternoon," he says, his face filled with wonder, like he'd just been shown how an instant camera works for the first time. It's an affected look, like most of N.J.'s looks. It's something he's able to call forth; he's a consummate mattress salesman pushing flawed goods.

N.J. has fair, wholesome looks, like that of an off-Broadway actor or someone who works at Banana Republic. He has the looks of someone who enjoys eating corn on the cob and collecting matchbooks, someone you can trust. It's his one talent, the ability to make nearly anything he says seem true.

"Mawmaw's?" Morris asks, distracted. His thoughts are on Stefani, and on his mother.

N.J. nods. "It saved me from The Cyndi, man," he says, lifting his beer.

"It saved you from what?" Morris glances about the bar, feeling he's being watched. The three other men are held rapt by an infomerical on TV for a product that stops perspiration. Mrs. Cruxo absently stares into a middle-distance while picking at her teeth with the corner of a folded dollar bill.

No one's watching him.

"The Cyndi, man," N.J. says, like Morris should know.

Morris and N.J. have been friends forever, or for at least a long time. Met when they were ten, at the Asser Levy pool during open swim. It was one of the few times Morris's mother let him go alone. He was practicing his crawl stroke, swimming from one end of the pool to the other. N.J. worked to stay afloat. He fought the water like a man trying to climb a broken ladder, grabbing for rungs that weren't there. Morris, gracefully slicing the water, saw N.J. mid-depth, halfway between the bottom of the pool and the surface. His eyes were open, blazing with terror, and his mouth moved like a snake's whose head was lopped off.

Taking a deep breath, Morris dipped down and grabbed N.J. by the arm, giving him a tug toward the surface. N.J. spun with fright, grabbed Morris by the head, and tried to use him to climb his way from the water.

They both struggled.

They both sank. Morris panicked, the air exploding from his lungs. He elbowed N.J. in the stomach, scratched at his face, and then, in a violent burst of energy, sprang from the pool's floor, rocketing both he and N.J. to the surface and the side of the pool.

The lifeguard, an obese girl with the face of a pumpkin and a thick back pinched in a faded red one-piece swimsuit, stood at the pool's edge, looking down at them. She blew her whistle twice, motioned at them both, and shouted, "Quit the horseshit rough-housing."

Yanking them by their gangly arms, she pulled them free of the water, dropped them onto the pool deck.

Coughing fiercely, N.J. shot a stream of chlorinated water and snot from his nose, spraying the lifeguard across the crotch. "Sorry, man," he told her between gasps, then turning to Morris, said, "Thanks."

They were banned from the pool for the rest of the day.

Morris's Adam's apple ached, his lungs felt charred by rubbing alcohol. Shaken, Morris toweled off and quickly dressed.

Heading out the door, Morris found N.J. waiting on the steps. "Man," he said, "that was weird. Like sleeping in a mound of mud. I guess I owe you my life or something like that."

"Forget it," Morris said. He meant it. The one time he goes to the pool by himself he nearly drowns. He didn't want it mentioned again.

N.J. trailed Morris home, talking a storm about anything and everything, finishing his tales with a story about how his father once shot him in the stomach with a Civil War-era rifle. "Should have killed me, man," he said, "but it didn't even break the skin. Did get an itchy rash, though.

"This your place?" he asked when Morris stopped before his apartment building. "I live on Fourth Street, next to the record store. Wanna check out my Spanish sword collection?" he asked.

Morris said no, but from that day forward, N.J. was a part of his life.

Leaving his building or coming home from school, Morris would find N.J. sitting in the low branches of the tree out front. "Wanna see where some woman's brains got exploded?" he'd ask, or, "Want me to show you where I saw two naked Mexican guys doing sick stuff to each other?"

Morris steered clear of him for weeks on end, thinking him irritating, bad luck. But N.J. didn't give up.

"Hey, man, I know how to get some free ice cream," he called to Morris from the tree one afternoon. "Want to come?"

Morris paused. What could it hurt? "Sure," he finally said. "Sure, let's get some free ice cream."

It wasn't free. Morris ended up spending his allowance on the both of them. Yet, like coffee, Morris slowly acquired a liking for N.J. Soon, he grew to need him.

"So what's The Cyndi?" Morris asks N.J, wondering what's real in his friend's life, what's not. Wondering if N.J. believes half the bullshit he spills. "What's a Mawmaw's?"

"It's all about economics, man," N.J. says. "How people spend money, what they spend it on. It's all about the way people spend *other* people's money."

"Like my buying you a beer because you're always broke?" Morris says.

"Not broke, man," he says, "just frugal." N.J. has an occupation but no job; he is a skip tracer, a bounty hunter, though his first and only catch happened over six years ago, and it was more by accident than skill or design.

N.J. bagged Chi Thomas, a tiny man with frail features who lived across the hall from him. Chi stood only five foot tall, and had a gut that made his gait more a waddle than a walk. N.J. and Chi had become drinking buddies, spent long afternoons that drained into evening sitting in N.J.'s cluttered studio sipping beer and listening to scratchy records N.J. found on the street.

One evening, after they'd split five forty-ounce beers, Chi drunkenly bragged that he'd been busted for robbing a grocery store, had jumped a twenty thousand dollar bail.

"Bullshit, man," N.J. told him.

"Scout's honor," Chi said, making a peace symbol with his free hand.

"Twenty thousand bail," N.J. said, pouring the last of the beer in Chi's McDonald's supersized plastic tumbler. "Where'd you get that kind of money for bail?"

"It's all Ceetle's, my bail bonds guy. Or most. My Ma threw down two thousand. Ceetle's Bail Bonds," Chi said, then sings, " 'When you're down, we get you out.' " He smiled. He was drunk. "That's their slogan."

"Tell me the story, man," N.J. said, opening the last beer and refilling Chi's tumbler. "Tell me the whole thing."

Closing time one Saturday night, with the grocery store near empty, Chi crawled onto a floor-level shelf of soups and hid by placing the cans all around him. "I was smaller then," he says, burping. He patted his hard, round stomach. "Not like now. I could fit anywhere, could fit inside a drier, a suitcase. Use to scare the shit out of my Ma by popping out of the oven." When the store closed and only the manager was left, Chi came out of hiding. "I threatened him with a bottle of Clamato juice," he said. "I once dated a Dominican who drank that stuff like Champaign. Drank it all the time with gin. Swore it was an aphrodisiac. She was beautiful, but her breath got so bad after a couple of those, like rotting vegetables on a tar beach, that I couldn't even kiss her." He shakes his head, remembering. "What was I talking about?"

"The grocery store, man."

"Right. Yeah, so I waved a bottle of Clamato juice at the manager and told him to give me the money or he'd be sorry. What a sad push-over. He gave me the money, something like seventeen hundred dollars and a bunch of food stamps. I grabbed two six-packs and walked out free and easy."

Chi started rocking, like he was on a subway rounding a bend. "I got tripped up at church the next day," he said, then finished off his beer. N.J. refilled his tumbler again. "The store manager was a member of my church, saw me the next morning. The cops came just as the collection plate was going around." Chi held up a finger, making a point. "I thought...I thought he looked familiar, but..." He fell silent, glanced about the apartment, confused. Taking a deep swallow of beer, his face went rubbery and empty of thought. "I need a nap," he said, and rolled heavily onto the floor. "Ten minutes. A quick nap," he muttered, then passed out.

N.J. prodded him in the belly. "Hey, man, don't get sick or anything." Chi vomited on N.J.'s shoe, across his floor.

"Goddamn it, man."

Chi vomited again, splattering N.J.'s bed.

Irate, N.J. found Ceetle's Bail Bonds phone number. "I got someone here you might want, man," N.J. told Ceetle.

He and Ceetle carried Chi down to the ninth precinct, turned him in. N.J. got a thousand dollars for the tip.

He's fancied himself a skip tracer ever since.

N.J. tugs at the lapels of his tux. "Like Medusa and a mirror, man, the economics of Mawmaw's broke the curse of The Cyndi," N.J. says. "Nearly had to use this monkey suit, man."

Morris feels drunk, uncertain. Extremely tired. He has no idea what N.J.'s talking about. "N.J., I have no idea what you're talking about," he says, standing to leave. All he wants is sleep, his pillow and home. "Call me tomorrow."

"Mawmaw's is a buffet up in Harlem, man," N.J. clarifies, finishing his beer. "The Cyndi was my fiancée."

Morris stops. "Your fiancée?"

"Why do you think I've got the tux for, man? I was getting married today." He pulls out a wad of papers from his pocket and hands Morris a folded document. It's a marriage license made out to Newton Ralph Jerzy and Cynthia von Swartz.

"Who's Cynthia?"

"The Cyndi, man, the love of my life—until I saw the viper's fangs at Mawmaw's."

Morris is pained. "You were getting married and you didn't even tell me."

"It all happened so quick, man."

"You could've called. You could've said, 'Morris, I'm getting married.' " He studies the marriage license. "How long have you been dating this woman?"

"The Cyndi," N.J. says, signaling Mrs. Cruxo for two more beers. "I've known The Cyndi since Sunday, met her at church."

"Sunday?" Morris asks. "Six days ago?"

"I like to think of it as a week, man."

"A week," Morris says, feeling displaced, caught in a joke. This is his best friend, a supposed known entity. He seems a stranger. "When have you ever gone to church?" he says. "And this woman, did you even have time enough to find out her middle name?"

"Von," N.J. answers. He points to the marriage license. "Her middle name is von. Cynthia von Swartz." Then he adds, "A week can be a long time. Rome was ravaged in less time. The Seven-Day War changed the landscape of the Middle East. A lot can happen in a week, man."

"A lot of destruction, you mean. And it was the Six-Day War that happened in the Middle East."

"God created the world in a week," N.J. says, then, "But what's important is that it didn't happen; I didn't get married. I was saved." He explains. "We had a four o'clock appointment with the judge to get married. The hottest state, man, The Cyndi and I. Really into each other. We were on each other like plaid on polyester, man. Morning,

noon, night. Her place is in Harlem, so we go to Mawmaw's for
lunch this afternoon, a pre-wedding meal. Mawmaw's is the best soul
food buffet in the city, man. No kidding. Four dollars and twenty-five
cents a pound buffet. Except for chitlins, which cost more. Great stuff.
So at the buffet, she loads up on rice and beans. Nothing else. Not the
ribs, not the greens, not the pulled pork. Nothing. Just the cheap,
heavy stuff, man. Her meal ended up being seven dollars, all for
beans and rice, man! And I was the one paying for it. We were
suppose to marry in less than three hours and I suddenly saw it all,
man, saw the true colors of The Cyndi. I broke it off then and there.
How could I marry a woman who has no problem paying seven and
change for a plate of beans and rice?" N.J. shakes his head.
"Mawmaw's, man, it saved me. The economics of Mawmaw's."

Two fresh beers are set before them. Mrs. Cruxo looks to Morris
for money. Grudgingly, he pays. Economics, Morris ruefully thinks.
The spending of other people's money.

"Who's the girl I saw you with, man?" N.J. asks, dipping into
his second beer. "She stalking you?"

"Stalking? No. Why?"

"She just seems like a stalker, man." He prods the Brie. "Was
this a gift or a threat?" he asks. "The thing stinks. Reminds me of that
one woman I use to date. She smelled, man. Not a specific, put-your-
finger-on-it stink, not like she wore too much perfume or used cheap
shampoo or even had one of those after-a-workout-sweaty smells.
She just smelled. You remember her?"

Morris shook his head. "No."

"It wasn't a really *bad*, bad smell," N.J. says. "It was subtle, man,
like something misted on her. Or no, something *in* her. Like in her
skin, you know, coming from her pores. A weird, spicy kinda smell,
like that soup at Indian restaurants that always upsets me. She
smelled like that. That, and fried butter. I kept having these stomach
and bowel problems each time we hung out, man. Ended up having
to see a doctor because of her smell. It was a part of her. She couldn't
get rid of it. Even if she showered, I could smell it. It was her—what
are they called?—Federalmoans."

"Pheromones," Morris corrects him, then adds, "You remember Jetski, that guy from high school?"

"Jetski? You mean that wiry kid with the hair lip who spit when he talked?"

"No," Morris says, unable to think of who he means.

"Oh, man, I know who you mean," N.J. says, rapping the bar. The three other patrons turn and look at him. "The guy who got his finger ripped off by that lathe in shop class. Frankenfinger. That thing never looked real after they sewed it back on."

"Yeah," Morris says, having forgotten about that. "That's him."

"Ol' Frankenfinger," N.J. says. "The guy's an asshole, man. Use to work at the movie theater on Twelfth Street. Once tried to sell me popcorn he'd swept off the floor. Real asshole, man." He downs the rest of his beer in a single swallow.

"Yeah, well, that girl you saw," Morris says, "that's his daughter."

"Your girlfriend is Jetski's daughter? Shit, man, how old is she, fifteen?"

"Eighteen," Morris says, flush with embarrassment. "And she's not my girlfriend."

"Well thank God for that, man." He orders a third round.

"Why?"

"If she was, I'd have to tell you to dump her, man," N.J. says, unwrapping the Brie. He takes out a small Buck knife, cuts a thin wedge of cheese. "My advice, man," he says, licking the cheese off the blade, "would be to dump her quick."

"Like I said, we're not dating," Morris says.

N.J. gives him a flat, perplexed look. "So you're not dating her?" N.J. asks, savoring the cut of cheese.

The light in the bar is dim and failing and somehow reminds Morris of Coney Island in the early morning hours. "Just dig in, feel free," Morris offers of the cheese, then, "No, I'm not dating her."

"But you slept with her."

"Listen, I met her today at—"

"Yes or no, man."

"Okay, yes. I did. But what's that have to do with anything?" he asks, but already know the answer. It has everything to do with it.

"I thought so, man," N.J. says. "I can tell things like that." The third round is set before him. N.J. cuts another slice of Brie, offers it to Mrs. Cruxo. "Give this a try," he tells her. She accepts, sniffs it, then takes a small bite.

"You know you can't mail maps in India," N.J. tells the both of them, pointing with his knife. "It's illegal, man. Isn't that crazy? If you get caught mailing a map in India, they throw you in jail for five years."

Morris gazes at N.J.'s marriage license. "I still can't tell what's real with you," he says. "Even after all these years knowing you, I don't know what to believe."

N.J. places a hand on Morris's shoulder. "One thing I learned when living in Cuba, man," N.J. says, "is that keeping a hundred percent true to a tale isn't what's important. It's the story that's important, the moral. Whether it lingers and lives on after it's been told. That, man," N.J. says, "is what's important."

All three are silent. N.J. looks to Morris. Mrs. Cruxo looks to Morris, waiting to be paid for the beers. Noise and exhaust from the street slide in the open front door. Morris examines the even face of his best friend, the trustworthy features. "When have you ever been to Cuba?" Morris asks N.J. "When have you ever even left the city?"

Eleven

It's after three a.m. when Morris gets home. He quietly slides into the apartment, not wanting to wake his father. The door to the back room is closed; his father's asleep. In his bedroom, Morris wrestles off his boots, strips his clothes, then heads to the bathroom for a short, cool shower. After, he slips on a pair of jeans, a T-shirt, laces up his tennis shoes. He's ready to hit the street if he wants. He doesn't want to.

He's ready for bed.

N.J. had repeatedly told Morris to break-up with Stefani as he and Mrs. Cruxo worked through the Brie.

"There's nothing to break up," Morris replied.

"Just tell her it was a mistake," N.J. advised. "Tell her it was an oversight, man."

"An oversight?" Morris said. "You make it sound like it requires a congressional investigation."

"Basically, man," N.J. said, "you had sex. Two fancy animals doing what animals do. An act of nature. I'd get out of the relationship before the emotions get tangled. End it before it gets messy, man."

But it's already tangled, messy. Everything looks the same, but some silent, hidden change has happened, a chemical reaction that passed unnoticed to the naked eye. Something has happened that Morris can't fully comprehend.

Morris sees the photo of his mother. It stares out at him from his bureau. Picking it up, he searches for Stefani in it. Even N.J. noted the similarity. But there's no likeness, he tells himself, studying the photo. None at all. Stefani is nothing like his mother. Still, he turns the photo face down, fearing that, like those determined to find the image of the Virgin Mary in a snowcapped mountain, he'll start seeing resemblances that aren't there.

Outside on the street, a woman brays a painful laugh, like she's been stabbed and found it funny. The city is still alive, awake and roaming, even in the last hours of the night. As a child, Morris believed everyone followed the same schedule as him, all around the world; when he slept, the world slept. When he ate, the world ate. Now he knows different.

The faded world map spans his wall, a map he's had since he was fifteen. He'd saved his money to buy it, ordered it via mail from Rand McNally. It was compact, orderly, and tightly creased when it arrived. The whole world folded down to fit in a pocket. Excitedly he unfolded it. The map spanned most of his floor, the longitude and latitude lines cutting black arcs from one end to the other. Seeing the map spread open, he knew he would never be able to put it back the way it'd been.

Now, twenty years later, the map's secured to the wall with hundreds of colored pins marking the places Morris plans to go. Morocco, Madrid, Malta. He's got the fliers and brochures describing the places; he's going to visit them. Italy, England, Ecuador. They're on his list. Lisbon, Lima, Labrador. Sometime this summer, or in the fall, or this winter. Paris, St. Petersburg, Prince Edward Island.

He studies the gray pin puncturing Prince Edward Island, Canada. Why'd he mark it? He thinks and thinks, hoping to recall. *Anne of Green Gables*. He'd read the book. It was set there, Prince Edward Island. But why'd he marked his map? He didn't much like the story, or the setting, or even the character Anne. So why was the pin there?

Gripping the head with his fingers, he wiggles the pin back and forth until it comes free. "I'm never going to go there," he says, flush with awareness. His vision runs the world. He pulls the pin from Jaco, Costa Rica, a place where the waves were supposedly incredible to surf. Or so Morris has read. But Morris has never surfed, never even rode a skateboard, doesn't have the balance for such sport. Guinea, Africa? The place sounds interesting, and the lobsters there are incredible, he's read, but he's allergic to shellfish and sunburns easily. Caracas? Too much crime.

The pins fall from the map, one city after another, one country then the next, leaving a small, dark hole where the pin once was. Morris doesn't stop, can't stop. Never going there, or there, or there, he says to himself, pulling and pulling and pulling one pin after another, until none are left.

The last pin out, he quickly steps back, frightened by what he's done. Nothing holds the map to the wall, but it holds. Sheer force of habit; it's been there for years, for two decades, why should it leave now? Then the reality of gravity grabs it. The upper left corner of the map softly folds down, like a bed turned down for the night. Then the middle comes away and the map flaps to the floor, a large pelt torn from a long dead animal. In its absence is a perfect rectangle where the wall's been protected, the paint a cleaner, lighter shade. Hundreds of tiny pinholes. A star field in negative, the black holes littering the whiteness. A constellation in reverse.

A sextant, Morris thinks. It makes him think of the sailors of old, charting their path by the dark sky. If only he had a sextant, then he could plot his course.

The map lay crumpled on the floor, punctured and old. He runs his hand over the tiny holes in the wall. They're random, scattered. His mother's photo is face down. In thirty-five years he's never gone anywhere. Still, he feels lost.

Twelve

It's early; dawn arrives expectedly. Morris slept poorly, fitful and restless, kicked about all night with bad dreams. He kept jolting awake, then slipping back into the haze of sleep. He dreamt he was trapped in the middle of a protest march filled with thousands of people. Everyone looked the same, the men, the women, the children. It was a face he didn't recognize but somehow knew. "What are we protesting?" he kept asking. "Not on the floor!" was the response. To his left, right, and behind, a unison voice. "Please, not on the floor!" Creaks and footfalls, the noise of Sofar's pacing in the apartment above, sound-tracked his dream. The marching mass with Morris in the middle. "Dear God, someone's here," the woman beside him in his dream loudly whispered. "Someone's finally come."

Morris jerked awake. There was no one, his room empty, silent.

He brushes his teeth, changes out of his sleeping clothes and tennis shoes. Thankful the night had passed, he heads quietly into the kitchen, his stomach foul from all the beers at the Old Homeplate. One beer had turned to four, which dented his wallet. He drinks down a tablespoon of baking soda in water to settle his queasiness.

On top of the refrigerator is a large Mason jar full of coins. Gingerly he pours change onto the kitchen table, separating the quarters and dimes from the nickels and pennies. It's the last days of the boiler being on, the season warming. The radiators call to one another, the pipes banging a comfortable note. The apartment's dim and warm, a safe house from the world.

Outside, all is different. The air is vibrant, crisp. The sun clips the sky. Saturday. People are sleeping in late, their regrets of the night prior not yet born. The streets are empty, an eerie calm over everything. The occasional car or cab snaps by, the road their own. The synchronized stoplights click from green to yellow to red then start again.

Morris stops at Marcelo's Hot To-Go-Go, a storefront coffee spot with windows blurry from fried food vapors. Getting a coffee and a bacon, egg, and cheese sandwich to go, he pays in coins, then wanders west then south down the Bowery, past the cheap, ugly furniture stores, the stained-glass and lighting shops, past used restaurant supply places whose gutters are greasy and black.

In a vacant parking lot with advertised parking rates of $12.38 per hour, tax included, a frail, Pakistani man scatters breadcrumbs from a powder-blue Tiffany's bag. He's missing half his left hand and all his lower teeth. Cooing and clicking, he patiently waits for pigeons to arrive. Against the fence is his bike, a rickety beast made with cannibalized parts from other bikes and held together with electrical tape, metal coat hangers, and faith. Attached to the back is a cart cobbled together from a baby carriage and a rolling file cabinet. Three empty banana boxes are stacked on it.

The gray, brown, and white birds drop on the breadcrumbs, pecking and flapping as they circle and circle the ground for their share. When a solid sized flock has gathered, the birds turning and turning in a random pattern, the man grabs up a blue nylon fishing net and masterfully swings it out and over the flock, trapping nine birds. The others lift for the sky, fleeing with a beat of their wings.

With a swift yank, the man collects the netted birds and stuffs them in the banana boxes. Then, the process starts again. The crumbs, the wait, then the whip of the net.

Morris thinks to ask the man what he does with the captured birds, then he thinks better of it. Their fate, he imagines, is oven roasted over a plate of rice pilaf.

Turning back, Morris heads toward home.

The morning's spiced with the scent of spring and dampness. On Fifth Street, Morris sees the men and the construction dumpsters out front of the police precinct, ready for the day's work.

The place is finally coming down.

Since the police left, the building's been locked down. The police cars are no longer parked about the neighborhood, half on the sidewalk, half blocking the street. There's no longer traffic in and out of the front door. It seems so peaceful, calm, like the warming moments between dawn and the morning's first car alarm sounding.

Inside, it's anything but peaceful.

Three months prior, a crew of seven squatters climbed a tree at the back of the building and got onto the fire escape. They took the building the way a virus takes a body, have since been thriving there in secret.

Pausing in front to study the building, Morris feels a sharp sadness. It's always been there, an anchor of the neighborhood. A part of his life. Now, it's being replaced.

Morris hears his name yelled. "Bliss."

Turning, he sees a big man in brown Carhartt cover-alls striding toward him in a straddle-walk, like his thighs are chaffed.

It's Stefani's dad. "Jetski," Morris says, surprised.

"Jetski?" he says. His face sours. "I should wax your fucking tugboat, Bliss."

He comes at Morris fast. Morris instinctually braces, but instead of a hammering of fists, he finds himself in a one arm half-hug. Jetski's face presses into Morris's chest as he slaps his back. He laughs. "Jetski," he says, his face lit up. "Sweet baby Judas, Bliss, no one calls me Jetski anymore. I should take you down for that. You know I hate that nickname." His face is red, like he's shaved off the first few layers of skin, and he smells of wet wool and rubbing alcohol. "Twisted Bliss. How you been?"

Stunned, Morris hesitantly answers, "Good." His body's still clinched.

"This is a reunion, my Bliss," Jetski says, excitedly. "This is great. How are things, things good?"

"Yeah," Morris says, relaxing slightly. Jetski doesn't know, Morris realizes. He doesn't know about him and his daughter, Stefani. "Well, it was good seeing you," Morris says, turning.

"I hear what you're saying, Bliss," he says, getting in Morris's way. "It's good seeing you, too. We should go out for a beer sometime. Or I should have you over, meet my family."

Morris sees it clearly; he, Jetski, and Stefani all in the same room. He sees the ugliness. "What are you doing over here?" he asks, trying to work past Jetski. Jetski keeps tacking, staying in front of him. "I thought you lived—" Morris pulls up short. He knows exactly where he lives. Stefani told him. "I thought you lived elsewhere."

"This is my show," Jetski says, pointing to the police precinct with his reattached finger. Frankenfinger. It's crooked, bent, points off the left of where he's indicating. "These are my men." He motions to the crew. "I'm the project foreman, Bliss. I'm in charge of taking the building down. Priority project stuff. Got us working Saturdays for the next few months," Jetski says, his red face still glowing with joy from seeing Morris. "They set a deadline, then make you wait and wait and wait. Then the assholes expect the deadline held." Jetski's gotten heavier since high school, gained thirty or so pounds; there's a hint that he might once have been handsome. He never was. Stefani's his girl, a concept that chills Morris. It's a small evolutionary step from the naked woman that was in his room yesterday to the man before him. Thankfully, Jetski and Stefani share only their hair color. They look nothing alike.

Jetski asks, "Whatever happened to you?"

"What do you mean?"

"We use to be tight, good friends. But after high school, you disappeared."

"Well, you know," Morris says. They were never tight. Morris hated him in high school. "Things happen. I've been—" He breaks off, realizing he's about to give an answer by rote—*I've been traveling.*

"Things happen," Jetski says, nodding. "That's solid fact. Things happen," he says, then, "Shit, you remember the Bloody Eagle Brigade? I tell my wife and daughter that story all the time."

"No," he says. "I don't."

"Oh, come on, Bliss. The Bloody Eagles." He playfully jabs Morris in the ribs. It hurts. "You and me. Remember? All the hi-jinx. You, Morris the Professor, coming up with the plot, and me, the axe man, getting the job done. Remember all the shit we use to pull?" There's a longing, a faint desperation in Jetski's voice.

"We never really hung—"

"Twisted Bliss and the Bloody Eagle Brigade. We were famous in high school. Shit, remember that time we put black shoe polish on the girls' bathroom toilet seats, or when you Super-glued Mr. Arnold's chair to his desk?"

"No."

"Yes you do, Bliss."

"Actually, no, I really don't."

"The Bliss and Stevie J. The Bloody Eagles, baby. You remember."

Morris relents, lifts his head, giving a noncommittal half nod.

"I really miss that, Bliss. All those times. But now's now, you know what I'm saying?" Jetski says. "Got a wife, a teenage daughter. But I make good money." His voice turns tired. He glances about, like he's gaining his bearings. "What are you doing now?" he asks, his initial excitement wearing down. "Where you working?"

"I'm between jobs," Morris says.

"Bliss, you should've called me. I could've gotten you on here. You should've talked to me last week," Jetski says. "Let's do some beers. How about tonight? Let's go have some drinks and catch up."

"Tonight?" Morris asks. "Ah, well, the truth is, I've got to watch my cash right now."

"Should've talked to me last week," Jetski says, shaking his head. "I'd've had a job for you." He pulls out his wallet. "Here's a tide-over," Jetski says, presses two twenties into Morris's hand. "Until you get going again."

"No, no," Morris says, embarrassed. This isn't the man Morris remembers. Jetski was never generous. "I can't take this." First his daughter, now his cash.

"Bliss," Jetski says, "take it." He gives Morris another awkward hug. The Frankenfinger digs into Morris's back. He feels sympathy and repulsion for Jetski. He's changed. "From one Bloody Eagle to another," Jetski says. "Hey, you up for seeing the precinct before I take it down?"

"Sure," Morris says, slowly pocketing the money. He'd spend a few minutes with Jetski, earn the money.

Hardhats on, they head up to the front doors of the precinct. Jetski pulls his keys.

"Finally taking her down," Jetski says. He runs his hand over the building's wall like he's petting an old horse. The building, a pale limestone quarried from Indiana, stands silent, large, as it has for over a century. "Haven't been in here for six months," he says. "Restrictions, permits, this person suing that person. A mess. Off limits to everyone. Couldn't do a thing until everything was approved. Well," Jetski says, "now there's no more bullshitting, right, Bliss? Got to do what the man says." Selecting a key on his overloaded key ring, he pops the large padlock off the thick, oak doors like he is christening a yacht. "Time to get dirty." With his steel-toed boots, he kicks the door open on the dark entry.

The smell of decay and dirty feet strikes them flat.

Morris's eyes tear. "Jesus, what is that?"

"Something dead, I'd say. The place needs some airing out," Jetski says, coughing. "Pretty bad, huh?"

Morris shakes his head. He pulls his shirt collar over his nose. "Not the smell. *That*." He motions to the pile of lockers, broken tables, and chair mounded in the center of the room. It's a barricade, a fortification built of items left in the precinct. "What's that?"

A voice sounds from the middle of the mess. "This is your one warning," a woman says, rising from the debris. "Leave, or suffer."

"Sweet baby Judas," Jetski says, startled by the figure. "Who the fuck are you?"

"We've been breached," the woman shouts, sending out the call. She strikes a flame with a Zippo lighter, holds it high above her head like she's at a rock concert. "Breach, breach," she cries again. There's a sound of scuffling as the others struggle from sleep and race to take up defensive positions. Two other squatters, bounding down the stairs, dive behind the barricade.

"You can't be in here," Jetski shouts at them. "This is a work site. Off limits." He steps into the foyer. Morris is right behind him.

"Remember the *Maine*," the woman yells, then dips down behind the barricade, the lighter still aflame.

"It's the Alamo, you asshole," Jetski says.

"Ignition," the woman shouts.

"Come on, Bliss," Jetski says, "we're cracking some heads." He strides forward, ready to drag all three squatters out on his own. But before he can take two full steps, an explosive wad of flaming red phosphorous tears across the dimness of the room and strikes him solid in the chest, like a chestnut fired from a crossbow. It scorches his cover-alls before dropping to the floor and fizzling out. "Mother of God," Jetski cries, slapping his smoldering front. "What the fuck was—"

Cheering, the squatters fire a second shot of burning traffic flare from their make-shift surgical elastic slingshot. The projectile clips Morris's pant leg then whizzes out onto the street, where it bounces into the middle of the waiting workers. They all scatter from the hissing spark.

"Jetski," Morris yells, dancing about. "I'm getting out of here." Another flare zings past, bangs against the front door.

"I hear you, Bliss." They cut a rapid retreat, hustle outside.

Trying to spark another flare, the woman fumbles her lighter, drops it on the stockpiles. A flare ignites, then another, the whole mound quickly bursting into a violent, blinding red. All three squatters roll from the barricade and stumble up the stairs.

The entire room is aglow in red, like a cut of raw tuna.

Jetski grabs the heavy oak doors and swings them shut. He loops the steel lock back through the chain, hammers the lock shut.

"The place is going to burn down," Morris says, terrified, exhilarated. He'd never been fired on. It felt like war, or what he imagines war to feel like.

"They won't be that lucky," Jetski says. The front of his cover-alls is charred black. "Burning to death would be a blessing for them, Bliss. It'd be the only way to kill the smell." He wipes his nose on his shirtsleeve, then flips open his cell phone to call the police. "Get the cops to clampdown on this," he says, then pauses. His red face lights up. He snaps the phone shut without making a call. "Pack it up for today," he yells to the workers. They look to each other, confused. "You'll get paid," he says. "Pack it up." They hurry off before Jetski changes his mind. "I got an idea, Bliss," he says to Morris, placing his arm on his shoulder. "I think the Bloody Eagle Brigade is going to pay someone a visit tonight," he says.

Thirteen ·

"Where you going looking like that?" Seymour asks, sitting at the kitchen table with a bag of peanuts and a beer. Dinner. Shells are scattered everywhere. The *Post* is open to the horse racing section.

Saturday night. Morris is clad in full black, his pants, T-shirt, shoes, and leather gloves. In his pocket is a ski mask.

Jetski had come up with the plan. "You fuck with a Bloody Eagle, you get the talons," he kept telling Morris. He'd sketched out the precinct on a waxy Dunkin' Donuts bag, the floors, stairwells, windows. He explained how they'd enter, how they'd proceed. "You're in with me, right Bliss? Tell me you're in," Jetski kept asking.

The plan was simple. It was absurd; it actually might work. "I just don't know," Morris said. Being with Jetski is something to avoid, but breaking into the police precinct is a rare opportunity.

"I need you on this, Bliss. The Bloody Eagles, baby," Jetski said, then, "I'll pay you for your time." He offered a hundred dollars.

Seymour works a peanut from between his teeth with a matchbook cover. "You go and paint your face white and you'd look like one of those French clowns," he says. He scrutinizes his son. "What do you got going on?"

Morris gathered his keys, a flashlight. "Work, Daddy. A job," Morris tells him, opening the front door. "I'm going to make some money."

Fourteen

Jetski and Morris peer over the edge of the roof of the building adjoining the police precinct. Jetski's afternoon bravado has evaporated.

"God, I hate heights, Bliss," Jetski says, sweating. The night's cool. "Heights and rats. Both make me freeze up."

"You can do this," Morris says, testing his flashlight. He accidentally drops it, picks it up, and tests it again. Jetski had brought the paintball guns and red laser pointers. "Just like that time you killed the rat with the mop. You didn't freeze up then," Morris says, regretting the words the moment they're spoken. Jetski hadn't told him that story. Stefani had.

"I told you about that?" Jetski asks, nervous. He's wearing a black *Got Beer?* T-shirt turned inside out and dark jeans. He wipes his face with a washcloth. "I told you about the rat?"

"Let's go over the plan once more," Morris says. "We'll both enter—"

"When did I tell you about the rat?" Jetski asks.

"Steven," Morris says, using his birth name. "We're Battle Eagles—"

"Bloody Eagles."

"If this is going to work," Morris says, "we need to be together, to focus. We've got to stay on plan or it won't work."

"We should rethink the plan," Jetski says.

Morris slips on his ski mask. "It's your plan. The plan's fine. It'll work," he says, not convinced it will. But it'll be a thrill, and Morris will make a hundred dollars, which he feels slightly guilty about. Not too guilty. He is doing a job. He's helping Jetski out.

Jetski tentatively picks up one of the paintball guns. A laser pointer is duct taped to the barrel.

"Let me hear you say the plan," Morris says.

"We go in and try to get them out," Jetski reluctantly answers.

"No," Morris says, handing him a flashlight. "We go in and attack. They nearly killed you this morning. If you were in the army, you'd get a Purple Heart for that. Fuck with a Bloody Eagle..."

"You get the talons." Jetski nods. "You're right, Bliss. You're goddamn right." His anger rises as he mulls it over. Morris can see the transformation happening. "This is my building, my project. We need to force them into the street like the rodents they are. Just like that rat."

"Just like that rat," Morris says.

Jetski greasepaints his face. "Laser sightings on," he says.

Morris pulls on a pair of clear workman goggles over his ski mask. Jetski flashes a few random hand signs at Morris, then jumps the short space to the adjacent roof, the police precinct. "No prisoners, no negotiations," Jetski says. "And remember," he says, emboldened, "aim for the face or the crotch."

Fifteen

The squatters occupying the precinct are lead by Hattie Rockworth, a thirty-two-year-old woman from Palm Beach, Florida, and a family of Real Estate money. Lots of money. Money that makes other money stop and stare.

Hattie's the heir to the Rockworth Real Estate Corporation, which owns sixteen percent of Montana, a chunk of Florida, over fifty buildings in Manhattan, and a small city in Luxemburg.

Her solid upbringing is exhibited by her fantastic teeth and her habit of speaking in compete, clear sentences. But she professes to have turned her back on all that, abandoned her family and its money right after her year traveling abroad. She's no longer Hattie Rockworth; now she's Hattie Skunk. Her fellow squatters—The Skunks—are her family now.

Hattie came up with the Skunk surname not in reference to the way they smelled—which they do—but as a shout of protest, a salvo at the City, a cannon blast at New York. The City and its policies stink. Hattie hates the City, hates everything it stands for. She hates the people that live here, the people that run-line to the hype, every drone in a suit or khakis or black turtleneck with a Jack Spade bag. She hates the people who wait in line for brunch to gladly pay twelve dollars for two eggs and toast. She hates people who think rebellion is getting drunk and dancing on a table, or having sex with their roommate's boyfriend, or sneaking into a second movie without paying. She hates the awful new buildings, the crumbling old ones, hates every inch of the poured concrete, tar, and rebar that hold the island together.

She wouldn't live anywhere else.

She refuses to leave. Hate is her and the Skunks' purpose, their calling. Without it, the Skunks' manifesto is void. In a city that stinks, the manifesto calls for the Skunks to stink right back, stink twice as much.

After this morning's battle, Hattie expected the riot police, the National Guard, and tear gas to come tearing through the front door. She expected flashing lights, sirens, and media coverage. Fox News, the *New York Times*, NPR. At least someone from the *Village Voice*. She was ready for the precinct to be stormed, the front door broken down. It was going to be a fight. The Skunks would make a stand, make a name for themselves.

But nothing happened.

All day, she and her Skunk crew stood guard, waiting for the imminent. The barricade was rebuilt, booby traps set. They stood on high alert. Now, at eleven p.m., their vigilance is wearing thin.

"This is bullshit," a Skunk named Torc tells Hattie. He's agitated, spoiling for action. They wait in the dark, on the top floor, watching out the windows. The street's busy though nothing's happening. No police, no media, no National Guard.

"They're not coming back."

"They're coming," Hattie says, inspecting the street. Maybe they'd send snipers, she thinks, then dismisses the idea.

"They're not coming," Torc says. "They pussed out and—"

A soul-shaking screech roils through the building. Torc blanches, the noise so inhuman. "What the fuck was that?"

A spike of fear taps Hattie's spine. "It's them," she says, steeling herself. It was starting differently than Hattie had envisioned. The police were to cordon off the block, use bullhorns and floodlights.

The noise rips through the precinct again, causing both Torc and Hattie to jump. "No cop sounds like that," Torc says. "It sounds like—"

"Revenge," one of the two black-clad men yells, bounding down the metal staircase from the roof. He shrieks again as he lets loose a barrage of paintballs. Blues and yellows and reds explode across Torc and Hattie's torsos and legs.

The second attacker, his laser pointer dancing a red dot on the ceiling and walls, doesn't fire. All he does is repeatedly sneeze.

For Hattie, all courage collapses. Fear takes over and she leads the rush to retreat, calling for the other Skunks to follow suit.

She and Torc stumble down the staircase, seeking exit as the sting of paintballs strikes their backs. In her haste, Hattie accidentally triggers one of the booby traps, spilling a box of glass and splintered boards on Torc's head. A bay of pain echoes through the building.

The other Skunks join them. "What's going on?" one asks. They all want orders, directives.

"Remember the Alamo, assholes," the attacker shouts, coming up behind the group. He executes a dive and roll before tapping a Skunk with three paintball rounds, two yellow and a blue. Spinning, he hits another Skunk in the back of the head with a red paintball. The Skunk snaps forward, looking like his brains have exploded. He squeals like a squeezed cat as he hobbles down the stairs.

"Abandon the squat," Hattie orders, her eyes tearing. The Skunks pile out the way they originally entered, via a second floor window and down the fire escape.

Sixteen

"You got them," Morris says, congested. He didn't fire a single shot. The stench and odor of patchouli—the Skunks' favorite deodorizer—irritates Morris's sinuses. He sneezes twice. "You cleared them out."

Jetski's lathered in sweat, is panting. "We did it, Bliss. The Bloody Eagles did it, baby," Jetski says, overjoyed. "They tasted our talons." He clumsily high-fives Morris.

"They tasted talon, all right," Morris says.

"Bliss, we should get tattoos with that," Jetski says. " 'Bloody Eagles. Taste our talons.' Get them right here." He punches him in the arm.

Morris sneezes again, and with the sneeze, accidentally discharges the pistol. There's a damp *thuuumb* as a yellow paintball hits Jetski in the stomach, doubling him over.

"Bliss," he says, the wind knocked out of him, "shit, that hurt." He sits heavily on the floor, his eyes pooling. He coughs for air. "That really, really hurt."

"Jesus, Jetski," Morris says, bending down to help him, "I'm sorry. It was an accident. The gun, I don't know, it just fired. I'm sorry. Jetski, I'm really sorry."

Jetski's eyes are the color of a newborn's tongue. "I should wax your fucking tugboat, Bliss," he manages the say between gasps of air. He pushes himself into a standing position, takes hold of Morris's arm. He leans his face inches from his. Morris can feel the heat wafting off him. "It's Jouseski, Bliss. Jouseski," he says, letting go. "No one calls me Jetski anymore. You know I hate that nickname."

Seventeen

Hattie runs and runs, her face lashed with tears. She'd failed her fellow Skunks, failed herself. When the time came, she collapsed instead of standing, turned tail instead of fighting. She was defeated. It's the first time she's not won out, gotten what she wanted. The shame stings worse than the paint ball bruises.

Certain she's not been followed, that she's shaken all the Skunks, she circles around at Avenue B and heads back toward the precinct. She needs time alone, time to think. Cutting down Six Street past First Avenue, she enters an Indian Restaurant. The waiter offers her a table. She quickly walks past, through the dining area and into the kitchen. She's out the back door and sprinting across the yard before the cooks and waiters can say anything. One fence, a second, she manages, zinging through the shabby gardens.

She stops at the back of Morris's building, gains her breath between sobs. The police precinct is ahead. It's over for her and the Skunks; the Skunks are no more. She can't face them, not after the brutal rout.

She scampers up the fire escape ladder of Morris's building and pops open an unlocked second-floor window. Pushing past the unsecured, wrought-iron security guard, she enters the cool, dark apartment. A sense of relief floods her. She closes the window, the guard, then wipes the tears from her face. She's safe. She's home. She's alone.

The apartment's hers, one of three she keeps in the city. Her family's business, the Rockworth Real Estate Corporation, owns the building. Morris's rent goes to them.

Laying out two trash bags, Hattie strips her paint-stained clothing.

Her hair is matted, her fingernails dirty, and her back's sore from the paintballs' impact. She runs a hot bath in her Jacuzzi tub, drops in a bath bomb of teatree oil and lemon peel, then, with a bottle of wine and glass, slowly slips into the warm, fragrant waters, letting the grime and stench and soreness soak from her skin. Letting the remnants of Hattie Skunk wash away.

An hour later, Hattie Rockworth emerges from the tub.

Hattie Rockworth's returned.

Eighteen

It's the hardest hundred bucks Morris ever earned.

After the beating he served up, Jetski wanted Morris to stay, sit out the night in the precinct with him, making certain the squatters didn't return. In the morning, two of Jetski's crew would take over.

Jetski had given him the money. Morris felt underwater, his head so clogged. He could leave, but he reluctantly agreed to stay. He felt he owed it to Jetski, especially after shooting him.

All night, Jetski wouldn't shut-up, talked and talked and talked about everything and nothing. "Remember that time..." he'd start out, then relate some stale tale from high school. High school was his world, the focal point of his life, all things referencing back to it. It saddened Morris to hear him speak of that time as halcyon days, brilliant and gleaming. Morris didn't view them that way, always felt high school was a placeholder, an action to burn time. He has no glowing memories, didn't really learn or experience anything special there. What he knows he knows from his own studies, from life.

Sunday finally opens, dawn slow to arrive. "My wife's the first woman I slept with, Bliss," Jetski confides in the grainy light. "Can you believe that? The first, and probably the last. She got pregnant that first time we did it, middle of senior year. What's the chances of that? When I'm lucky, it's always with bad luck. But you should see my daughter now," he says, "a beauty. But she's grown up now. I don't feel the same around her anymore, you know? She's a woman now, which is weird. My baby girl a full grown woman." Jetski pauses, pondering. "You got a girlfriend, Bliss?" he asks.

"You hungry?" Morris asks, uncomfortable with the conversation. Uncomfortable with Jetski talking about Stefani. He wipes his nose. "I could slip out and grab something," he says, his clogged sinuses making him sound like he's speaking through glass.

"I'm a smart guy, Bliss," he says, ruminating. "I could've done things, but I had responsibilities. My girlfriend was pregnant so I had to get married. At nineteen, I had a wife, a child. I had to work. It's hard to get past stuff like that, Bliss. You got to believe me on that. I'm a smart guy, but that's some hard stuff to get past."

"You've got a nice family," Morris says, wanting to leave, to get some air. Jetski's confession, his desire to bond, makes Morris ill at ease. It reeks of desperation. Morris stands. "Steven, I've got to go."

The front of Jetski's shirt is splattered yellow; his face is black with grease paint. He looks like an abstract bumblebee. "Yeah, well," he says, visibly disappointed by Morris's leaving. He stands, too. "You said you're hungry." He checks the time. "You know, the crew's to be here in an hour to take over," he says. "The place is probably all right for an hour, don't you think?"

Morris sees where this is going: Jetski asking him to breakfast. "Should be fine," Morris says, thinking through excuses.

"What do you say to breakfast, Bliss? Head over to the Double Dog Diner? My treat."

"I'd love to," Morris lies, "but I've got to get ready for church."

"Right, Sunday. Church." He nods his head. "All right, then."

Morris offers his hand. "Well…" Morris says. "It's been good."

Jetski firmly shakes it, his Frankenfinger burrowing into the back of Morris's hand. His smile's wan, distant. "No, Bliss," he tells him, "it's been great."

Nineteen

Some lies are fine. Others eat at Morris.

Having told Jetski he's going to church, Morris now feels obligated.

He takes four antihistamines, drinks a cup of coffee. Showered, he takes his one suit from the closet. Wool, it has the smell of trapped space and candle smoke. His fingers keep fouling his tie's knot. It keeps coming out wrong.

Morris goes to church. St. Barbara's Greek Orthodox Church. His church. The one he and his mother attended when he was a child.

It'd been two years since he'd last attended a service, the twenty-year memorial of his mother's death. He came and lit a candle for her, prayed a prayer he felt hypocritical for praying, then left. God had never revealed Himself to Morris. It was foolish to call upon an entity that didn't exist, or if existed, was malevolent. Yet the church, the Greek Orthodox religion, with its rituals and customs, held a mystical sway over Morris. He liked the idea of it, not the actual.

Built in 1921, the church originally was a synagogue, a temple for a small, divisive community of eastern European Jews. But immediately upon its opening, an innocuous debate over strength of faith grew into a heated argument, then a full blown battle. The community split into three camps, each attacking the other on their interpretations of the Torah, family bloodlines, and who the true leader of the synagogue was. No one would give ground. Fisticuffs would erupt on the Sabbath, one group of men descending on another with slaps and kicks and yanks of the beard, screaming that the others were devils or gentiles or uncircumcised cretins who flouted rabbinical law. Boycotts of businesses were decreed by one group on another, and returned in kind. A newly married young woman was abandoned by her husband, his family angry at hers. Another woman had a miscarriage when she was knocked down a flight of stairs. Friendships of twenty years were dissolved, weddings suddenly called off because groom-to-be's family wasn't "pure enough." Each group fought for control of the community, the vitriol and attacks increasing with each passing week. Slowly, the temple was driven into debt and ruin.

By 1926, the congregation disbanded, unable to resolve their issues. The building was shuttered and put up for sale. It remained abandoned for two years.

Flush with cash from questionable stock deals, Manos Fousli, a young Greek immigrant, bought the building outright in 1928 and donated it to the Greek Orthodox Church. He did it to raise his standing, to appear magnanimous and good, and to be able to hold something over his neighbors. "Are you going to church?" he'd ask, with the real meaning understood. "Are you going to *my* church?"

He enjoyed bragging rights for only a short period. Just one week after the church's consecration, the stock market collapsed. He lost everything. Ruined, Manos Fousli found himself falling in front of an approaching subway train.

The church grew in the thirties, forties, and fifties, reaching its peak in the mid-sixties, then started its slow decline as families aged and children moved from the city. Now it struggles to fill even a quarter of the pews.

Standing in the street, Morris gazes up at the solid structure. He's always found the building ugly. Lodged alongside the Williamsburg Bridge overpass, the Star of David is still large and visible in the stone above the front door, but now it serves as symbol of Christianity's Old Testament. The heavy, oak doors are propped open, welcoming. Morris mounts the stairs, planning on having a quick visit, paying respects. Halfway to the door, the thick scent of incense envelops him. The odor sparks a mix of memories: his mother making him say the Lord's Prayer in Greek; the grainy, bittersweet taste of *koliva*; the priest's thick, callused hand he'd have to kiss after communion, a hand that always smelled of bacon.

Entering, he stands toward the back of St. Barbara's, near the candles and icons and Soula Nicolouspolis, the ancient, bone-and-gristle widow who tersely greets everyone as she stands guard over the worn wicker donation baskets. She's stood watch since Morris's childhood. The woman never takes a break, a Sunday off, never goes on vacation. No one else stands there. No one else is allowed.

Guarding the near empty basket, Soula welcomes him like a regular, with a curt nod of her head and a croak that sounds more like "God deal with you" than "God be with you." Morris drops a few dollars in the donation basket, lights a lean candle and crosses himself.

Nothing's changed about the building, the church. It's like he's a child again.

He's not staying, plans on only a moment of silence then he is out the door, but the hard pull of obligation pulls him in. A need to show respect to his mother. Five minutes, he thinks.

Quietly, he moves down the side aisle and sits heavily in the last pew on the right, the pew he and his mother used to always occupy. It was their pew. The congregation knew. This is where the Blisses sat. No one else.

The pew's hard, sharply angled, and while uncomfortable, Morris feels a reassurance in its familiarity. It's stained with a sense of his mother, his life with her. Like home, he thinks. Nothing has changed, the place untouched by time. A place of peace, meditation, held safe from the weathering of the world outside. It's an incorruptible touchstone.

He takes it all in, the gold painted icons, the warm smell of smoky incenses. Nothing's changed.

But after a few minutes, he notices a large crack running the length of the wall, and a pane missing from the stained-glass window. The liturgy book is marred by coffee and the woman in front of him noisily chews gum. A cell phone rings, a man answers it. "*Oriste?*" he asks. "*Oriste?* Speak up." The cantor's chanting is sharp and off, like he's being poked by his wife's knitting needle. And the priest, Father Dennis, when he finally steps into view, with plumes of incense smoke wrapping him, looks defeated, old. He'd aged in the last two years, his beard turned from a dark brown to all gray, and his robes, once flowing, now tightly hug his huge body.

It isn't the same. It isn't home, Morris admits to himself. The incorruptible has been corrupted.

At least the bench is the same, he thinks, running his fingers over the smooth wood before he rises to leave. At least that's still here. His and his mother's pew.

Stepping into the aisle, he notes there are multiple sets of bolt holes in the worn, hardwood floor behind his pew. Bolt holes where two other pews once stood. Where he and his mother's pew once stood.

He realizes his mistake. His pew no longer exists. Even that is gone.

He crosses himself and quickly leaves.

Pausing on the steps outside, he breathes the cool air and wipes a stray tear from his eye. Feeling light headed, he loosens his tie and takes off the suit jacket. From just inside the doors, hidden in the dimness of the church, the antique voice of Soula Nicolouspolis calls to him, low and looming: "God deal with you."

Twenty

At four-thirty Sunday afternoon, Morris takes the F train up to Thirty-Fourth Street for the focus group Andrea Angel set up, a focus group for a new salsa.

Sundays are the worst at Herald Square, the masses pushing from Macy's to the Gap to the discounted perfume and tie shops to the wholesale gadget stores with their overstock of the Statue of Liberty lighters and World Trade Center bottle openers. Buy, buy, and buy more. Everything's cheap, fleeting. The stench of stewing hotdogs and caramelized peanuts hovers over the sidewalk like mustard gas; no one escapes a lungful.

Morris finds the address.

Inside the building's lobby, signs posted everywhere announce that everyone must show I.D. before entering. Morris pauses at the front desk, pulls out his stitched wallet to shows his license to the security guard. The guard waves him on without even looking up; he's more intent on solving the last entry of his "The Bible and You" crossword puzzle.

The elevator snaps Morris to the twenty-first floor, rising swiftly then slowing. He's still wearing his suit from this morning, minus the tie. The doors open on the offices of New Day Focus Group.

"What's your name?" the receptionist asks Morris as he signs in. She has the odor of Aqua Net hairspray and has a slight hair lip. She lisps.

"Morris," he answers. "Morris Bliss. I'm here for the salsa session."

"Sombrero Salsa," she says. "You're the first to arrive. Small group. Sundays usually are," she tells him. "Just you and" — she glances at a print out — "three others, women. This way, please," she says, and leads him down a hall to a room with corporate brown carpets. One wall is all mirrors, like in a police interrogation room.

Morris studies his reflection, corrects his posture and decides he needs a haircut.

"There're some snacks," the receptionist says, pointing to a small spread of warm cans of Guavatini, a milky fruit drink, and a basket of well-picked over Doritos. "Help yourself—pack it in, if you like—and then have a seat. The others should be here soon."

Morris motions to the mirrored wall, asks, "Is that one of those mirrors with someone watching on the other side?"

The receptionist turns to the mirrored wall, like she's noticing it for the first time. She gasps. "*Woooooo*," she says, then, laughing, strides out of the room, closing the door behind her.

Aside from the lingering smell of hairspray, Morris is alone.

The room, sparse, looks like a conference space for a law office that specializes in divorces. Set about a large, round table are six chairs crafted more for design than comfort.

To the side of the table stands an easel. A dark blue cloth covers it, concealing presentation boards. Morris meanders the room twice, then, curiosity taking him, he walks over and slowly lifts the corner of the cloth, wanting to see what is underneath.

"Step away from the easel," a lisping voice commands from the room's speakers.

Morris steps back, startled, then turns to the mirrored wall.

"I see you, Mr. Blister," the voice states. "I'm watching. *Wooooo*."

"It's Bliss," Morris says. He's talking aloud to an empty room. "The name's Morris Bliss."

There's no response, no reply.

He tries leaving, but the door is locked. "Hey," he yells. "Hey, I'm locked in." No one answers, no one comes.

He stops rattling on the door, walks up to the mirrored wall. He presses his face to it, trying to see through. "I know you're back there," Morris says. "I know you're watching."

"Are you talking to yourself, right?" Andrea Angel asks, standing in the doorway. The door's now open. Three women are behind her.

Seeing Andrea, Morris's tongue turns thick, like it's been soaking in salt all night. "Hi," he says. "No, it's just, I was locked in."

"Right, well," she says, testing the knob, the door. "There's no lock on this door, so that's impossible." She motions the others in. "Why don't we all have a seat."

Morris sits, feeling like an idiot.

"You look nice, right? Good to see you," Andrea says, coming around the table to touch him on the shoulder. "Great. Okay, right," she says, passing out name-tags. "I'm Andrea Angel," she says, "and —"

"We're being watched," one of the women, Nancy, says. She has the face of a professional poker player, her mouth and eyes non-committal, betraying no thought. She nods to the mirrored wall. "This guy here was talking to the people behind those mirrors," Nancy says to the group, to no one in particular.

"She's right," Morris says, vindicated. "There's someone back there."

"It's that fat man with gray hair and a lopsided goatee, and the woman who reeks of hairspray and lisps. The fat man's touching his nose right now."

"You can see them?" Morris asks, seeing only himself and the room in the mirror.

"Yes, right," Andrea answers, her hand gesturing toward the reflective wall. "This session's being observed. There are people taping this —"

"A fat man with a lopsided goatee — he's scratching is neck right now — and the young woman who reeks of hairspray," Nancy repeats, her voice flat. "She lisps."

Morris is intrigued and slightly frightened by Nancy, her ability to see through the mirror. He shifts his chair so he can keep an eye on both her and the reflective wall.

"Right. Yes," Andrea says, "but let's not worry about them." She moves around the table, unable to keep still. "They're only here to record your responses. Just act like they aren't there, right? So. As I was saying, I'm Andrea Angel," she says, and by rote, gives her background, and the history of New Day Focus Group. She's wearing a tight, black silk crewneck and form fitting black pants with a blue, yellow, and orange Pucci patterned scarf tied around her hips. Her "fling into spring" attire, she likes to say. Morris misses the entire background and case history of the product they are going to discuss, Sombrero Salsa. His thoughts are on the people behind the mirror. They're laughing at me, he worries, sitting up straight in his chair.

"Okay, right," Andrea loudly says, pulling Morris back to the moment, "any questions so far?"

"Are we going to get to taste the salsa?" asks Maria, a woman who looks like she's just woken up from a prolonged nod on bad heroin. "How can we judge an ad campaign if we don't know what the product tastes like?"

"Right," Andrea says, staying in motion, like she fears she'll be attacked. "Good question. And no. We aren't tasting salsa tonight. What we are doing is looking at some ideas for print ads and seeing what your thoughts on them are, right? Seeing if the ads make you *want* to buy the salsa."

"I don't like the name," the third woman, Nadine, says. She squints. Both profiles, her right and left, are clean and attractive, but viewed from the front, her face is incongruous. She has the look of a wounded groundhog, a look that is interesting but ugly.

"Right. Okay, duly noted," Andrea says to her, forcing a cheerful voice. "You don't like the name. We'll get to talk about that, the name, in a bit. But first, let's have a look at some print concepts."

Nancy glares at the mirrored wall, her head moving slightly like she's tracking prey.

Morris is uncomfortable with the group, feels ill at ease with these women, these strangers, the fact he's being watched.

"Are all the ingredients in this salsa free-range?" Maria asks, her head rising to attention like she's channeled a spirit. "That's one thing I look for when I go to buy something, if it's free-range."

"Right, well, no," Andrea says. "There's no chicken, no fish, no meat in this salsa."

"Can't buy it," Maria says, determinedly. "For me, all ingredients in a product have to be free-range."

"Okay," Andrea says, looking to Morris. Their eyes meet and she smiles a smile so slight, no one but Morris notices. He feels a secret connection with her. "Right, duly noted," Andrea says, keeping things moving, the session going.

She sets out a sample jar of the salsa on the table, a jar that's shaped like a sombrero, with a small, silver-dollar sized lid sealing the top. Andrea says, "This is the product we are going to discuss tonight."

"Are we going to taste it?" Maria asks.

"Right, and like I said earlier, no," Andrea says, moving to present the first print concept. "We're here to look at ads to get your thoughts on them, like this one." She removes the blue cloth from the easel to reveal a presentation board with a photo of a jar of Sombrero Salsa, a bowl of corn chips, and ad copy. Andrea reads it out loud: " 'Take your hat off to the best salsa in town. Sombrero Salsa, Heads Above the Rest.' "

"Is that supposed to be funny?" Nancy asks. Still, she stares at the mirrored wall. " 'Sombrero,' 'Heads'?"

"Right, well, catchy," Andrea says. "Do you think it's catchy?"

"I don't speak Mexican so I don't know what the name means," Nadine remarks, baffled. "What does it mean?" She squints at the print ad. "I mean, what's the name again, Sand Burro? What is that, a desert donkey?"

"There's donkey in this?" Maria asks, having drifted a moment. "My God, I can't eat donkey, even if it *is* free-range."

Andrea fights to corral the group back to order, to bring them back to the topic at hand. "Right," she says, commanding the moment, "so this ad, does it make you want to run out and buy Sombrero Salsa? What are your thoughts, Morris?"

"The ad's got a humorous—"

"I wouldn't buy it," Maria interrupts.

Andrea holds a tight smile. "Right, thank you, Maria. Nancy, your thoughts?"

"I don't eat salsa," Nancy states, matter-of-factly. "It messes with my menstruation."

"But in the interview you said you did, right?" she says, controlling her voice. "You said you eat salsa and that you'd be *glad* to comment on a new product. Am I wrong or did you not say that? Am I wrong, right?"

"I stated I've *eaten* salsa," Nancy says, her palms laid flat on the table. "But I don't *eat* salsa. Messes with my menstruation."

"Right. Okay, duly noted," Andrea says, resigned. Again, she asks Morris his thoughts.

"Like I started to say," he answers, "it's humorous, the bottle eye-catch—"

"You know," Maria interrupts again, "I wouldn't buy the stuff, but I dated a Latin American studies professor in college so I can appreciate the whole Central American vibe, the echoes of a proud heritage, the work, the harvesting, all of which is represented by the sombrero, the 'mascot,' if you will. But, listen, I just got a great idea."

"I was speaking," Morris says, irritated.

"Think about this," she continues, ignoring him. She holds her hands out before her. "A TV ad showing Inca Indians high in the mountains of Mexico, show them toiling under the crushing sun, sweating, struggling with rudimentary tools made of fallen trees or ox bone or something, all to produce the perfect tomato, the perfect pepper that will go into the making of Sombrero Salsa. And," she says, "and they can be wearing sombreros." She raps the table. "That's the tie-in. The Indians will be wearing sombreros. 'From the sweat of our brow to your dining room table' can be the tagline. Or something like that. I could see it working. But I'd recommend dropping the donkey meat from the product, even if it is free-range."

"What's this?" Nadine asks, entering the conversation like she's just happened upon a murder. She glances around the table, her head tilted back so she can see better. "Indians?" she says to Maria, slow to grasp the concept. "You said Indians. I don't get it. Why would Indians sell salsa on TV? Turkey, Stovetop Stuffing, cranberry sauce, yeah, okay. The whole Thanksgiving thing I can see, but salsa? What do Indians have to do with salsa?"

For the next fifty minutes, Andrea corrects, cajoles, and tries to control the group as she covers five concepts for print ads, each featuring the sombrero-shaped salsa jar.

The three times Morris tries to offer his opinion, he's interrupted by Maria's new concept. The session concludes with him not having said a thing.

"Right. Okay, great," Andrea says, visibly relieved that the time is up. "Got some really good thoughts and I appreciate your time," she tells everyone. "You can pick up your money at the front desk on the way out. Again, thank you, right? Any last comments?" she asks, looking to Nancy, Maria, Nadine, then Morris.

"Actually," Morris says, wanting to offer his one thought, "I did want to comment on bottle design."

"I agree," Maria says, picking up her purse, "it's great. It'll stand out on the shelves."

"What I wanted to say," Morris says, "is there's a problem with the design."

The four women look to Morris like he made a vulgar comment. The room's achingly silent, and Morris swears he can hear the hum of the video camera behind the mirrored glass.

"Right?" Andrea finally says. "A problem?"

"Yes," he says. "Think about the chip."

"Right, yes, the chip," Andrea says, then shakes her head. "What about it?"

He walks to the snack spread. "The bottle designer didn't consider the chip." Morris finds an unbroken Doritos and holds the chip up for them to see. "See how big it is?"

"Right. And?"

Stepping back to the table, he takes the sample bottle of Sombrero Salsa, pops off the small lid.

"We're sampling the salsa?" Maria asks.

"No," Andrea says, holding up a hand to silence her. "Go on," she says to Morris.

"The chip doesn't fit," he says, showing how the bottle's opening is too small.

The women all look to each other, then look to Morris, hoping for clarity.

"The chip won't go in," Morris reiterates. But it's like speaking arches and angles to infants. They don't understand what he's trying to say, why the chip would need to fit. No one here would ever think to eat salsa straight from the jar.

Twenty-one

"This is rustic, right?" Andrea says, glancing about the Old Homeplate as she and Morris enter. It's seven p.m. and the first time Morris's ever brought a woman with him to the bar. Mrs. Cruxo throws Morris a glance, a look that says, *Good job*, or *Not in here*, a look he can't decipher. "I just love to go to places like this," Andrea says, her face pinched in a thoughtful manner. "Makes me appreciate the life I have. Can we sit at the bar?"

After Morris had collected his hundred and twenty-five dollars from the hair-lipped receptionist who acted like she didn't know who he was, Andrea had stopped him. She asked, "You're heading home, right? Let's share a cab." While he didn't want to waste his windfall, he didn't want to seem cheap either. He said sure.

Bunched together in the back of the cab, Morris's knees pressed to the hard, bulletproof partition that divided the driver and them, Andrea kept tapping his arm as she spoke, like she translating everything she said into Morse code. He was acutely aware of her every touch, her closeness, the thick, tangy sense-dulling smell of her perfume. It was like he'd entered a sweltering sauna filled with eucalyptus leaves; she enveloped and overwhelmed him.

"So, right, I think to myself," she said, clicking her fingernails on the partition and telling the cabbie to pull to the northwest side of the street. "I'm good with people, I like to shop, so this is the perfect job, right, doing focus groups? It's not." Andrea paid for the fare and deftly slid out of the cab, like she'd been practicing for years. Morris struggled to get out, his leg trapped.

On the sidewalk, Andrea told him, "I don't want to go home yet." She suggested a drink, somewhere close. "You choose," she said.

The Old Homeplate came to mind. It's the only place he's familiar with, and the drinks were cheap.

Perched on the battered, red vinyl covered stools, Morris asks Andrea what she wants. "A Latino Temper, hold the salt," she says.

Mrs. Cruxo sets down two draft beers before Morris can even order.

"Beer all right?" Morris asks, relieved he didn't have to negotiate a Latino Temper. Morris has never heard of the drink, and he knows from experience that Mrs. Cruxo's cocktailing repertoire doesn't include drinks with more than two ingredients.

Morris *tinks* his glass to Andrea's, says, "Cheers, and thanks for the focus group."

"Right, of course," Andrea asks. "Know why we do that? Know why we clink the glass together before drinking?"

From what he'd read, Morris explains, during the medieval times, the host would always poured a bit of his drink into the guest's chalice, and vice versa, thus insuring that if one is poisoned, the other was too. It was a sign of trust. Now, the touching of the glasses' rims signifies the act. "As a show of good intentions," Morris concludes, then asks, "Is that what you heard?"

"Right, well, no," she says, "I hadn't heard that. I'd heard it's done to make the beer's foam go down."

"It does that, too," Morris says.

Andrea suddenly looks stricken, ill.

"Are you all right?" Morris asks, and touches her shoulder. He's surprised by his action, that he'd reach out on his own.

"Yes, of course. Of course, I'm fine," Andrea says, her eyes growing glossy and wet. "No. I'm not. I'm not all right."

"What is it?" Morris asks.

"Did you know I almost didn't marry George, right? I almost got married to someone before him, a guy named Carl."

"No, I didn't," he says. "What happened?"

"Nothing happened, that was the problem. Carl was a good guy, but a Hydrox, right?"

"A Hydrox? You mean like—"

"The cookie," she says. "Right. The cheap, knockoff Oreo. He wasn't an Oreo, you know, wasn't real. He looked pretty good, had pretty nice teeth, right? Had a pretty good job and was a pretty solid guy all around. He was—" She searches for a word. "What's it called, to be in between? When a person is neither too much one way nor the other?"

"Indecisive?"

"Moderate," she says. "Carl was moderate. In everything he did, right? Ordered his steak medium, his latte with one-shot decaf, one regular. Folded his dirty laundry before putting it into the hamper," she says, "which is plain strange. But I liked him, right? I guess I liked him. I didn't *dis*like him. We got along fine. No arguments. Nothing, right? And that was the problem. Who wants to spend their life with someone they *like*. Who wants to be just *fine*? This is my moment, my life. I want better than *like* and *fine*. But the longer I dated Carl, the more *fine* we became. It was terrible, right? Like one of those movies you sit through and can't remember a thing about the moment it's over. If it had been a bad relationship, okay. Then at least I'd have something to remember. I mean, if he'd beaten me, or cheated, or had the habit of picking his toes—which I can't stand—just something, then well... Really, you don't know how awful it is to see your future and be bored with it. I saw my skin sagging and no excitement to show for it. But what made it worse was that I *knew*, I knew it wasn't getting better, but I kept on, for nearly a year and a half, I dated him, thinking, 'Well, maybe...' Things moved too quickly." Her eyes, glossed, hold Morris's. He can't look away. "I lost a part of my twenties to him," she says. "I allowed him to steal my life, right? I've learned that there are no maybes. There is a yes, there is a no. More nos than yeses. But no maybes. Cut your loss, move on. Don't pretend that the soy hotdog you're eating over your kitchen sink filled with dirty dishes is a Nathan's and you're at Coney Island. It's not, right? You're not. Anyway"—her hand flickers before her face, like she's trying to disperse a foul smell—"lesson learned. And I was fortunate to be going through my demented beige stage while I was with Carl. I don't know what I was thinking. Beige isn't my color. It isn't a color; it's a symptom, right? I'd have been miserable if I'd been trying to date, trying to find a boy, while wearing beige."

"Then you met George."

"Right, then I met George," she says. "We dated six months, then got married. Been married three years, and I can tell you one thing, unlike Carl, George and I aren't *fine*. We're anything but *fine*. I don't *like* him." She breaks off, realizing what she's said, that she's disparaging her husband. "Right. Well, you know what I mean. Still," she says, her hand trembling, "I don't want to go home right now, right?" she says. "Had a terrible, terrible fight with him last night." The clack of the pool balls bumping into each other sounds behind them. The jukebox plays a gentle, pleasant song from an album that failed to generate any interest. "Why can't things be clear and clean with smooth edges?" Andrea asks, speaking softly, quietly, like she's waking from a sleep. She stares at herself in the mirror behind the bar, stares straight ahead.

Morris senses the sadness, the searing loneliness of being surrounded by people.

"I stormed out of the house, right," she continues, her voice firm, sure again. "I stayed with my friend who lives on Eighty-Eighth and Lexington in this tiny place she claims is a one bedroom but is really just a glorified studio with a Pullman kitchen." She drinks her beer quickly, like she's filling something empty as fast as she can.

"I'm sorry," Morris says, not knowing what else to say, then motions to Mrs. Cruxo for two more beers.

"You know what frightens me the most?" she asks Morris. "Not being appreciated. At home, I don't feel appreciated, right? That, and turning shabby. I'm twenty-eight and fear I'll never look better. I don't want to be like a couch, don't want to get worn and run down and lumpy. I don't want to wake one day and realize I look *used*. You know what happens to shabby couches, right? They get junked. You've seen them, right? On the street. They're thrown out."

Two fresh beers are set before them. Both Morris and Andrea are silent. Andrea runs her finger around the rim of the glass. "Tell me something interesting," she says, after a minute. She turns to Morris. "Something about yourself that few people know."

"I'm half Greek," he says, not certain that is even interesting.

"I knew there was a reason I liked you," she says. "Mediterranean men know how to handle women, right? You have a way with women."

"No, no," Morris says, awkward with the shift of attention, the way Andrea's studying him.

"Tell me something else," Andrea says, scooting her stool closer to him. "Tell me a story. Tell me about your first concert."

"My first concert," Morris says. "Well, my *first* first concert was Liberace."

Andrea laughs, clear and hard and bitter. "Right, great," she says, "no, really."

"Really," Morris says. "Liberace, Bob Hope, and for some reason, Bruce Jenner. All three on one stage, one night."

"Bruce Jenner, you mean the guy from the Wheaties box?"

"The Olympian," Morris says, "yeah, him."

Andrea's face sobers, then she breaks out laughing. "You almost had me, right?" she says. "I thought you were serious."

"I am serious," he says. "I was twelve. My mother took me." The three were the closing act for a teacher's conference in Staten Island, and though Morris's mother wasn't a teacher, she'd somehow got tickets for the conference. "I was too young to appreciate the oddness of the whole thing," Morris says. "I didn't understand who these people were, what we were going to see. That, and I was angry with my mother then." His mother had returned from her three-month absence, had tried to double her attention on Morris to make up for the time.

"I can't think of a time I *wasn't* angry with my mother," Andrea says, leaning on the bar. "Then she died, right? Now I don't know who to be angry with."

"How'd she die?" Morris asks, a cheerlessness fluttering over him. His mother had returned, had come home, to spend her last months with Morris, her family. And Morris had been angry with her, angry that she'd left in the first place.

She was to leave again, for good.

"How does anyone die, right?" Andrea says, lifting her beer. "Something stops or something won't stop. Cancer, a car wreck, a coronary. Something stops or something won't stop, right? But enough," she says. "All's good." She sits up straight, forces a smile. "I'm not complaining, right, not saying things are bad." She takes his hand in hers, laces her fingers with his.

Something thick and coagulated breaks in Morris blood stream, like cold syrup heated over a flame. He feels it rise in him, slowly push through his body, warm and dizzying.

"Why can't things be clear and clean with smooth edges?" she asks him, leaning in. "Like in a novel or a movie. Why can't I bolt off witty lines and responses when I need to?"

"You speak well," he says.

"I speak well," she says. "Right. But tell me something," she says. "Tell me something you like about me." She holds his hand to her chest, his palm flat to her sternum.

"I like...I like your blouse," he responds, the fabric at his fingers.

"And I like you, right?" she tells him. "I like you a lot." She pulls him to her, kisses him hard, hard and ferociously.

Twenty-two

"Mors," Seymour calls the moment Morris enters the apartment, "get in here."

"What is it, Daddy?" Morris asks, distracted. He closes the front door, locks it, then lifts his hand like he's reaching to touch his nose or rub his eyes; his fingers settle on his lips, as if feeling them for the first time. Still, he's bewildered by the make-out session, by Andrea kissing him. Disappointed in himself for responding to her meaningless affection.

"We can't do this," he remembered telling her, breaking from her embrace. His breath was short, shallow. Flustered, he didn't want to stop but knew he must. There were a million reasons why it was wrong; none of them readily came to mind. She's married, he thought. That's one. "This, us, we can't do this," he said, experiencing a multitude of emotions—everything from scorching exuberance to a trouncing sadness.

Her lips joined his in another bruising kiss. He couldn't stop her. She pulled back a moment, her mouth glossy with spittle. "What can't we do?" she asked, then pressed in again.

Morris's pores opened and a vigorous sweat covered his body. He wanted to take her on the bar, or the pool table, or on the sticky floor, his animal impulses overpowering his brain. Finding her thin body, he held it fast, drawing it tightly to him. And as he kissed her, breathing an air she'd already breathed, the words "Half the evil in the world comes from people not knowing what they like" rose to his mind like a sunken buoy that's broken free from its trappings.

Ruskin's *The Stones of Venice*. He'd reread part of the book this afternoon, his copy worn and frayed. It was on the shelf in the back room, next to a copy of Gail Sheehy's *Passages*, a book of his mother's. And while his recollection of Ruskin's line wasn't exact, Morris knew he wrote about the curse of not knowing. Simple clarity, clean truth. *Half the evil in the world.*

Andrea was in his arms, desired; she was not what he liked. A difference he'd be hard pressed to define, but a difference he intrinsically understood.

Stefani clambered into the back of his mind. She, too, was wrong. They both were wrong. Nothing could come from either, except damage. Remorse.

Reluctantly wresting free from Andrea the second time, he felt the presence of someone else, a hard stare. Turning, he found Mrs. Cruxo on the other side of the bar, barely two feet away, her head propped in her hands and an expression of boredom lining her face, like she was watching a poorly produced TV commercial for a local butcher's shop for the hundredth time in a row.

"Right, like, can I help you?" Andrea asked. Mrs. Cruxo's lumpy, baked-apple face turned from Morris to Andrea, examined her closely, then turned back to Morris, where her eyes settled on him with a look of pleading.

Clearing his throat, Morris wiped his mouth on his shirt sleeve and said, "Another, please." He motions his hand like he was conjuring a coin from thin air. "Another two beers."

Mrs. Cruxo slowly lifted herself from her propped position and lumbered to the beer taps, moving like gravity dealt with her differently than others.

"Hasn't she ever seen two people kiss?" Andrea asked, her hand resting on Morris's neck. "You need a hair cut," she told him, lightly tugging at his hair.

"This isn't right," Morris said, confused. *Half the evil in the world comes from people not knowing what they like.* He studied Andrea, her black hair, the lines guiding the skin around her eyes and mouth. Her lips were lopsided, the lower one thicker. Morris looked for answers in them, hoping the sight of them alone would settle and calm him. This is not what makes me happy, he thinks. "Andrea," he said, "I feel — what? I just — "

"Right, I know," she replied. "Guilt. It's so nice to finally feel something."

"I'm not myself these last couple of days," he said. Stefani, Jetski, Andrea. He felt his life had been yanked from him like a bear ripping a baby from a stroller; fierce, forceful, unalterable. "What I mean is, we just can't—"

"I know we can't, right? But I know we have," she said. Her cell phone rang. She looked at the number. "George," she said, her voice flat. "He's sorry now, that's why he's calling." She answered it. "Right," she said to her husband. "Right, right. No, I know, right." She hung up. "I hate to go," she told Morris, "but I have to go. I have to face what needs facing, right?" She popped a cinnamon Altoids in her mouth and stood. "We'll talk," she said, and dropped a twenty-dollar bill on the bar. She then gave Morris a passionate parting kiss and walked out.

Morris stared at the bar's door, at the point Andrea last occupied before stepping out into the world and night, unsure of what had taken place. Two fresh beers sat before him, two half drunk ones. Morris slid the twenty toward Mrs. Cruxo. She slid it back, as if to say "On the house," or "You need it more than me."

"Mors, damn it," his father calls, "get in here."

He finds his father standing in the middle of the room, fresh from the nightly shower, one he takes prior to bed. A towel's wrapped around his waist. The phone's in one hand. The other holds a pair of yellow panties. Stefani's. From Friday. Her surprise.

"Who's on the phone?" Morris asks, ignoring the panties.

"Some girl," Seymour says. "Been calling all evening." He shakes the panties like they're a bloody cat's pelt. "Something you want to tell me?" he asks.

Morris takes the panties from his father, stuffs them in his pocket. "I need some privacy, Daddy," he says, handling the phone. He covers the mouthpiece. "I need a minute," Morris says.

Seymour doesn't move.

"Alone."

Seymour doesn't move.

"In private," Morris says.

Seymour grudgingly leaves. "We need to talk," he tells his son. His voice is tinged with something like pride. "We need a good talk."

Putting the phone to his ear, Morris says, "Hello?"

It's Stefani. Her voice is strange, ragged. "Mr. Charlies tried to kill me."

It takes Morris a moment to register what she's said. "What?"

"This afternoon, Mr. Charlies tried to run me down with a white stretch limo."

"You sure it was him?" Morris asks, unable to picture Mr. Charlies driving. "You sure it wasn't someone else driving a limo?"

"He wasn't driving," Stefani says. "He was in the back, being chauffeured." She'd been at Central Park, she explains, was crossing Fifty-seventh Street toward the Plaza Hotel. "I hear this screech and this limo roars right at me. I had to jump out of the way, you know. Like really jump."

"Mr. Charlies was being chauffeured?" Morris doesn't believe it. "Stefani, I think—"

"It's 'cause of that cheese I stole," she says. "He's out to kill me."

"He's not going to kill you over Brie," Morris says, but then isn't so sure.

"His driver nearly ran me down. And when I go to yell at him, the driver just ignores me, walks around to the other side of the limo and opens the back door. That bitch Mr. Charlies steps out, dressed in an all-white suit like that guy from that old TV show with the midget, *Fantastic Island* or whatever. I just wanted to spit on him."

"So you're telling me Mr. Charlies was chauffeured to the Plaza?"

"Yeah."

"In a limo?"

"Yeah, a white one. And you should've seen his driver," Stefani says. "Huge, like he had that disease where you grow and grow and can't stop growing. A freak. And black. Like really, really black. I'd have gone at Mr. Charlies myself if it wasn't for his driver. The guy scared me."

Morris doesn't respond, can't respond, his head soaked with images.

The issue of Stefani's panties, Seymour somehow finding them, is a twig in a swollen river; the currents have already carried it off and around the bend.

"Mr. Charlies," Morris says aloud. "Outside of his store." It wasn't an impossibility, but like a sighting of the South American quetzal, it was something rare.

"That bitch Mr. Charlies will pay. But listen," Stefani says, "I got to get off the phone. Promise me two things, though."

"Yeah, sure," Morris says, half listening.

"Are you listening?"

"Yes, yes. I'm listening. Two things," he says.

"First, meet me after school tomorrow. Ray's Pizza."

"Tomorrow?" he says. "Okay, I can do that."

"Promise."

"Ray's. After school," he says. *Half the evil in the world.* Tomorrow he'll tell her, "No more." He'll tell her they can't keep on. "What's the second?" he asks.

There's a hesitation on the line. He can hear Stefani breathing. "Prom," she finally says. "Promise to take me to Junior Prom."

Twenty-three

Sunday night and the city is quiet, people recovering from their weekend, gaining vigor for the coming Monday. Morris walks down the East River Park to South Street Seaport. The empty fishmongers' stalls reek of old catch. He heads further south, to Liberty Park, then up the west side of the island to Forty-second Street and over to Times Square, where the neon lights tear up the night, giving the place a look of day.

He walks for hours, trying to clear his mind of Stefani, of Andrea, of Jetski, and of his mother.

Prom. The concept's so distant, so old-fashioned to Morris, like the idea of war bonds or moustache wax. Proms seem like something that would have gone the way of gauchos with knee-high tube socks, something that is an embarrassing memory.

When Morris was a senior in high school, he wanted to go to prom. There was one girl he planned to ask. Lacy Laimey. She was studious and plump and had shiny, blond hair that reflected light. She sat beside him in Latin class, always faced rigidly forward, her profile soft and engaging. "Going to prom?" Morris asked, summoning the courage to talk to her one day after class. The dance was two weeks away. Lacy looked to the floor, then to Morris. "I can't find a dress I like," she said. "I don't want to look at prom pictures twenty years from now and think 'God, what a terrible dress.' "

"So you've…" Morris felt his chest tightening, like he'd been wrapped in a wet sheet. He was too late. "Someone's already asked you?"

"I can't find someone I like," she said, then looked to the floor. When she lifted her head again, she caught Morris with a direct, stunning look. It was like being hit with mace; Morris was immobilized, choking. "If someone I liked asked me," she told him, "I'd go. I'd find a dress I liked."

"Yeah," Morris finally mustered. "Yeah, I know what you're saying." They both stood there, like they were waiting for a bus, or for the start of an eclipse, or for a helium balloon to finally descend. Waiting for something they knew would happen. Something that must happen.

Morris was going to ask her to prom.

They faced each other until they could no longer face each other. "I…" Morris said. He didn't ask. His courage failed. "I know what you're saying," he said, then turned and left, leaving Lacy and her wet, eager eyes.

Now, Stefani wanted him to go to Prom. "Promise," she kept saying on the phone.

He agreed to meet her after school the next day.

Morris pauses at the window of a travel agency. Posters of Greece, the cutting blue waters, the majestic ruins, hang in the window. Mom must have family there, he thinks, then wonders why he doesn't know. For all his years of talk of traveling, he'd never once thought to see if he has family elsewhere.

He's tired of himself, of the illusions he's held for so long, tired of saying and not doing. All the tales of travel are tales he's annexed, stolen. Books are good, up to a point.

He thinks of Stefani. "I can't wait to see you tomorrow," she said, before ringing off.

"Patience," Morris said, more to himself. He'd tell her tomorrow, "No more."

"Yeah, patience," she replied. "Patience is a vulture."

"Virtue," he said. "It's virtue."

"You sure?"

"Yes."

"I think you're wrong."

"I'm not."

"Well, okay. If you say so. Virtue is a vulture," she said, then hung up.

Twenty-four

Confidence is the congealer. Stand straight, keep your hands out of your pockets. Move to a person before they move to you. Convince others you are what you say you are, even when you're not.

Hattie knows these lessons, learned them from her father and her father's father, both who closed multi-national deals with little more than words and poise. They affected economies with their decisions, and handled millions and millions of dollars daily, like it was something natural, common.

People want to believe, will bend backward to believe. Hattie knows first hand. The Skunks believe Hattie's the true call. She formed the group, founded it as the antithesis of the societies her father and her father's father belonged to. But her family also believes Hattie's a Rockworth, through and through. She'll run her wild oats and fall lovingly back into the Rockworth fold.

Until now, her conviction held both lives together, like vinegar and oil in the same jar, touching but never mixing.

Now she's shaken. The precinct debacle rattled her confidence, cracked her façade. She feels exposed, a fake. Every action she now questions. Would Hattie Skunk act or speak that way? Would Hattie Rockworth?

A swampy paranoia has taken over. She's afraid to leave her apartment.

The welts on her back have blossomed into a lovely purple. Multiple baths with Epson salts and lemon-pine bath bombs did little to help. She's burned Navaho hand-crafted incense, and sipped thyme tea in hopes of relaxing. Still she's a mess. She needs to regroup and take inventory of who she is, reassess what she wants.

No more Skunks, she tells herself, pacing her apartment. That life's dead. Too dangerous, too crazy for her. She could get hurt; she is hurt. It is minor, but the next time…

She contemplates becoming an elementary school teacher, or starting a literary magazine, or following the summer yacht touring circuit. What she needs is a rest, she determines, no demands or distractions.

What she needs is half-and-half, can't drink her Peruvian Platinum Blend coffee without it. And she desperately needs a cup of coffee, needs it terribly.

For twenty minutes she mounts her confidence to step outside, builds the courage to shrug off the worry that she'll be recognized. A quick trip to the deli, she repeatedly says to herself, like a mantra. She checks then rechecks her front door's peephole, checks and rechecks the street below by pulling back the curtains and peeking out.

Sunday. Night's taken hold, the day's light collapsed. "The world moves and keeps moving," Hattie says aloud. "Whether I'm with it or not."

She slides on a pair of silver Gucci wraparound sunglasses, a Yankees ball cap. "I'm with it," she say, then repeats, "A quick trip, a quick trip, a quick trip."

She turns the front door's bolt, opens the door. The hall smells of rotting apples and burnt fish. It's clear; no one around. With the stealth of a leopard, she moves down the stairs, fast and quiet.

Out the front door and into the night. Arms folded to chest, head down. Hold close to the buildings. Striding along at a brisk, powerful pace, she looks no one in the face.

Mr. Charlies is out of half-and-half, has only nonfat or buttermilk. She has to walk an extra block, to a bodega with *papa rellenos* and crusty bottles of Goya Malta, to get her half-and-half. The clerk rings her purchase, gives her change, all without exchanging a word.

Rounding the corner back onto Fifth Street, her half-and-half in hand, she thinks, "Home free." She has to hold herself back from breaking into a run. She pulls her keys out, readying.

Then she hears him, his voice a flush of boiling bleach through her heart.

"You," he says.

Looking up, she finds a man in her building's doorway, held by the shadows. He leans against the front door, blocking her way.

She stands stock still, like she's been impaled by a pole from behind. The welts on her back flare with pain. Hit him in the face, she thinks. Jab in the eye with her keys. Then run, run, run.

"I was hoping," the man says, his voice clear and direct. He doesn't move, makes no effort to get out of her way. Hattie steels herself for the worst, for a fight of all fights.

"I was hoping you could help," he says.

Twenty-five

It's Monday afternoon and Morris waits for Stefani at Ray's Pizza, sits at a table out front on the sidewalk, drinking a coffee, watching the crowds slide past. Across the street is the brown stone building of Cooper Union's Great Hall, where Abraham Lincoln sealed the Republican presidential nomination in 1860. Such history so near the tongue piercing stands of St. Marks Place.

Morris has practiced. "Stefani," he'll tell her, "no more." He isn't going to Junior Prom. He's ending it. Cutting it clean.

That morning, the trucks where back out front of the precinct. A clamor and banging and tearing echoed from within the building. Work had finally begun. The Skunks were gone. He and Jetski ensured that. The Bloody Eagles had ensured that.

The day's damp, overcast. The fake marble table Morris is at wobbles. He shifts it, rams a folded napkin under the leg to stop it from rocking. Still, it rocks. The traffic pushes north and south along Third Avenue. Taxis stop, blocking the cars and trucks and other taxis behind them. People cross against the light, dancing through the traffic like capeless matadors.

Saint Benedict's Ukrainian Catholic School lets out.

A group of boys in navy blue slacks, white button down shirts, and plaid school ties amble by, their faces oily with adolescence and anxiousness. Their laughs are forced and loud, laughs boys laugh when something isn't all that funny. Then come girls in packs of three or five or silently by themselves. Then the stragglers.

Soon, they've all passed. But no Stefani. He waits five minutes, then five minutes more. He waits until twenty after three when finally, one of Stefani's classmates, a gawky white girl who's already gone home and changed into a Triple Five Soul tank top, low-riding skirt, and put on a pair of rattling roller blades that sound like a shopping cart with a broken wheel, comes skating up and tells him, "She's not coming, 'kay?"

"Who?" Morris asks, hoping that Stefani hadn't told anyone about their appointment. Knowing she probably told everyone.

"Ah, shit," the girl says, then snorts. Her face is like a pickle sliced lengthwise, long and awkwardly colored. "Yeah, right. 'Who?' " she says, grabbing the edge of Morris's table for balance. It shakes and his coffee flips to the pavement, spilling. "Shit," she says. "Like, 'whoops,' 'kay? Listen," she says, still grasping the table and taking small, faltering steps to stay standing, "she isn't coming. She told me to tell you that, and to tell you to meet her tonight at the Ukrainian Festival, out front of McSorley's pub. Seven o'clock, 'kay?" She pauses a moment then says, "And she said for you to buy me a pepperoni slice and a large root beer."

Morris waves her off, tells her no. "I'm not buying you anything," he tells her, wanting to pry her hands from the table.

She lets go of the table. "Personally," the girl tells him, unsteadily rolling backward toward the street and the racing traffic, "I think you and her are perfect together." She catches herself at the last moment, hobbling forward before she slides off the curb and into the path of an approaching ice cream truck. "You're both really gross," she yells, wheeling off.

The Ukrainian Festival. Not something Morris wants to attend. He heads home.

Out in front of his building, N.J. is waiting. With a bright orange cashmere scarf loosely looped around his neck, he leans against the bark-stripped tree he used to climb as a kid. Morris's never seen him in a scarf.

"N.J., hey."

"Morris, man," N.J. tells him, "I've got news, and news, and more news, man. But first, let me tell you, I just saw your cheese girl."

"You saw Stefani?" Morris asks. "Where?"

"At Norman's Sound and Vision. She didn't look happy."

"She didn't look happy? How do you mean?"

"I mean, like not happy, man. But listen, this is important: I've found the One," he says, sounding sincere. His voice vibrates with excitement, like God has whispered a new testament in his ear.

Morris shakes he head, not understanding. "Why wasn't she happy?" he asks, thinking of heading over the Norman's to see if she's there. Then he thinks not. He asks, "So what did you find? And what's with the orange scarf?" He tugs at it.

"Cashmere, Bergdorf's," N.J says, then, "I found the *It*, man. The woman. My life. The reason to go on."

A flash of irritation rifles through Morris. He's heard this before and isn't in the mood for it again. "Two days ago you were planning to marry. What happened to *that* woman, that love of your life?"

N.J. waves off the comment. "Listen, man," N.J. says, "that was yesterday, years ago, but listen. Two things have happened since then, two important things. The first," he says, holding up his thumb. "No, wait, man, I'm starting wrong. I'm about to ruin this before I've even begun. Hold on. Just hold on, man." N.J. trots down the street with the air and confidence of a winning quarter horse coming off the track. He rounds the corner, toward Mr. Charlies.

Morris stands motionless a couple minutes, then thinks, Why am I waiting? Exhausted, he wants to rest. He didn't sleep all night, spent the time wandering the city, thinking. Keying his front door, he heads into his building, slowly starts up the stairs.

Behind him, there's a rapping on the door. N.J. with a plastic bag in hand.

"What's wrong with you, man?" N.J. asks when Morris opens the door for him. "You're as touchy as Liz Taylor out of Diet Coke. I'm trying to tell you something important and you ditch me, man. What's that about?" He pulls a forty-ounce bottle of beer from the bag and takes a swig. "At least celebrate with me," he says, holding the bottle out for Morris. Morris takes a drink.

N.J. takes another drink, wipes his mouth with the scarf. "Lend me your tired, your poor, your huddled masses, man," N.J. says, then, "So, yeah, man, you're right. The Cyndi thing, a fiasco. Stupid of me. But this is different, man. It's real."

"Okay," Morris says, sitting on the steps. He's trapped. He'll listen. "Five minutes," he tells N.J., "then it's my turn to tell you something. And I want you to listen, really listen."

N.J. nods. "Always, man, always. When you speak, my ears are turned on for you. You know that. But listen, man," he says, "me first. Let me tell you my tale first."

Morris places his elbows on the stair behind him, leans back in preparation for a long tale.

Ever since eighth grade, N.J.'s progressively increased the pace he moves through the field of women, dating one then another, positive the latest is the perfect match. Each time it ends in damp disappointment.

From his first real girlfriend, Mary Dally, the daughter of a Middle-Eastern snack food deliveryman, to The Cyndi, his near wife, N.J. has become a skilled hand. He claims he craves a functioning, genuine relationship. He truly believes this.

It isn't what he wants.

He wants the *prospect* of a functioning, genuine relationship. Yes, he says, yes, man, I want love. But his terms come from a bastardized dictionary. He wants a love that's continually seething and heady, capricious. He wants non-binding blind promises. He wants to know someone without getting to know them, without having to deal with the idea that there are faults. He wants the form of love that's corrosive to a long-term, serious relationship.

With each new girlfriend, he's aflame, alive, heated with a euphoric anxiousness and unquestioning certainty. She is *It*, he says.

Then she isn't it.

The next woman absolutely is *It*.

A week or two passes; she fades like an item left in a blighting sun.

Once a relationship's over, N.J.'s free to start new. And there have been many, many new ones. There was the artist, who knew everything about art except how to make it; the judicial clerk who'd constantly grill N.J. over any topic; the claustrophobic who, when visiting the Annette Messager exhibit of yarn hung from the ceiling in dense clusters, got tangled in the art work and had a panic attack. Then there was the tattooed barista, who explained the intricate meanings and symbolism of each of her fifteen tattoos. They represented important events in her life, altering moments, metamorphoses that no other person could fully understand. Later, under the influence of four lemon Vodka Twirlers, she confessed that all the important events in her life—all the events she'd gotten tattooed for—actually weren't, in hindsight, important. "It's so hard to tell what's important and what's not," she told N.J., running her fingers over her stained skin. "How do you differentiate? They're nearly the same."

After the barista, there was the mystic from Staten Island who smelled like she'd doused herself in patchouli then rolled in incense ash; the accountant who chewed her fingers until they were raw and bleeding; the thin-haired hairstylist with an immensely bad dye job; the rabbit farmer from Long Island who smelled fecal and tangy and liked to wear thick, tarnished bangles; the advertising copywriter who spoke in mottos and catchphrases and consumed only peanuts and Coke; the physical therapist who constantly cracked her knuckles; the graphic designer who broke into tears every other day because her computer crashed; the sous chef with the diet pill problem; the broker who carried four cell phones and rang off, "Peace and pray the Dow up ten"; and the dental assistant with inflamed gums and a lifetime supply of Scope. And then there where the others. All the others, all the ones that were *It* and now aren't.

Now, it's happening again. N.J.'s animated.

Morris is tired of the routine.

"I found her, man. But listen to this," N.J. says. "The best. I've got to tell you the best. Two words, man." He opens his arms wide and clicks his tongue. "Mister. Charlies," he says, smiling.

"Mr. Charlies?" Morris asks. He sits up. "What about him?"

"Mister. Charlies," N.J. says again. "Last night, or, no, man, really, really early this morning, I was in Chelsea—" N.J. breaks off.

"I'm listening," Morris says, sitting forward. "You were in Chelsea…go on."

"No, wait, man," N.J. says. "I'm starting wrong. I'm about to ruin this before I even begin." He pauses a moment. "Chronology, man," N.J. says, pointing his beer. "That's how it's got to work. Let the story be told the way the story happened, man, in the order of its order."

He takes a long draw of beer, then sets the bottle down next to Morris. Rubbing his hands together, he begins: "Okay, man, listen. After we hung out Friday night, after you bought me those beers, I started thinking—I mean, really thinking deep—and I got depressed. That whole thing with me getting married, man..." He shakes his head. "I really bent myself to become something I wasn't, all for The Cyndi." He leans toward Morris, their heads nearly touching. "I have to tell you something," he solemnly says. "I think I might be a phony, man." He holds up his hand, indicating he doesn't want argument from Morris.

Morris isn't arguing.

"No, listen, man, I am. I fear I'm a real phony. And I hate it. My driftlistness—"

"Driftlistness?" Morris asks.

"Driftlistness, man. You know, drifting around listlessly. No goals. No real purpose. I hate it." He takes a swig off the bottle. "Plus, man, it doesn't help that you're such a good friend."

"Now you're complaining I'm too good a friend?"

"Not complaining, man, stating fact. You're too good to me. You're an enabler, man. You enable."

"What the fuck are you talking about, Newton?" Morris asks, angry. "Are you paying me a compliment or insulting me?"

"It's a compliment, man," he says. "Just not a good one. I have to be honest; you're an enabler. All those drinks you bought me Friday night," N.J. says, "enabled me to get drunk." He nips off the bottle.

Morris stands. "You sound like you're in A.A. or something."

"I kinda am, man. Or was," he says. "Come on, Mors, sit down. I'm not finished."

Morris studies his friend. "Hurry it up," he tells N.J., sitting back down. "I've things to do," he says, though his afternoon's open.

"Okay, listen, man, Friday night, after all those beers, and after thinking through The Cyndi mess, I felt I'd lost control of my life." He looks wounded, sad. "I thought about it all Saturday and it was killing me. Couldn't sleep at all Saturday night. So yesterday," N.J. says, "I decided to become a 'Friend of Bill.' "

"Friend of Bill?"

"Yeah." He tilts the bottle to his lips, then offers Morris a drink. He accepts. "That's how fellow A.A. members identify each other," N.J. continues. "They say, 'Are you a friend of Bill's?' It's like the secret password, asking if you're a friend of Bill, the founder."

"N.J., this is—"

"Listen," he says. "I'm opening up to you here, man. I need you to listen." He pauses a moment, like he's recalling lines. "There's a bunch of A.A. groups in the city," he continues, "but none that meets down here on Sunday. And anyway, man, I knew what kind of people would show up to the meetings down here in the East Village: down-on-their-luck kinds, man, losers, old hippies, atheists who think cleanliness is next to Godliness. Know what I'm saying? I didn't need that. Always," he tells Morris, taking the bottle back from him, "surround yourself with people better than you."

"That's the reason you hang out with me?"

"So I thought," he says, ignoring Morris's question, "what type of alcoholics do I want to associate with? Who do I want support from? People better than me, man. Rich, successful people."

"Rich, successful alcoholics," Morris says.

"Exactly," N.J. answers. "That's what I'm thinking, man. People who are accomplished and come from good families. So I went to a meeting on the Upper East Side and man, did I hit jackpot. Seventy, eighty percent of them were women, young women, right-out-of-Sarah-Lawrence young. And they're all good looking. I thought, Hey, there's something to this. And so I get up and do my 'My name is N.J., I'm an alcoholic,' and all the girls responded, man, said, 'Hello, N.J.' It was beautiful." N.J. rubs his chin, his smile large and bright.

"So you met some young, rich drunk and now you're getting married?" Morris asks. "What do you have to tell me about Mr. Charlies?"

"Chronology, man. Order in its order," N.J. says. He pulls heavily on the bottle, taking two or three large gulps. "So after the meeting, this woman—no, man, this girl, twenty-two, twenty-four years old—comes up to me and she says, 'Your story was so touching—'"

"Which story is this?"

"The story about how I'm in this vicious cycle because my best friend's an enabler."

"Jesus, Newton," Morris says. "Here, let me enable you to stop drinking," he says, taking the beer. He drains it in four drinks, then hands the bottle back.

"No, man," N.J. says, looking mournfully at the empty bottle. "All I'm saying is I'm a phony. All I'm saying is that you're generous and nonjudgmental, man, that, you know..." He stops, lost in the midst of his fumbling compliment. "Listen, man," he explains, "I threw out your name just as an example—"

"You told them my name?"

"You're safe, man. I used a code name. I called you Boris, Boris Miss, not Morris Bliss," he says, then, "So this woman, this girl, and I get to talking, and—"

"She's the one, the *It*," Morris interrupts. He stands. "Well, good," Morris says, his voice clipped. "Maybe this time it'll work. And if you get a chance, maybe I can meet her before you get married."

"No, man, she's not the one," he says, settling his hand on Morris. N. J.'s face is filled with hurt, like he's overheard his mother making fun of him. "I'm telling you something here and you're not listening."

N.J.'s a nuisance, but he's still a friend. Morris's only long-term friend. He sits down again, feeling bad about being rude. "Go on," he says, "I'm listening. You met this girl at A.A. and nothing happened."

"Well, man," N.J. says, "something *did* happen; I spent the night with her, or spent most of the night. I left about two a.m. And, man, she was great—as a person, I mean. And in bed, too, I'm not saying she wasn't. You should see the place she has," he says, his voice lighting up. "Huge three bedroom on Fifth Avenue and Sixty-seventh with this view of Central Park. Man, she has some money—"

"So she *is* the one?" Morris asks, confused.

"No, man, she isn't," N.J. says. "At first I thought it was happening, but then I realized it couldn't happen."

"Why?"

"She's got problems," N.J. says, glancing at the empty bottle he still held.

"Like what?"

"Well, man, for one, she's an alcoholic," N.J. says. "And then there are other things. She has no concept of money, its value." He holds out his scarf. "Two hundred and ninety dollars," he says. "I know this girl three hours and she buys me this scarf. Listen to this, man," he says. "After the meeting, we went for a coffee, and after a half an hour or so of talk about our families and problems, she takes my hand in hers and says in this incredibly sad voice, 'Your face is so beautiful; it should be framed in a halo of flame.' That's the way she spoke, man, all educated and weird like that. Almost poetic. But I don't really know this girl, so I'm thinking, 'Great, she's going to torch me with lighter fluid.' " He extends his forefinger. "Number one rule I learned in Hostage Negotiation training is—"

"In what?" Morris asks.

"Hostage Negotiation training, man," he repeats. "Took a two week intensive course last summer, late June, in Nigeria. They got a whole university there, man. It's both a terrorist and law enforcement training school. You can study anything, man, from stopping a riot to crafting explosives out of toothpaste and ground-up mango pits to making an assassination look like a heart attack. It's all good stuff to know in my line of work."

"Late June," Morris says, "you were visiting your aunt in Yonkers. And what 'line of work' are you talking about?"

"I'm a skip tracer, man. A bounty hunter," he says, insulted. "Why are you so down on me, man?"

"I'm not—" Morris pauses. "I'm uptight. It's got to do with Stefani," he says. ·

"Fifteen-year-old cheese girl you're dating?"

"Eighteen," he says, "and we're not dating. But yeah," he adds. "Her. And now," he says, nodding upward, "Andrea Angel."

"Who?"

"The woman in apartment five," he says, his voice low. "And on top of all this, I ran into Jetski, Stefani's dad. Ended up spending the night with him in the police precinct."

N.J. looks like a carp pulled to land. "His daughter wasn't enough, man?"

"Not 'spend the night' like that. We were—" Morris breaks off. "Just...go on with your story."

"That Stefani girl's a nasty rash," N.J. says, unwrapping then rewrapping his scarf with a flourish. "I'd take care of it quick," he says. "Before it spreads and gets real ugly."

"I'm working on it," he says. "Tonight."

"Good, man, good," he says, then launches back into his tale. "My face in a halo of flames, man," he says. "Pure poetics. That's what she said she wanted to see. So I played along, keeping calm, keeping the options open. That's what I learned at the Nigerian Hostage Negotiation school: You've got to float like a leaf on a river, man. Just keep going. But be alert. Be ready to kill." He then recounts the rest of the evening, how they kissed in the cab heading up to Bergdorf's, how, even though the store was closed for the night, the security guard knew her by name and let them in, how she took him to the men's section of the store, stripped his clothing, and wrapped the flaming orange scarf around his head. "A face of fire, man," N.J. says. "She made me leave it on the entire time. She said I was a saint. I *felt* like one of those saints, man, like an icon made of gold leaf. She promised me everything, anything, as long as I remained her saint. Or maybe she said her martyr," he says, thinking. "I think she said martyr." N.J. then lifts his head and intones: " 'For I have known them all already, known them all: Have known the evenings, mornings, afternoons, I have measured out my life with coffee spoons.' She kept reciting that, man, while we were doing the—"

"Who wrote that?" Morris asks. "That's T. S. Eliot, isn't it?" The lines are familiar, like something he was once forced to learn in school or a pop song incessantly played on the radio.

"Prufrock, man," N.J. says. "A guy named J. Alfred Prufrock. But listen, man," he says, continuing, "after all that, after the Bergdorf's, the scarf, the kisses and promises, I was down in Chelsea around three a.m. and guess who I saw."

"Mr. Charlies," Morris said, his interest piqued.

N.J. nods, tilts the empty bottle to his lips, hoping for remains.

"Where exactly did you see him?"

"This gay club called the Leather Muskrat. I was going to the bathroom—"

"The Leather Muskrat? What kind of name is that?"

"I don't know, man, but the place was like an UPS convention," he says. "Everyone was trying to handle my package."

"What were you doing there?"

"I just told you, man," N.J. says. "I was going to the bathroom and in walks Mr. Charlies."

"But, I mean..." Morris lets it go. "You're positive it was him?" he says.

"Yeah, man, it was him."

Two sightings in twenty-four hours. What were the chances? "Did he see you?" Morris asks.

"Oh, *man*, did he see me." N.J. shivers, tightens his scarf around his neck. "It was sinister, man, him checking me out like that. Never noticed it before, but his eyes are like a lizard's, all green, man. And he wouldn't stop looking at me. Had my pants unzipped but couldn't go. I got stage fright. He just kept staring, like one of those starving African kids you see in the Sally Struther's ads; he was hungry, man."

Standing, Morris says, "Give me a call tomorrow." The news is important, Morris just doesn't know how. His mind's bustling with thoughts. *Half the evil in the world comes from people not knowing what they like.*

"Hold up, man," N.J. says. "You haven't even asked me who it is."

"Who what is?" Morris asks.

"*It*, man. The one," he says. "The woman. My life. The reason to go on."

"Who is it?"

"Her," N.J. says, pointing up the stairs to Apartment 4. Hattie Rockworth's place. "It's her," N.J. says, his voice choked. "Hattie Rockworth. I met her last night, man, out front." N.J. stares up at the door, like it's a newly discovered gem mine. "I stopped by to see if you wanted to get a drink before I went to my A.A. meeting. And there she was, man, a vision with a pint of half-and-half in hand. She's the one, man, the one."

Twenty-six

N.J. follows him up the stairs to Hattie's door. "We'll talk tomorrow, man," N.J. says, rewrapping his scarf. Hair smoothed. "Tomorrow, man," he says, then opens Hattie's door without knocking and strides in, like the place is his own.

Morris heads on, pauses at Andrea's apartment, contemplates knocking, but doesn't. George might be there.

Two flights up.

Home.

Keying his door, Morris finds his apartment is quiet, empty. Seymour's still at work. Dishes still need washing. Laundry needs doing.

He checks the messages, sees if Stefani, if anybody, called. No one.

In his room, a blank wall waits. His Agenda of Travel, some twenty years of planning, is no more.

His mother's photo is face down.

He uprights it, so that it faces him, then sits on his bed. Everything's shifting, sliding out of his control. He no longer knows what is what. His safe, set bounds have cracked.

He lies down for a rest, closes his eyes for what feels like a moment, then jerks awake to the rhythmic steps of Sofar's in the apartment overhead. 5:45 p.m. He's slept over an hour. The day's light wanes. Disoriented, he's uncertain of the day, if it's morning or evening. "Daddy?" he calls out. Seymour's still not home.

Sitting up in bed, Morris finds his feet are bare. He must have taken his shoes, his socks, off. He doesn't remember. Quickly, he puts them on, feeling exposed, vulnerable. Not ready.

Above, he hears Sofar hit one end of his apartment, turn and head back. The noise has become a part of Morris's life. Like the bathroom door that doesn't fully shut, it's something he's gotten used to. He no longer notices.

He's to meet Stefani at 7 p.m., in an hour or so, in front of McSorley's Ale House on Seventh Street.

Standing, the idea of visiting Sofar takes hold. "I'll visit Sofar," he says to himself, the floor creaking above his head. It's more out of curiosity than kindness. Morris hasn't paid him a visit in years, not since Sofar tried to get him to wear a dress.

"I'm going to visit him," Morris says, for no other reason than it seems the right thing to do.

Twenty-seven

Sofar is an anchorite, confined to the worn rooms of his small space. He lives on delivery, never leaves the building, paranoid that the moment he steps outside, he'll be booted from his rent-stabilized apartment.

His fears are well-founded.

The last time he stepped out, his place was broken into and Hambone was dognapped. Everything was left a mess.

It was Hatfield, the then-owner of the building, that broke in. He desperately wanted Sofar out, wanted his rent-stabilized apartment back.

For thirty-seven years Sofar's lived here, moving in when he was a young man of twenty-eight, a man willing to try anything. At that time, the neighborhood was broken. Even with the police precinct a few doors down, the street was scary. It was cluttered with car batteries and three-wheeled baby carriages. Rats stalked the sidewalks like hyenas on the veldt, whistling out sharp-pitched choruses during their nightly trolls. Sofar wanted to be a painter, or a composer, or someone who did something so cutting-edge that it earned him multitudes of praise, even though no one understood it. He needed a cheap place to live, a place to launch his life's endeavor, once he finally determined what it was. Apartment 10, the sixth floor apartment he took, had no rooms, no walls, was like an open boxcar or an empty cracker box when he moved in. Torn and dark, the hardwood floors looked like someone had tried to ice skate on them. Exposed pipes ran the walls, dropped from the ceiling, like veins ripped from the skin. The glass in the windows was spider-webbed with cracks and the toilet, yellowed with grime, stood strangely alone near the back of the place, attached to the wall. No shower. No kitchen. No oven.

"What's the rent?" Sofar asked Hatfield, looking the space over.

"Fix it up a bit, at your own expense," Hatfield said, chewing his fingernail, "and it's yours, rent-free, for a year. No," he said, instantly retracting his statement. The walk-up to the sixth floor had made him light in the head. He didn't know what he was saying. "Six months," he told Sofar. "Let's say six months then we can talk leases."

If Sofar was going to do the work, he wanted a lease, something binding. "I want a lease," he said, "something binding."

Hatfield glanced about, like he was viewing a meteorite crater or trying to locate the source of a howling baby. He cared nothing for the building, had inherited it from his father, a man whose death he was neither happy nor sad about. For him, the building was capital. The meager rents were gravy, a bit of extra cash each month. "What are you willing to pay?" he asked.

"Fifteen dollars a month," Sofar ventured. It was nineteen sixty-eight; no one wanted to live there. Still, fifteen dollars was extremely low. "And I'll do all the repairs. Put up some walls, the kitchen, find an oven, all of it." He waved his hands about the room, painting the vision.

"A hundred," Hatfield countered. "And no repairs."

After fifteen minutes of negotiations, Sofar and Hatfield agreed on a lease of forty-two dollars, with Sofar building the place out, making repairs, improving.

Sofar got a home. Hatfield thought he'd gotten a chump and free renovations.

Even before Hatfield left the building, before he made his way down the dilapidated stairs, he was thinking of how he'd kick Sofar out. Let him make the repairs, he thought, and after the year's lease is up, he's out. The place could be rented for more.

Hatfield was disabused of this notion three months later when he finally got around to dropping off the signed contract with his attorney. That apartment, the attorney explained, was rent stabilized. A tenant's rent could only go up by a certain percentage, a percentage dictated by New York State Rental Guidelines Board. "You make your money by having turnover," the attorney said. "Someone leaves, make some basic improvements to the place, up the rent by twenty percent."

"Basic improvements?" Hatfield owner said. "Like re-flooring the place, getting a new refrigerator?"

"God no," the attorney said, laughing sharply. "I said basic. You throw a little fresh paint on the walls, wipe down the oven, flush the toilet."

"And then I can up the rent?"

"There's some forms to fill out, some 'work related' receipts we need to provide," he said, "but yes, essentially, that's all you do."

"Then I just kick him out once I'm ready, once I think I can get more for the place."

"You can't," the attorney said. "You can't kick him out, unless he doesn't pay his rent or does something egregious."

"Egregious?" Hatfield asked, having a hard time saying the word. "What would that be?"

"Setting the place on fire, definitely," he said. "Shitting in the hall, possibly. Murder," he said, then, "Well, maybe not murder." He'd have to get back to him on that one. "But the longer he stays," the attorney informed him, "the worse it is for you. If he stays, say, twenty years, until nineteen ninety, he'll still be paying something like a hundred dollars."

"A hundred isn't bad for that hole," Hatfield said, not fully thinking it through. "And he's making repairs for free."

"We're in the space age," the attorney countered. "We're in the future. A hundred sounds fine right now, but think about what the place will be worth in twenty years. I'd bet you could get two-fifty a month for it," he said with confidence.

"Maybe three hundred," Hatfield said, getting excited.

"Let's not slip into fantasy," the attorney said. "It's a walk-up, remember?"

"I'll get him out," Hatfield said. "As soon as it's worth it, he'll be out. That you can be sure of."

But two weeks later, he met a woman named Lawrence, got married, and moved to Wyoming, officially becoming an absentee landlord, collecting rents and doing little else.

The Blisses moved into their apartment the spring of nineteen sixty-nine, signing a lease for a hundred and five dollars, over double what Sofar was paying. But their apartment, which was directly below Sofar's, was in better condition, had appliances, was livable. Which was important: the Blisses were going to have a baby. Morris was arriving.

Sofar and the Blisses became friends, each visiting the other. Seymour, needing to escape the moods of his wife and the cries of his baby boy, would take a six-pack of beer up to Sofar's, spend the evening talking things instantly forgotten. During the day, with Seymour at work, Sofar would venture down to visit Stavroula and the newborn, Morris, pass a couple hours chin-wagging. Sofar doted on Stavroula, brought her small gifts, and helped with the baby. He fell in love with her.

"Tell me about your family?" Sofar once asked her.

"My family?" Stavroula said, busying herself. "Seymour and Morris here," she said, picking up her baby, "they're my family."

"I mean, do you have siblings? A brother, sister? Are your parents still alive?"

"Seymour and Morris," she repeated, "are my family."

It was the first and last time Sofar asked. Family, he could tell, was not something to speak of.

The seventies passed. Sofar searched for his calling, studying sculpting, then dance, then Tai Chi. He went to bad art openings that served hang-over inducing wine and dated extremely thin women who had the habit of leaving the bathroom door open when they used the toilet. He got a dog, named her Hambone, and found an odd pleasure in collecting porcelain Hummels. His love for Stavroula grew.

Morris grew. By age eight, he was walking Hambone for Sofar. He ran errands, picking up eggs or a pound of blood oranges for him, always getting a tip for his work.

Hatfield returned to the city after a decade in Wyoming. He'd grown tired of raising polo ponies, tired of the severe weather and explaining to others that Lawrence, his wife, was a woman. He left her and their small ranch.

Having hemorrhaged half his assets from the wound of divorce, he went about rebuilding his holdings. He took an active role in the running of his building, wanting to turn the highest profit possible.

It was time to clear the deadwood. Sofar had to go.

Hatfield made evening visits to his building, five forty-five daily, roamed the halls with a tool belt loaded with tools that had never been used. He was a Superintendent of sorts, though he never fixed a thing. He'd knock on Sofar's door with the sole purpose of knocking, of rousting him from whatever he was doing. Hambone would set into barking.

When Sofar answered, Hatfield would say, "Aren't you ready for a change?" or "Staten Island has great views," or "You're taking advantage of me, paying so little." Five to six times a week, between five forty-five and six o'clock, he'd hammer on Sofar's door in the hopes that Sofar would finally relent, give in and say, "Okay, okay, I'll move."

He never did, never would. Sofar stayed. Time passed.

Hatfield didn't bother the Blisses; he knew better. The one time he knocked, Seymour greeted him with an eight-inch Bowie knife. "Rent's paid," Seymour said, cleaning his nails with the blade. "No other reason you should be knocking."

Hatfield didn't bother the Blisses.

He kept up his assault on Sofar, though. The entreaties and threats tapered off for a couple years when Hatfield became involved with Nana, the North American sales representative for Ciao Pussy products, a shoddy knock-off of the Hello Kitty cartoon. But when that relationship flamed-out, he turned his attention back to his building. He started in again with Sofar, now offering a handful of twenties for him to move. "To cover your moving costs," he'd say, or "I need this apartment back" or "Come on, for Christ sake, let someone else have a turn."

Sofar wasn't moving.

In the spring of 1982, there was a change. The Bliss family wasn't the same. Sofar could sense it. The air in their place was heavy and somber, a miasma of tension and unhappiness, but each time he asked either Seymour or Stavroula, he was told, "Everything's fine."

It wasn't.

Then one evening, there was a knock at Sofar's door. It was after six, so he knew it wasn't Hatfield. That, and Hambone didn't bark. She always barked at Hatfield, knew it was him at the door.

It was Stavroula. She'd come to say goodbye.

"Goodbye?" Sofar asked, upset. He was losing his neighbor, one of the few people he'd come to love. "You're moving?"

"I'm leaving," she said, her voice charred with resignation. "For a while."

"What do you mean?" he asked. "What's happened? Is it Seymour? What's he done?"

"It's me," she told him, then kissed him on the cheek. "It's something in me," she told him.

With the burn of her kiss still on his cheek, Sofar realized that her family was his. He loved her, had lived a vicarious relationship through her, experiencing all the problems and joys of a family. Had lived a life not his own. "I don't want you to go," he told her, taking her hand. He struggled for words, wanting to say more, say something consequential, affecting.

"I don't want to go," Stavroula said, her eyes pooling. "But I need to go." Her hand broke from of his. The door quietly shut.

That night, Sofar sat in a dark room, his chest feeling hollowed out by a hand axe. His fabric of Hope, the cloth that kept the cold of the world from chilling him, slightly tore.

~~~

All things, good or bad, come in threes. With Stavroula gone, the bad began. Hatfield's increased his assault on Sofar, his tactics turning malicious.

Using a screwdriver, he bored a hole in the building's roof above Sofar's apartment. Rainwater seeped in, damaging the ceiling.

The plaster turned a teabag brown, sagged like the flesh of a flabby arm.

While he hated to do it, Sofar called Hatfield, had him come take a look. "A lot of work, a lot of work," Hatfield said when he finally got around to examining the damage a week after the call. The one time Sofar wanted him, he wasn't around. It'd rained three days straight. Chunks of the drywall had come loose, fallen to the floor. A saucepan sat on the floor, collecting the rainwater. Hambone was locked in the bathroom, to keep her from biting Hatfield. "Looks like I'm going to have to take the whole ceiling down, find where the leaky pipe is."

"Leaky pipe?" Sofar said. "It's the roof. There's a hole. All you got to do is patch it."

"I'm not certain of that," Hatfield said, his head cocked as he stared at the ceiling. "I'm thinking it's a pipe. I'm thinking I'm going to have to take the entire apartment's ceiling down, just to make sure." Pausing a moment, he added, "Probably a seven week process." He clicks his tongue, shakes his head. "Maybe longer. Sure wouldn't want to try living here when the work's going on. The dust," he said, "the mess," then asks, "When's your lease up?"

The next morning, the sun came out. Sofar bought a can of tar sealant and some shingles. Finding the hole in the roof, he patched it himself, then repaired his ceiling. The whole project took him less than ten hours.

"We can get started on your place Tuesday," Hatfield told him when he stopped by at five forty-five.

"It's fixed," Sofar said.

"Fixed?" Hatfield asked.

Sofar showed him the work. "A hole in the roof," Sofar said. "Looked like it was done intentionally."

"Intentionally?" Hatfield asked, feigning concern. "I don't like the idea of someone damaging my property," he said. "Do you have any enemies, someone who's out to get you?"

"I can only think of one," Sofar said, glaring at him.

"Now listen here Sofar," Hatfield said, angrily, "if you're implying that I was the one who took a screwdriver—"

"Screwdriver?" Sofar asked. "Who said anything about a screwdriver?"

Hatfield stammered. "You did."

"No, I didn't."

"Well, it's good…" He gestured at the ceiling, backed up toward the door. "Good, I'm glad it's fixed," he said, then left.

Having called Hatfield's bluff, Sofar thought the harassment would stop. He was deluded to think so.

It got worse: a can of pink paint was spilt outside of Sofar's front door; the master fuse for his apartment, the one located in the basement of the building, went missing four times; random phone calls in the middle of the night would wake him; a foul odor of rotting, like that of death and cabbage stew, hovered in the hall out front of his place.

And still, the owner banged on his door every few days at five forty-five p.m., wanting nothing more than to irk Sofar.

Sofar's life ground down, his immunity and defenses beaten and bruised by the owner's continuous badgering, by the absence of Stavroula. He'd kept up with Seymour, with Morris, gave the boy errands. But he'd felt awkward, unwanted, whenever he popped in to see Seymour and the boy. His visits grew infrequent, rare.

Then Stavroula returned. He was overjoyed, but his joy was short lived. She was quite ill. It was obvious the moment he saw her. It was in her eyes. They were no longer as dark as they once were, no longer shiny and glowing and vibrant. Her eyes said it all; something was killing her, silently gutting her every moment of the day. Hambone whimpered, turned circles. He knew the woman, but her smell wasn't the same. She smelled of bad things to come. "Stavroula," Sofar said, trying to sound cheerful. He took her hand, though he wanted to hug her, to wrap his arm about her. "You look—" He broke off, the words lost. "I'm glad your home," he finally said.

She died on a Thursday, early morning, in the hospital. Hatfield pounded on the door at his regular time. Sofar answered, his mind clouded with grief. "Stavroula died," Sofar said before Hatfield could speak.

"What happened?"

"Mrs. Bliss," he said, "apartment eight. She died."

"Oh…well, sorry to hear it," he said, caught off guard. He'd never seen Sofar emotional. "When's the funeral?"

"Sunday. Four p.m."

Hatfield nodded, his mind churning with thought. "Sunday," he said, "at four."

The funeral was long, solemn, and saddening. Sofar felt as though it was his wife who died. His fabric of Hope frayed more, the ragged edges catching in the gears of life. He was brimming with sorrow, confusion. He didn't understand anything anymore. It was all a mess, a joke, what he called life, what he did day-to-day. He had no calling, no purpose.

None of Stavroula's family showed. Only Seymour and Morris. They were all Stavroula had. Now all they had was each other. It couldn't get any worse, Sofar thought, offering a prayer before leaving the funeral parlor.

He was wrong.

Returning home at around seven that evening, he found his front door ajar, the hinges broken. His place was a mess, all his items, including his Hummels, smashed or stolen.

Hambone was gone.

Twenty-eight

At five-thirty, Sofar sets three egg timers, one for five minutes, another for fifteen, and the third for thirty minutes, then sits on a turned milk crate and files his fingernails, then his toenails, then his fingertips to the point of rawness, making certain there's nothing left to file. Five-thirty to five thirty-five. It's the same every day. All in preparation for Hatfield, battle. Five minutes, the first egg timer chimes. Sofar lies on the floor, closes his eyes. Fifteen minutes, he tells himself, that what he's got to make it through. Fifteen minutes. He concentrates on his breathing, on pulling all things from his mind. He tucks away his thought of Hambone, his longings for Stavroula. He packs it all away. Ten minutes of slipping into the right state of mind.

After Stavroula's funeral, after his loss, Sofar had a meltdown. The woman he loved was dead, his dog gone, his apartment ransacked.

Morris visited a few days after the funeral. "Mr. Sofar?" Morris called. His door was open, ajar. Morris walked in to find Sofar standing in the middle of the wrecked room, running the jagged head of a broken Hummel along his lips. They were bleeding. "What happened?" Morris asked, frightened.

Sofar slowly turned. "Stavroula," he said, staring at Morris.

"You okay? Where's Hambone?"

Sofar dropped the Hummel head and walked into his bedroom, returned with a yellow and orange dress, the colors vibrant and nauseating. He'd bought it for Morris's mother, as a gift for when she left the hospital. "Stavroula," Sofar said again, a near chant. He pulled the dress from the packaging, walked it to Morris.

"You okay, Mr. Sofar?" Morris asked. He backed up a step. "You seem kind of not well."

Sofar paused a few feet from Morris.

"Why's your place a mess?" Morris asks. "And where's Hambone?" Morris called for the dog. It didn't come.

Sofar grabbed Morris, pressed the dress to him. "Stavroula," he said again, and started crying.

Morris stood still, terrified.

Then Sofar pressed his bloody lips to Morris's.

Morris flailed, knocking the dress and Sofar to the floor. Morris backed out of the apartment, leaving Sofar, dress in hand, weeping.

It was the last time Morris visited.

The *ding* of the second timer sounds. 5:45 p.m. Sofar stands, shakes out his arms and legs like a runner reaching for a world record. If Hatfield's coming, he's coming now, in the next fifteen minutes. Hatfield's like some incubus of the late afternoon; he only attacks during that that fifteen-minute window. Outside that realm, Hatfield doesn't exist.

In the reality called now, Hatfield doesn't exit either. Not anymore. A month after he turned over Sofar's apartment and stole his dog—which was some twenty-two years ago—Hatfield sold the building to the Rockworth Real Estate Corporation. He'd grown tired of it all, the work, the running around. He took the cash he got for the building and bought a golf course in Louisiana that sat on top of an old landfill. A year later, he developed strange red boils around his anus and died in a matter of weeks.

Word got back. Sofar heard the news: the building had been sold; Hatfield was dead. But it was a ruse, Sofar was certain. Just another way Hatfield tried to make him lower his guard, to get him out of his apartment. Hatfield was alive, alive and plotting. He'd be back, and when he came back, it'd be between 5:45 and 6:00 p.m.

Wearing his best black wingtips, shoes that have never touched the street, Sofar begins his path, pacing from one end of his apartment to the other at a rate of three lengths a minute, forty-five lengths total, for a total of fifteen minutes.

He has it measured out perfectly. He just had to stay in motion, that's what matters, to be in motion, to have movement. Fifteen minutes, then the threat will have passed. He'll be safe for another day once that third egg timer rings. The threat will have passed.

Four minutes pass, then seven, then fourteen. It's the same everyday. Sofar paces, the soles of his shoes clicking against the worn hardwood floor. He reaches the front of his apartment and sharply turns about. Home stretch. He feels the end approach. The last distance is the most difficult. He wants to run, to reach the other end of his apartment. He wants the timer to chime. Then the elements of his world will once again align for another day.

Counting down, he enters the middle room. Nine steps, seven, four steps remaining. He's done it so often his steps are synchronized to the timer. Touch the bedroom wall, the chime will sound. Just like yesterday, and the day prior. Just like always.

And as his hand goes out and as his fingers brush against the drywall, he hears the sound. He hears two sounds at once, one familiar, one foreign.

The timer offers its comforting *ting*.

The front door offers a resounding knock.

Twenty-nine

The twenty-seventh annual Ukrainian Festival to benefit St. Benedict's opens with a flutter. It's a week-long event of mediocre music, tepid food, and poorly planned festivities. At a quarter to seven, Morris wanders the sparse crowd, looking for Stefani. On an elevated stage that resembles gallows for public hangings, a priest offers a prayer, blesses the small gathering of people and the charity raffle, which anyone can enter for a dollar. Only a dollar a ticket, the priest repeats, and it's for a good cause.

All of Seventh Street is cordoned off between Second and Third Avenue, battered blue police barricades standing at each end, allowing no traffic through. Rickety framed booths with rain-proof tarps tossed over the top are manned by elderly women with hands as rough as a salted street before a winter storm. It's all for the church, the school, the motherland, and the museum that will never get built. They sell anything and everything—small store-bought snacks, poorly crafted Ukrainian tchotchkes, individual sticks of gum, and cold, hard pierogies—all at exorbitant prices. The name of Christ allows them to gouge.

The festival's never advertised, never publicized. Most people come across it accidentally, stumble onto it on their way for a beer at McSorley's or Burp Castle or the all-you-can-eat early bird buffet at Terry's Thai Land. Still, in the church's newsletter, the event is always reported as a wild success.

Waiting in front of McSorley's for Stefani, Morris watches as the Young Krainers, a traditional Ukrainian dance group comprised of eight and nine-year-olds, take the stage. They're costumed in the clothing of the people from the old country, peasant clothing. The costumes cost a mint.

The music's cued. The needle drops on the worn, black record, and the first notes jump, cutting and loud; then the music rolls, uneven and pitching, a dingy on roiling seas. The sound rips down the street, echoing off the old tenement buildings and hitting the heavy brown stones of Cooper Union hard and flat. The music bounces, shooting back to mangle its approaching self.

The volume is adjusted just as the young dancers start their steps.

The children, dressed as little men and women, move about the stage with little joy, little feeling for what they are doing. It's obvious they don't want to be here; it's an activity their parents make them do. Culture. Heritage. All the things that are to be remembered and held close to oneself; all the things youth wants to bury and forget.

The boys pull colorful handkerchiefs from their pockets and hold them high above their heads. The girls grab the free end of the hankies and spin and spin, their white dresses with red and yellow embroidery flaring like dying tulips. It's a traditional mating dance, or an ancient harvest dance, or a worshipful funeral dance. It's a dance of celebration or mourning, Morris can't tell. All he sees is the awkwardness of the young dancers, their clear desire to end the show as quickly as possible and get off stage, get back into regular street clothes.

Morris had knocked and knocked on Sofar's door. No answer. Sofar was inside. Morris knew he was inside, had heard him pacing his apartment, but the man refused to come to the door. He'd called through the door, said, "Mr. Sofar, it's Morris Bliss from downstairs. Stavroula's son." He wanted to see the man, talk with him. Vanquish the sour memory of Sofar turning freaky on him.

For three minutes, Morris knocked, then gave up. Sofar wasn't going to answer his door.

After the Young Krainers complete their routine, an older group takes the stage. They're dressed exactly the same, dance the exact same dances, only this group is taller, larger. It's like the Young Krainers have been miraculously transported five years into their future.

A hand slides on Morris's shoulder. Stefani, Morris thinks. He turns to find Jetski.

"Jet...Steven," Morris says, nonplussed.

Jetski's been drinking; his face is an odd shade of purple and his lips like that of a horse's, large and rubbery. "Shit, Morrie, old buddy," he says. He laughs a laugh that kicks out spittle from his wet mouth. "I didn't know you were into this stuff," he says, waving a hand about.

"Oh, I'm just waiting," Morris tells him. "For someone," he adds, then, "Nice seeing you." He tries to wander off.

"Where you going?" Jetski asks, taking his arm. "Bloody Eagles, baby. We've got to have a drink."

"I would, but I—"

"Who you waiting on?"

"A girl," Morris says, reluctantly.

"She Ukrainian?" He slightly lists, working to stay balanced.

"Down the line," Morris says. "Yes."

"Does she have big—"

"I should get going," Morris says.

Jetski won't free him, won't let go of his arm. He leans in to Morris. "What's she like?" he asks.

"How do you mean?" Morris asks, but he knows how he means. His kidneys ache; he has to urinate like he's never had to before, like it's never been an issue until now.

"I mean," Jetski says, his breath hot, "how is she—"

"Who's been naughty?" a voice interrupts.

Both Morris and Jetski turn.

There stands Andrea Angel, rigid yet beautiful. Like a stuffed pheasant. Her arms are akimbo, a smile on her face. "Morris, you never called like you promised," she says.

Morris never promised.

Her hair's different. She's cut her hair, cropped and dyed it a deep, brick red. Combed high and back, it is styled like a lion's mane that's been blow-dried and over-moussed. She gives Morris a kiss on the corner of his mouth, a kiss that is a near kiss, but not quite.

"Andrea," he says.

"You like the hair, right?" she says, pirouetting. "A new me." She speaks to Morris like they are alone, just she and he. Like Jetski's the autistic sibling: acknowledged but not included.

Jetski stares at Andrea like she's veal and he's starved. His breathing loud, a near snore.

"You look nice," Morris says.

"Right, nice," Andrea replies, expecting more.

"You look fantastic," Morris counters, meaning it. "Really fantastic. What's the reason for the make-over?"

"After last night, after our drinks, right, what you said really sank in," she tells him.

"What did I say?"

"Right," Andrea says, and laughs. "Like you've forgotten. No, your words cut me to my soul."

"No, really. What did I say?"

"You know, that whole thing about all those things, right? So this morning I said, 'Andrea, something new.' I went to Bumble and Bumble beauty salon and here I am, right." She rounds her arms about Morris's neck and braces herself to him. "Just like you said, and you were right, right?" she says, dragging him a step or two in time with the warped music. "I was so happy last night."

"That's great," Morris says, a thread of heat yanking through him. Her body next to his. "Andrea, I'm—"

She gives him a kiss, her lips crushing his. She pulls free, lets him go. "Got to run, right. Drinks again sometime this week?"

Morris vaguely nods, etherized by her kiss.

"Oh, hey, right," she says, before heading off. "Know who I saw when I was getting my hair done? That guy who runs that horrible deli around from us."

"Mr. Charlies?" Morris asks.

"Right, him. He was in the chair next to mine, getting his hair done. The whole package, dye-job and all. Never thought a man so ugly could spend so much and still look so ugly, right?"

"Mr. Charlies?" Morris asks again, incredulous. "He was getting his hair done?"

"Got George to deal with," Andrea says, turning. She heads off. "Drinks again, right?"

Jetski sides up to Morris, panting. "*Blood*-ee Eagle, baby. Morrie, that was solid," he says, watching Andrea work down the street.

"No, it wasn't," Morris says, riled, confused. He feels unstable, a combustible element listed high on the Periodic Table, one ready to explode from the slightest improper handling. Andrea's kiss. Another Mr. Charlies sighting.

"It was solid, Morrie," Jetski repeats. "First, the taking of precinct nine, now the women," Jetski says, excited. "Just like old times, Morrie, like way back when."

"No," Morris tells Jetski, "it's not."

~~~

Stefani snacks on a frozen Snickers bar and a bag of Cheesy Curls, chasing it down with a can of Mountain Dew as she sits on the curb outside of Love Saves the Day on First Avenue and Seventh Street. People pass. The festival stumbles to life. Morris is waiting for her down the street, out front of McSorley's. She saw him there, is making him wait. "Absence makes it hard to throw farmers," she tells herself. She heard the adage somewhere, in a movie, maybe, and liked how it sounded, though she has no idea what it means. All she knows is she's going to make Morris wait.

Bright orange crumbles of Cheesy Curls drift down onto her white Baby Phat jeans as she fills her mouth with two or three at a time. The music from the festival pitches and rises, sending an off-tune wave of noise. Some girls from her class stroll past, girls who look at her but don't acknowledge her. Stefani stares straight through them, knowing it's better to be aloof and remain unhurt than venture a "Hey" or "What's up?" and be snubbed.

Finishing her soda, her candy bar, and her Cheesy Curls, Stefani stands. Prom is on the agenda, though she no longer plans to go with Morris. She dampened on that idea since Robby Robinovitz, the boy with the sticky touch whose father owns a Subway sandwich shop, asked her to prom between English and Biology class today. Only

Robby's touch was no longer sticky. And he'd grown, filled out and become less chunky and more strapping. He'd been out of school for over a month, been in the hospital for an operation on something deep inside him, something that wasn't working the way it was supposed to work. "I'm not even sure myself," Robby told Stefani when she'd asked. "They explained it to me, but I didn't understand. All I know is that it was painful, and that I have a scar across my stomach. I have to go in for another operation at the end of summer."

"Are you going to live?" Stefani asked, intrigued. The idea of dating someone terminally ill held a perverse appeal. She envisioned herself wearing black and crying over his casket, envisioned all the attention she'd get.

"Probably not," he said, and shrugged. "But I'm good for now." He then asked if she wanted to go to prom with him.

She said yes, on one condition.

"Name it," he tells her.

"I want a kiss," she says, testing him.

He dove in passionately, grabbed her head in his cool, dry hands and stroked his tongue to hers.

A passing student hooted, yelled, "Go, go, go."

They ignored him.

Pulling back for air, Stefani said, "Yeah. Yeah, okay. Prom." They made out until the bell rang.

Morris is nice, Stefani thinks, but he's nice the way librarians are nice: quiet, helpful, reserved. And who wants to date a librarian? She'll let him down easy, tell him she changed her mind, isn't going at all.

She brushes the faux-cheese dust off her pants, applies some grape-flavored lip-gloss, brushes her hair, then strides down the street toward McSorley's and the dancing Ukrainians.

It's through the sparse crowd, past the stands selling undercooked meat products and warm cans of Coke, beyond the clattering old women in knitted shawls, that Stefani sees Morris.

She stops some distance away.

Her father's with him, his arm around Morris's shoulder. Seeing this, she grows angry. Morris is mine, she thinks, seething. Her father can't have him back; they can't be friends like they used to be. Morris is hers.

"He'll pay," she says to herself, watching her father laugh.

Then she sees the skinny woman with red lion's mane, sees Morris dance with her. Sees them kiss.

"That son of a bitch," she says. "He's cheating on me." She's jilted. Hurt. Enraged. "He'll pay, too," she says. "Goddamn it, they'll both pay."

Thirty

Stefani never showed. Morris was thankful. He couldn't shake Jetski, and if Jetski saw him with Stefani, if he knew what had happened between the two, he'd be infuriated. Most likely violent.

At home, Morris finds Seymour watching TV. He hasn't seen him all day. "What happened with that job talking on phones?" his father asks, his voice aggressive. "You need to get a job, get some money going."

"I visited Mr. Sofar today, Daddy," Morris says.

"Why?"

"I wanted to ask him about mom," he says, then, "Why did she leave us?"

"You know why she left," Seymour says, immediately subdued. He doesn't cherish the topic. "She was sick."

"That's not a reason. Why'd she leave?" he asks again, intent on an answer.

"You were there," Seymour says, tersely.

"I was twelve."

Seymour's mouth works like he is chewing a fistful of twigs. "She left 'cause she left," he finally says, then falls silent, a look of discomfort settling over him.

Morris knows that his father believes that what's done is done, and all that can be affected is now and what happens after now.

Seymour won't look his son in the face, his eyes wandering. "You never explained the woman's underwear," he says, shifting topics. "You aren't wearing them, are you?"

"You haven't answered me about mom," Morris replies.

"What'd Sofar tell you?"

"He didn't answer the door," Morris says, then, "Why'd mom leave?"

"She left 'cause she left," he says again.

"But why?"

Seymour turns from Morris. He looks at his hands like they hold the answer. "To see her father and mother, your grandfolks. She tried to see them and make them accept us. Accept me."

"For three months?" Morris asks. The fact that Seymour was once Morris's age snaps into his thoughts. The idea strikes him as odd, like when first realizing that the sun is stationary. It is us who move around it. "Three months is awful long for a visit," Morris says, continuing his questions. "Why didn't she come home? Why didn't she take me? What was she doing that entire time?" His mother's mother and father; these are people he knows of but has never met, people that exist as words. Grandpa, grandma. He had no family beyond his father. His paternal grandparents had passed away before he was born. It should all seem sad and strange to him, but it isn't. It's something he's never had, never known. The ghost of something missing.

"She was doing nothing there," Seymour says. "Or everything. They refused to see her," he says. "Wouldn't even acknowledge her. So she" — he pauses, swallows — "she followed them around for three months, went everywhere they went, trying to get them to understand, to accept her back. To accept her family, you and me."

"She stalked them?"

"I'm to blame," Seymour says. "They disowned her because of me." He turns his attention back to the TV, like the conversation is over, or has never started.

Morris turns the TV off. "What'd you do?"

"Nothing. I didn't do nothing."

"You must've done something."

"I loved her," Seymour says, his tone edged with hurt. "That's what I did."

"They disowned her because —"

"Mors," he says, "there's things I can tell you because I know them. Then there's things I can't tell you 'cause I don't know. Your granddad didn't like me," he says. "I don't know why."

"Have you tried to talk to them lately?"

"They're dead," Seymour says. "Died soon after your mom did."

"I—" Morris breaks off, realizing he doesn't know what to say.

"What I know," Seymour says, speaking loudly, steadying his voice, "is I loved your mother more than anything. And even when I didn't, when she'd get all moody and crablike and angry at me, even then, I loved her. I loved her," he says.

Morris is silent a moment, then nods. "Okay," he says.

Seymour looks to him. "Okay what? What's okay?"

"Just…okay. You, us. Mom," Morris says. "Okay."

Thirty-one

"I'm moving to Montana," N.J. says over the phone, his voice tinny and thin like he's calling from there. It's ten p.m. After their talk, Seymour went to bed, his energies exhausted. Just living, it seemed, took Pyrrhic effort.

"Montana?" Morris asks N.J., standing in the kitchen. It needs cleaning.

"Montana, man."

"What's in Montana?"

"Me, man, or soon I'll be," N.J. says. "Or rather, us. I'm in love."

"In love," Morris says, switching the phone to his other ear. He picks up a damp dishrag, runs it over the kitchen counter then drops it in the sink. "Who are you in love with now?"

"Now?" N.J. says, his voice fading then gaining strength. "Hattie," he says. "It's always been Hattie."

"The woman from downstairs?" Morris asks, shifting some items about, the salt-shaker, a cutting board, then shifting them back. He can't think of what she looks like, can't recall ever seeing her in the building. "You mean the woman you met last night?"

"Montana," he says. "We leave Tuesday."

"Tuesday? Like in tomorrow?" Morris pinches the phone between his shoulder and ear. "What are you going to do, hunt down fugitive buffalos?"

"Buffali," N.J. says. "The plural of buffalo is buffali, man. And no, man. I'm not hunting them down. I'll be ranching them."

"Ranching them?"

"Yeah, man, raising them on a ranch. Just Hattie and I."

"That's great," Morris says. Like N.J.'s other ideas, it's all banter. N.J.'s gone everywhere without ever having left. And I've gone nowhere while always planning to leave, Morris thinks damply.

"Listen, N.J.," he says, wanting to clean up a bit, "I've got to go. Talk to you tomorrow."

"I'm coming over," N.J. says.

"Why?"   ·

"I'm coming over," he repeats, then rings off.

Morris drops the phone on the hand rest.

The door buzzes, startling Morris. "Yeah?" he asks, pressing the talk button. He hits the listen button.

"N.J., man," N.J. replies.

"How did you get here so fast?" Morris asks, speaking into the intercom. He toggles between the talk and listen button.

" —at?"

"How did you get here so fast?" he repeats, not understanding.

" —ike I said, man. What did I say, man?"

"I asked," Morris says, then gives up, hits the door button, letting N.J. in.

There is a knock at the door a moment later. Morris opens the door. "How'd you get here so quick?"

"What are you talking about, man? I said I was coming over. I'm over," he says, then, "Let's go."

"Where?"

"Who is that?" Seymour calls from his room.

"It's N.J., Da—" He pulls up short, nearly saying Daddy. "N.J., Dad," he says.

"Good evening Mr. Bliss," N.J. calls. "How are you doing this evening? I was just telling Mor—"

"Shut up in there. The both of you," Seymour yells. "I'm sleeping."

"Good night," N.J. calls, then quietly says to Morris, "Got to show you something."

"It's late. Show me tomorrow," he says.

"I'm gone after tomorrow," N.J. said.

"Gone?" Morris asks, already having forgotten. "Where?" N.J. talks so much heat that his words are steam; they instantly dissipate, leave no stain of what was said.

"Montana, man. I told you, on the phone."

"Right, Montana," Morris says, his voice flat. "To raise buffalos with this Mattie woman."

"Buffali," N.J. says. "And her name's Hattie, not Mattie. She's the one who showed me."

"Showed you what?"

"The signs, man. They're everywhere, hidden notes and symbols saying things to the people who know what to look for. It's like a whole world of Masonic handshakes and backroom deals brokered by guys who shave all their body hair."

Morris glances about the kitchen. He doesn't feel like cleaning. "All right." He relents. The evening's pleasant. He'd enjoy a walk. "Show me," he says, grabbing his keys.

N.J. leads him south, toward Houston Street. After a ten-minute walk, the entire time of which N.J. talks of the West, the rolling hills, his plans for the ranch, they stop at the corner of Rivington Street and Essex. "There," N.J. says, motioning to the Essex Street Retail Market building. "That's it."

Morris looks at the dirty, mustard yellow building with dragon red doors. He'd only been in the building once, and found all the stands, all the stalls, selling useless items at an inflated price. The butcher shop's meats looked fouled and old, like they'd been left in the sun for an afternoon. There was a kosher wine shop inside that was offering a sample taste of their product. Morris tried a small glass, which he struggled to keep down. "How do you like?" the Hasidic owner asked. His side locks were long, longer than Morris had ever seen, reaching to the middle of his chest.

"Well," Morris said, setting the plastic cup down. "In all honesty, it's bad."

"You don't like it?" the owner asked. "You don't like?"

"No," Morris said. "It's pretty sour."

The owner's face blossomed into a smile. He relaxed. "Pretty sour?" he said, sounding pleased. "Good. I'm glad to hear. All my Jewish customers tell me that. But I'm glad to hear a Gentile tell me that, too."

"Good?" Morris asked. "You want it to taste bad?"

"Yes," he said, then placed a kind hand on Morris's shoulder. "A secret," he said, stepping near. He smelled of basil and old wool, a smell Morris found comforting. "It tastes sour," he tells Morris, "so you drink only a little. If it tasted better, you'd drink more." He explains. "My customers are my people, Jews. Only Jews buy kosher wine, and yes, I want them to drink my wine, but not drink too much, you see?"

"No," Morris said. "I don't."

"Winos don't drink kosher wine, do they?" he asks. "Have you ever seen one of my people drunk? Have you ever heard of an alcoholic Hasid?"

Morris thought. "No," he said, "I haven't."

The owner patted his shoulder. "Then you see. No one can become an alcoholic off kosher wine. It's too sour."

Staring at the closed market, Morris asks N.J., "So, what are you showing me?"

"By all appearances, a nice, little market, man. It's not."

"It's not?"

N.J. takes Morris by the arm, leads him halfway down the block. They stop at a streetlamp. "What is this?" N.J. says, tapping on the metal pole of the lamp.

"A streetlight." Different from the other streetlamps, it's cast iron, ornate, like those from the early twentieth century. The only one of its kind on the block, it pours its buttery glow over the sidewalk, the street.

"Exactly, man. And what do lamps do?" N.J. asks, patronizingly.

"They light up," Morris says, growing tired of the game. "Show me what you want to show me. I've got things to do," he says.

"They illuminate, man," N.J. says.

Morris lifts his hands, acquiescing. "Okay, great," he says. "They illuminate. What does *this* particular streetlight illuminate?"

"The truth, man. The truth."

"Which is?"

"Sometimes showing the obvious, man. Know what I'm saying?"

"No."

"Stand right here," he says, placing Morris right in front of the pole. "Okay, man," N.J. says. "What's that sign say there across the street?" He points to the market. On the building, embossed on the concrete wall, read the words:

ESSEX STREET

RETAIL MARKET

"Essex street retail market," Morris says, his view partially blocked by the pole.

"That's not what you see, man," N.J. says, disappointed. "You're seeing what you think you should see, man. You're not seeing what you're really seeing."

"I'm seeing what I'm seeing," Morris says, annoyed. "Tell me what I'm not seeing?"

"Look at it again, man."

Morris stands less than a foot from the pole and looks up at the sign across the street. "Essex—"

"No," N.J. says. "Not Essex. That's not what you're seeing."

Then Morris sees. With the view blocked by the streetlamp, the sign no longer reads:

ESSEX STREET

RETAIL MARKET

but

SEX STREET

TAIL MARKET

Morris says it out loud. "That," he says, "is just stupid."

"To the layman, man, yeah. I thought it was stupid, too, when Hattie was showing me. But check this out, man," N.J. says, then bends down and points to a symbol tooled into the base of the streetlamp. Made of a metal that looks like rose gold, the symbol is a looped rope, its ends pointing skyward.

"What's that?" Morris asks. "A tapeworm?"

"A sign, man. A sign."

"Okay, so…you stand here at the light pole with a little—I don't know—thing, and then the sign reads Sex Street Tail Market. You dragged me down here for that?"

"It's a Red Thread, man," N.J. says. "And this place happens to be the biggest sex bazaar on the east coast, man. They bring girls in from all over, Asia, the Middle East, Alabama—"

"Alabama?"

"It's a clearinghouse for sex, man."

"I've been in there," Morris says. "There's no sex going on. All there is in there are overpriced stores and stuff people don't want to buy. And who are 'they'?"

"They, man. The Red Thread. The secret cartel. The people who run the world. The Red Thread runs through everything, man. Businesses on Wall Street, Dakar, Gillette, Wyoming—"

"Why Gillette?"

"Coal, man. Fuel. Power."

"I'm heading home," Morris says.

"Tell me, man, how can a market that sells stuff no one buys stay open?"

"I don't know," Morris says. "Don't care, either." Then he says, "Someone must sell something in there." He thinks of the Hasid with the foul wine, how proud he was to make it taste awful.

"Oh, they sell something in there, man," N.J. says. "They sell sex."

Thirty-two

Morris doesn't argue. It's too ridiculous to argue. It's like racing for closing elevator doors; catch it or not, you look like an idiot. "Listen, whatever," he tells N.J. "The market can be whatever you want it to be." The Red Thread. The Bloody Eagles. Colors and birds. Jetski and N.J. are playing with me, Morris thinks.

They're working together, he thinks, then realizes that it's impossible. Jetski isn't that smart; N.J.'s too erratic.

"Got to run, man," N.J. tells Morris. "Gotta meet Hattie." He takes off, jogging down the street.

Morris waves him on. "We'll talk tomorrow."

"My flight's at noon," N.J. calls over his shoulder. "I'll stop by early."

"Right," Morris says, shaking his head. Tomorrow's noon will arrive. It'll pass. N.J. will still be here, talking the next plan, the next woman, the next day.

N.J.'s lies aren't lies to N.J. They're all hope, a true innocent belief. He believes he'll do what he says he'll do.

At least he still believes, Morris thinks. Still hopes.

Not wanting to go home, Morris wanders a bit, then decides to stop in Mr. Charlies. See if he's there.

He's there.

"Mr. Charlies," Morris says, walking in.

Mr. Charlies glares at Morris, his eyes tight. "Yes, Mr. Charlies, hello, Mr. Charlies."

"I've heard you've been out and about, doing up the town."

"I'm here, twenty-four hours, yes, everyday," Mr. Charlies says, wearily studying Morris.

Mr. Charlies' hair looks the same, foppish and black. It looked like it hadn't been combed in days. Morris asks anyway. "A friend said they saw you getting your hair done."

"There's something you need, Mr. Charlies?" he asks. "Anything you need you tell me, Mr. Charlies. I'll get it for you."

"I was thinking tea, Mr. Charlies," Morris says. "Something nice, fancy, something like what they might serve at the Plaza hotel," Morris says, watching Mr. Charlies closely to see if there is a reaction to his mention of the Plaza. "You ever been to the Plaza, Mr. Charlies? Ever been in a limo?"

"Tea, yes, Mr. Charlies," Mr. Charlies says, coming from behind the register. "We have tea. Fancy tea, Mr. Charlies, I have that," he says, coming back with a large, orange and yellow box of tea. It's Lipton's. "Fancy, fancy, like they serve in the Hamiltons," he tells Morris.

"The Hamiltons?"

"Yes, Mr. Charlies," Mr. Charlies says, ringing up the box of fifty tea bags for $3.99. "The rich, rich. They drink it iced in the summers."

"What's the Hamiltons?" Morris asks.

"Where the rich, rich drink the tea, Mr. Charlies," Mr. Charlies says. "The movie people and the rich people. The place they go in the summer, on the island, Mr. Charlies."

"You mean the Hamptons?" Morris ventures.

"That's what I said, yes," he says, bagging the tea. "Anything else, Mr. Charlies?"

"A dance club," Morris states. "In Chelsea. My friend saw you there. And you apparently saw him, too," Morris says, recalling N.J.'s tale.

"A club of dance, Mr. Charlies?" Mr. Charlies asks, a look of confusion on his face.

"One of those" — Morris searches for a word to describe it — "macho places."

"Macho, Mr. Charlies?" Mr. Charlies asks. "What is a macho?"

"The Leather Muskat," Morris says, naming the club.

"Ah, yes," Mr. Charlies says, his face lighting up. "Yes, yes, of course, Mr. Charlies." He comes from behind the counter. "I know, I know what you speak of."

"So it's true?" Morris is surprised.

"Yes, very true, Mr. Charlies." He passes Morris and heads to the back of the store. "Very true and very popular. A lot of men like it," he calls. "I, myself, like it, Mr. Charlies."

Lurid images of Mr. Charlies jigging on a dance floor in the midst of young, shirtless men shoots painful through Morris's mind. "Does Mrs. Charlies, your wife, know?" Morris asks, watching him scoot down an aisle.

"She knows. She insists on it," he says, coming back to the counter. He hits the cash register for $6.50. "This makes them wild, Mr. Charlies," he says, placing an item on the counter. "You'll like very much, Mr. Charlies," Mr. Charlies says, tapping a dusty bottle.

Morris picks it up. *Leather Musk*, the label reads. Cologne.

"Ten forty-nine," Mr. Charlies says. He snaps out a plastic bag, puts both items in.

"No," Morris says, "I wanted to know if you'd ever been to a gay club—"

"Yes, Mr. Charlies," Mr. Charlies says. "Ten forty-nine."

"I don't want this stuff," Morris says, realizing what he's just purchased.

"Ten forty-nine, yes."

"I don't want it."

"Yes, ten forty-nine."

Morris gives up, hands Mr. Charlies a ten, then sees if he has change. The tea he'll drink. The cologne he'll give to N.J. A going away present for not going away.

Morris doesn't have change. All he has is another ten, and twenties, money from the focus group. "Can I owe you, Mr. Charlies?" he asks.

"Ten forty-nine, Mr. Charlies," he says, pointing to the register. "Ten forty-nine. Ten forty-nine, please, Mr. Charlies."

Reluctantly, Morris hands him another ten-dollar bill.

"Out of twenty," Mr. Charlies says, ringing out the till.

The drawer pops open. Mr. Charlies places the two bills in, then shakes his head. "Oh, problems, Mr. Charlies," he says. "No change."

Thirty-three

Bag in hand, Morris steps out onto the street. He decides on a beer. The Old Homeplate instead of home.

There are four people in the bar, a crowd for a Monday night. One of them is N.J. He's sitting at the bar. "Hey," Morris says, surprised. He left him twenty minutes prior. "What are you doing here?"

"Waiting for Hattie, man," N.J. says. He's decked out in a leather cowboy shirt, black leather pants, and blue, red, and orange detailed cowboy boots. He looks stiff and unyielding, like he's been sprayed with a thick coating of sealant.

"How'd you change so quick?" Morris asks, touching the shirt. He smells of a tannery, rich and woodsy and strong. "And what's up with the outfit, you kill a cow?"

"When in Rome," N.J. says, waving Mrs. Cruxo over and ordering Morris a beer.

"What do you mean, 'When in Rome'?"

"Montana, man. This is what they wear in Montana. This is what I'll be wearing when I herd, man."

"You're really going?"

"I'm going, man. Hattie and me are going." N.J. motioned to Morris's bag. "What'd you buy, man?"

"Things," Morris says, placing the bag on the bar. "Got you a present." He takes the cologne from the bag. "To go with your outfit."

"Thanks, man," he says, sincerely touched. He splashes some on. "Hattie loves this stuff," he says, then, "I'm going to miss you, man."

The beer comes. Mrs. Cruxo sets it down in front of Morris. "I got this one, man," N.J. says. His pants are so tight he has to stand to get his hand in his pocket. "This one's on me."

"The enabled is now the enabler?"

"No, man, I just owe you a round or two."

"Or two hundred."

"Or two hundred," N.J. concedes, pulling out a roll of bills the size of a horse's leg. He peels off a hundred dollar bill, sets it on the bar.

"My God, N.J. Where'd you get that?"

"Hattie, man. She set me up. And check this out, man." He reaches down the front of his shirt and pulls out a medallion on a thick platinum chain. The medallion has a design, round and painted red. It is the symbol N.J. had shown him on the lamp pole across from the Essex Street Retail Market. "That whole thing I was just showing you, the Red Thread, man," N.J. says. "I'm in the cartel."

Morris stares at the pendant, not comprehending.

"Hattie introduced me to her parents, man. The Rockworths. Her father and I hit it off and he inducted me into the club, as a junior member."

"When did this happen? I saw you a half hour ago."

"This morning, man. Didn't I tell you? Flew down to Florida and had breakfast with them. And they loved me, man, said I was the best thing that's happened to their daughter since Yale. Good people, really nice. Really rich, too."

"The guy who's always broke is now a member of a cult?"

"Not broke, man, just frugal," N.J. says, offended. "And I'm not yet a member, man. I'm a junior member, on trial probation. I've got to go through a rite of passage, man. An initiation."

"Like what, sitting naked on a block of ice for an hour?"

"This isn't some tree house gang, man. This is real," N.J. says, irritated, then, in a softer tone, "The initiation is to prompt a coup in some African or Central American or Asian country, man."

"And if a cult member can't pull off the coup?" Morris asks, playing along.

"Even if he can't kick the country over, he can still be let into the club, man. Style counts for a lot, man. A guy can get in strictly on style."

"Style counts with this cult."

N.J. shakes his head. "Open your eyes, man, listen to the world, read the papers," N.J. says, then, "A guy's going for initiation tonight. And it's a cartel, not a cult. Fordie, Hattie's dad, is sponsoring me. So I've got to go to some meeting in Brussels next month and meet the other members, then I've got to go through some sort of rite of passage, man."

Morris lifts his beer then sets it down. The story's bluster, but the cash is real. "The money—"

"Yeah, I know, I know, man," N.J. says, standing again. He pulls the roll out again and peels off five one hundred dollar bills. He sets them before Morris.

"Five hundred dollars." Morris is stunned. "You're kidding."

"Okay, man, Christ." He lays out two hundred more. "I thought you said you weren't keeping a tab, man."

"Seven hundred dollars."

"Don't get greedy on me. I can't owe you more than that, man. No way I drank that much over the years." N.J. sits down. Mrs. Cruxo brings N.J. his change from the hundred, a wad of dirty bills, sets them before him.

N.J. tips her a twenty. "I'm going to miss you, man," he tells Morris again.

"No, really," Morris says, staring at the money. "Where'd you get the money?" He pokes the bills on the bar like they're alive, like they might bite him. "Tell me the truth," he says. "The money, the Red Thread club, seeing Mr. Charlies at the gay club, this Hattie woman and you moving to Montana—tell me the truth."

"I've told you the truth."

"It's all real?"

"What's real is real, man. I'm sorry you're not able to see that." N.J. nods to the door. "Is that that asshole from high school?" he asks.

Morris turns, looks.

In the doorway stands Jetski, his face aflame. He's in a fury, and pointing his crooked Frankenfinger, yells, "I'm calling you out."

"Yeah," Morris tells N.J., "that's Jetski."

"He looks like shit, man," N.J. says. "Gained a ton of weight. And who's he pointing at anyway? I can't tell with that finger of his. Is he pointing at you or me or Mrs. Cruxo? Hey, man," N.J. calls to Jetski, "who are you pointing at?"

"Bliss, I'm calling you out," he says, his voice raw.

"He's calling for you, man," N.J. tells Morris.

"Yeah, thanks, I heard."

"You going to want some help on this?"

"No," Morris says.

"You sure, man?" N.J. asks, though he's visibly relieved Morris isn't counting on him. "I mean, he seems pissed. But then, I'd be pissed if you fucked my fourteen-year-old daughter, man."

"Eighteen," Morris corrects him.

"Still, man, I'd be pissed."

"Bliss," Jetski yells again. He seems smaller, heavier, like he's gotten denser in the last couple of hours. "I've got a score to settle with you. I've got your number. I'm going to punch your ticket. Are you coming out or am I going to have to drag you out?"

The few people in the bar turn and look at Morris. Mrs. Cruxo turns to Morris with a look he's never seen—a look of either compassion or terror, he isn't sure.

" 'Punch your ticket'?" N.J. quietly says. "He sounds like Mrs. Smithdangler, man, our elementary school lunch lady. Remember her, man?"

"Easy, Steven," Morris says, standing. "I'm coming. And quit your yelling," he says, "you're bothering people."

"Yeah, man," N.J. adds, feeling emboldened, "cool your jets, Jetski." He grabs Morris by the arm before he can leave. "One word of advice, man," N.J. tells him, folding the seven hundred-dollar-bills and stuffing them in Morris's pocket. "Something I learned in Calcutta. He's going to take a swing at you, man, and when he does, lean into the punch. Go at him like he's his daughter, like you want a kiss."

Morris studies his best friend, a person he's known nearly a quarter century, a friend who knows more about Morris than anyone else. "Newton," he says, looking him in the eyes, "when have you ever been to Calcutta? When have you ever left New York?"

~~~

Jetski's waiting, his body swaying, an alcohol-powered rhythm. "She told me everything," he shouts when Morris makes it to the sidewalk. "Told me all about the two of you." He seems more unsettled than angry. "You betrayed me. A fellow Eagle and you betrayed me. My own daughter, Bliss."

"Steven, listen, I—"

"You swore," he says, shaking like he's at the onset of cerebral palsy, like he realizes he's lost control and can do little about it.

"Steven, listen, it was never my intention to—"

Jetski laughs a high, sad laugh, one that is filled with pain. "Bloody Eagle or not, Bliss," he says, "you fucked me. And know what? She doesn't love you."

The patrons of the Old Homeplate crowd the doorway, staring out. All except for N.J., who sits calmly at the bar, sipping a beer.

"She doesn't love you," Jetski shouts. Spittle flies from his mouth, sprays across Morris's shirt.

Morris starts to speak then stops, having nothing to say.

Jetski pulls a waded sheet of paper from his pocket, throws it at Morris. It strikes him in the chest, falls to the sidewalk. "Read it and weep, fellow *Eagle*," Jetski says.

Morris picks it up. Carefully, he unfolds the sheet.

It reads: I don't love you.

It's signed by Stefani. Her "i" is dotted with a smiley face heart.

The postscript reads: I told my dad about us.

Morris awkwardly folds the paper. "Okay," he tells Jetski. There's nothing more to say.

"Okay what?" Jetski says, enraged. "What's okay?"

"Just, okay," Morris says. He could go on, try to explain, tell Jetski how they met, how he didn't know she was his daughter, but he'd be saying nothing. There's nothing to say.

"What's okay?" Jetski demands.

"You, us, Stefani," he says, putting the note in his pocket.

"Stefani," he says, visibly shaking. His daughter's name riles him sober. He's lucid, strengthened. "Don't say her name."

"I just meant—"

"Don't try taking my daughter from me."

"I haven't taken anything," Morris says, trying to calm him. "Steven, Stefani and I—"

"Don't take her from me," Jetski shouts, then powers back, calling forth his decades of destroying buildings.

Morris feels it coming, feels the swing before it's in motion.

And before he even thinks, he leans in. Like N.J. instructed. He floats to Jetski like a mother to a returning son.

Jetski's swing circles around Morris in a graceless embrace. Morris pushes him off, breaks free, but then catches a fist to his face as Jetski launches into a windmill of punches. Morris head snaps sideways and his eyes tear. Another punch finds his left eye. Morris lowers his head and tackles Jetski, grabs him in a bear hug. He lifts him off the ground, neutralizing the attack. Sweaty and reeking, Jetski radiates an intense heat, a foul odor of loneliness and anger.

He flails, pounding Morris on the back, but with little effect. Morris has him tight. They dance a few staggering steps, a silent symphony leading them, then stumble to the ground, land heavily on the concrete sidewalk, their limbs wrapped about each other.

Morris pins Jetski to the pavement. He can't fight.

"Don't take her from me," Jetski shouts, his face to Morris's. He struggles, trying to lash free. He can't. Morris is crushing him. "Don't take my daughter," he cries, then breaks down into rasping sobs. He cries for air, cries for understanding. "Don't take that from me."

Thirty-four

It's over in three minutes, Jetski reduced to a weeping heap. Morris helps him to his feet. "Steven," he says, "I really—"

Jetski slaps him. "Shut up," he yells, and lurches off. He jags down the street, howling like an injured cat. At the intersection, he turns back. "Stay away from me and my family, Bliss," he yells. "I'll kill you. I swear, I'll kill you."

Morris watches him round the corner, then studies his hands, his thin fingers, and wonders what they are meant for. Wonders what he's meant for.

Reentering the bar, he's met with cheers. Four beers now rested before him, drinks bought in congratulations by the other patrons. "Waltzing Matilda," a withered man of twenty-two calls Morris. "The most beautiful dancing I've ever seen." He, too, is a veteran of fights. His two front teeth are missing. He smiles a smile that looks like a broken door. "Waltzing Matilda kicked some ass!"

The entire scene leaves Morris humbled, embarrassed. He feels terrible, like he's gained something at another's expense.

Morris takes Stefani's note from his pocket, smoothes it out on the bar. He slides onto a barstool. What's happened these past days? He tries to trace his actions back, to find out how it first all went wrong. But the cause, the root, is a culmination of factors. They run too far back, run too deep.

"That was weird, man," N.J. says to Morris, not having moved from his stool. "You got something on your face." He touches his own cheek, indicating where.

Morris takes a cocktail napkin and wipes.

"No, man, the other side," N.J. says.

Morris wipes the other cheek. The napkin comes away stained with blood.

"Jesus," he says, seeing his own blood. It sets him off balance. He's confused, feels a need to cry, to be alone. "I'm heading home," he tells N.J., wanting to crawl into bed, to hide. Four days prior, his life was monotonous but safe; he had his map pinned to his wall, his travel plans, and his delusions. Now he has over eight hundred dollars cash, a bleeding face, and no idea of himself. *Half the evil in the world...*

N.J. rises from his stool in what Morris thinks is an offer to walk with him home. It's not. "Hattie," N.J. says, looking to the door.

A woman in wraparound sunglasses and a Yankees ball cap confidentially strides toward N.J.

She smiles a business smile, her teeth straight and large. "Let's go," she says to him, ignoring Morris.

N.J. gives her a display kiss, one for others to see. "You just missed the excitement, man," he tells her. "My boy Morris here just served some serious beating a la carte."

N.J. introduces them.

Morris holds out his hand. She doesn't take it. "Your face is bleeding," Hattie says, then she turns to N.J. "Time to go."

Morris studies her in profile. She seems familiar. He knows her somehow. They've met her before. "I think we've met before," Morris says, wiping his face again. "You live in my building, right?"

"It's her building, man," N.J. says.

"N.J.," she says, "we don't—"

"She owns the building, man."

"You own the building?" Morris asks her. He can sense her irritation.

Pausing, she states: "I own some things." She hasn't taken her sunglasses off. Morris can't see her eyes, can't tell if she's looking at him. "My family owns other things," she informs him.

"Hattie's family, man, owns a big chunk—"

"N.J.," Hattie says, stopping him. People with money don't speak of money. "We don't speak like that. That's something we don't speak about."

"I know you," Morris says, trying to place her. It's her voice, her attitude.

"No you don't," she tells him, then, "Your face is still bleeding."
She takes N.J. by the hand. "Let's leave."

Then it hits Morris. It's her. The woman from the precinct, the
one who'd opened a fusillade of flares on him and Jetski. The one
who got pounded in return by Jetski's paintball gun. "The precinct,"
Morris says. It's like playing charades; he guessed correctly.
"Saturday. That's how I know you."

Once the words are spoken, he wishes he'd held them. He'd
worn a ski mask to hide his identity. Now she knows who attacked
her.

Hattie halts mid-motion, looking taxidermied.

N.J. turns to Morris, then to Hattie. "What happened Saturday,
man?" N.J. asks.

In a burst of action, Hattie snatches an empty beer glass from
the bar, points it at Morris like it's a knife. "Don't move," she yells,
then grasps N.J. like he's a hostage at a failed bank robbery. "Don't
anyone move." She waves the glass like it's threatening. It's not.
Everyone in the bar turns, looks at her curiously. N.J. serves as a
shield as she crabs the both of them backward toward the door.

"Guess we're heading out, man," N.J. says to Morris, being
pulled.

Morris nods, watching the both of them.

"Tomorrow, man," N.J. says at the door. "Before we leave."

"Yeah," Morris says. "Tomorrow."

Then they're gone, out into the cool night.

The jukebox randomly fires a song, some friendless melody
about a dead brother. Mrs. Cruxo's behind the bar, silent and
guarding. Morris's face is already bruising from the fight. The
bleeding's slowed. He looks about the Old Homeplate. He's been
coming here for years, knows this place, the people in it, the songs on
the jukebox, the worn stools and scarred bar. All is familiar. It all
seems so foreign.

Thirty-five

After the precinct trouncing Saturday night, the Skunks, *sans* Hattie, regrouped at Tompkins Square Park. No one was sure of what next to do. All they were sure of was that they had just gotten their asses kicked. That, and Hattie was missing.

When she didn't show by Sunday, the group was in disarray. Word started that she'd been arrested, or that she'd committed suicide by licking the charged third rail on the F subway line, or that she'd found God and was now a part of a cult that served free lunches of rice and macaroni throughout the state of Indiana.

Word was that Hattie was gone.

The Skunks searched the usual spots—the park benches, the public library, the places easy to shoplift from—but they didn't find her.

Sunday night, an argument broke out as to where to look next, what to do. No one could agree. The Skunks broke apart, splintered into two groups, one of four people, the other of two. The group of four dubbed themselves the New Skunks and fought over who'd be the leader. May and Torc, the remaining two, sorted through restaurant trash and had sex in a stairwell of a building on Avenue C.

By Monday morning, the New Skunks had splintered again, then once more before noon, until there was no longer a group, only four individuals, each seething at the other.

After a meal scavenged from the trash of a Mexican restaurant, May and Torc announced their love for each other. "I don't know how to say this," Torc told May as they curled up together under the FDR viaduct running next to the East River Park. "I don't know how to tell you, but I've never been happier than I am when I'm with you. And it isn't just the sex," he told her, rubbing himself against her. "It isn't just the sex," he said, reaching into the seat of her pants.

They talked of settling down, getting tattoos of each other's names across their chests and moving to Austin, Texas, May's home town, once they got enough money saved. "It's great down there," she told Torc. "Always warm, and everyone carries a gun."

All evening, they planned for a future in Texas, a future together.

Now, heading down First Avenue toward Houston Street, Torc and May come upon McDonald's trash, bags upon bags of it stacked on the curb. They tear them open, searching for food. "I hate what it does to my thighs," May says, pulling out the remnants of a Big Mac, "but I just love the special sauce." Torc laughs. They make each other laugh. Dirty and stinky and grimy, they make each other happy.

The McDonald's manager rolls out of the restaurant, a broom in hand. "Get the fuck out of there," he shouts, taking a swipe at them. They both spring back, out of reach.

"I want a refund," Torc says, holding up a half eaten Chicken sandwich. "I asked for no mayo. This has got mayo." May finds that funny. The manager swings again, brooming Torc across the face.

"Ouch! All right, Mayor McCheese," Torc says, retreating. Both he and May have an armful of scraps, burgers and fries and watery sodas. "Don't get all Grimace on us, we're just looking for a snack."

The manager raised the broom. "Out. Before I call the cops."

Torc and May head off with their carry-out.

At the corner, May stops. "Look," May says, sticking two stale fries under her upper lip to form tusks. "I'm a walrus."

"Guess what I am," Torc says, taking in a mouthful of chocolate shake. He holds it in his cheeks.

"I don't know," May says, unable to figure it out. "What?"

He spits the shake out, arching a foul brown spew into the street. "Lactose intolerant," he says, his chin covered.

May howls, doubling at the waist. Coming up for air, her sight lands on something down the street. A couple. Approaching.

Her laughter chokes to a stop. "Jesus," she says. The approaching man's in leather, looks like he's headlining a western band at a gay bar.

The woman she knows.

"What?" Torc asks, turning to see what she's staring at.

"It's Hattie," May says, amazed.

Torc looks. "Holy shit," he concurs. "It's Hattie."

Thirty-six

Morris sleeps nude that night. Sore and beaten and bruised, he removes his shoes, strip his clothing, and curls up in bed.

He no longer feels a need to be ready. He has nothing to be ready for.

Since his mother's death, he's been preparing, waiting for something.

None of it matters. His planning didn't matter. The last days have shown him that.

He wakes to the gray light of the coming dawn, feeling like he's been rolled through a thresher. The cut on his face has closed. So has his left eye. It's swollen shut.

Five-thirty a.m., Tuesday. He hears his father rattle about the kitchen, making his pot of coffee, three scoops of grinds per cup. The smell sifts through the apartment like a gas leak, faint at first, then overwhelming.

Rising from bed, Morris puts on some pants, and heads to the kitchen.

Seymour looks at his son but says nothing about the eye.

"Morning, Daddy," Morris say.

"Today's my birthday," Seymour says. "Turn fifty-eight."

"That's right," he says, having completely forgotten. "Happy birthday." He'd wanted to get a gift, had gone to Norman's Sound and Vision on Friday for an album of Greek folk music, but he'd been sidetracked.

Stefani.

Seymour sips his coffee. "You were asking about your mother the other day," Seymour says, then is silent.

Morris looks to his father. Seymour keeps his focus cast down, won't meet Morris. "Yeah," Morris says. "I was."

Seymour nods, and exits the kitchen. He returns with a worn bundle of manila envelopes tied with twine. "I was your age now when she died," he says. He hands him the bundle. "Don't think you've ever seen this stuff."

Morris takes it.

"Mostly pictures and letters and things," Seymour says, kneading his hands together like he's washing them. "Things of your mother's I kept," he says, sounding tired. "Thought you might like 'em."

"Thanks," Morris says, sincerely appreciative. It's a rare gesture on his father's part. Morris unties the twine, pulls out a photo of his mother, one similar to the photo on his dresser. He studies it a moment. "Who took this picture?" he asks.

Seymour looks at the photo, looks at his son. His eyes are bright, gleaming, like they've been freshly shellacked. "I'm sorry you didn't have any other family," he says. "No grandparents or nothing."

The statement catches Morris off guard. "What do you mean?"

Seymour clears his throat, wipes his mouth. "You remember on your sixth birthday, your mom asked you what you wanted to be when you grew up?"

Morris shakes his head. "I remember having chocolate cake."

"You had chocolate cake every birthday."

"That's probably why I hate it now," Morris says. "What did I say?" he asks. "What did I want to be when I grew up?"

Seymour looks to his son, looks to his one good eye. "A stranger," he says.

A silence laps the room.

"I said that?"

Seymour nods, then says, "Your Aunt Christina, your mom's sister, took that picture."

"Oh," Morris says. He knew his mother had a sister, knew he had an aunt, but he was aware of her like one is aware of air; it's there, but not often acknowledged.

Seymour puts on a jacket, readying for work. "You've been living here now how long?" he asks Morris.

"All my life," Morris says, studying the photo. "Thirty-five years." How he saw traces of Stefani, he can't imagine. What he sees are traces of himself.

"Know what I want for my birthday?" Seymour asks, opening the front door to leave.

He looks up from the photo, looks to his father. "What?" His father never asked for gifts. "What do you want?"

Seymour stands at the threshold, at the cusp of their home. "I want you to find your own place," he tells his son. "I want you out of the house and on your own."

Thirty-seven

Sofar was furious, despondent. "Morris Bliss my ass," Sofar said. "Like I believe that! Morris Bliss!"

Twelve hours had passed since the egg timer rang, since the terrifying knock at his door. He hadn't moved the entire time, the hollow thump at his front door congealing his blood. The sound delivered a shot of lead to his heart. Everything stopped.

Hatfield, the building owner, had finally returned. Sofar was positive. It's Hatfield, it's Hatfield, it's Hatfield, was all Sofar could think.

"Mr. Sofar," the person knocking had called. "It's me, Morris Bliss from downstairs."

Morris Bliss. Sofar wanted to laugh. Impossible. Morris was only a boy, Sofar thought. Right? Last time he saw him he was, what—thirteen, fourteen years old? And that was how long ago? Sofar couldn't recall. But Morris definitely wasn't a man yet. And it was a man at his door. The voice, the force of the knock. It was Hatfield trying a new trick.

"Mr. Sofar," the man called again. "It's Morris, Stavroula's son."

Stavroula! Hatfield had no shame, evoking the name of the woman dearest to Sofar. A woman now dead.

Anger rose hot in Sofar's throat. Still, he was immobilized, his limbs grounded. Stavroula, he thought. A poison of grief leaked from a place he'd long sealed shut. Stavroula, he said to himself, longing to say the name out loud.

The knocking finally ended. Hatfield had left. For now. But he'd be back. Sofar knew he'd be back.

Still, Sofar stood motionless the entire night, his mind mincing through his life.

Now morning.

He is no longer human, he realizes, has turned into an animal in hiding. "It wasn't worth it," he decides. He can't endure. "Hatfield can have the place."

With this decision comes the realization that Sofar has nothing more to live for. Keeping his home had been his motivation, the reason he woke each morning. Now, he no longer had that.

A strange liberation settles over him, a quiet relief. He is now responsible for nothing.

He showers and shaves, dresses in an old navy-blue suit with a yellow collared shirt and a burgundy striped tie. He breaks out a new pair of socks, sheer silk socks, socks he'd saved for a special day.

Today is that day.

He slips on his wingtip shoes, shoes that have never felt pavement.

The hall is empty, has a faint odor of talcum powder and mildew. The florescent light flickers overhead. Sofar closes his door, rattles out the right key to lock the deadbolt.

There's no use locking it; he has nothing to lose.

He heads down the stairs, heads out into the bright, brilliant morning.

The street has changed in the years since he's been out, the trees taller or no longer there. He strolls to First Avenue. It all looks so different. Sofar takes it in.

He walks down Sixth Street, past all the Indian restaurants with name like Gandhi's House or Gandhi's Garden or Gandhi's Buffet and the thick smell of spice that reeks of body odor, strolls to Second Avenue and finds that the Fillmore East, the club where he saw so many great bands, is no longer. It's now a bank. The businesses, the people, have changed.

Sofar has remained.

Heading down Fifth Street, he walks past the police precinct. It's being gutted.

Jetski stands in front of the building, yelling orders to his men. He holds his hardhat in his hand, unable to wear it; there's a knot the size of an apricot on the back of his head. The fight with Morris.

Hung-over, he is in an exceptionally foul mood. His home life is crumbling. After the rumble with Morris, he went home. Stefani wasn't there, was out with her new boyfriend Robby, the heir to the Subway Sandwich shop and her date to prom. Jetski drank more, then got into a fight with his wife over his erratic behavior. She didn't understand him, he screamed, breaking his wife's favorite Princess Diana commemorative plate.

He was kicked out of the house, told not to come back until he was sober, calm. When he'd gotten a replacement plate.

For Jetski, coming to work is the highlight of his day. He is actually glad for something to occupy him. It serves as a grounding, a reprieve from his chaotic life.

Sofar pauses in front of the building. "What are you doing with the place?" he asks Jetski.

"I'm taking it down," Jetski says. He claps. "Gutting it then ripping it apart."

"What's going to go up here?"

Jetski shouts at two workers, tells them to pick up the pace. "Same thing," he says. "But it'll be better. It'll stand forever."

Sofar nods. He offers his hand.

Jetski takes it out of habit, takes hold of every hand offered him.

There's a violent ripping noise from inside the building. Two workers drag a large chunk of wall out the front door, break it into small pieces, then toss it in the Dumpster.

Sofar holds Jetski's hand for a long while. Jetski tries to pull loose but can't. Sofar's grip is too firm.

"All right there, Tiger," Jetski says, wanting free. "You can let it go."

"I already have," Sofar says, then, "Good luck."

And with the ease of the drowning breathing water, he lets go.

Thirty-eight

"You look like panda, man," N.J. says, seeing Morris's swollen eye. He's stopped in to say goodbye, is on his way to the airport with Hattie. "It hurt?" he asks, lighting touching Morris's cheek.

Morris jerks back. "Yes, it hurts," he says. "Don't poke at it."

"Got into a scrap myself last night, man." He hitches his thumbs in his pants. He's wearing his leather cowboy attire, but has added a bolo tie, the gold clasp stamped with the Red Thread symbol.

"With Hattie?"

"With a couple of Skunks."

"Skunks?" Morris asks.

"A couple of the squatter friends of Hattie's. After I slapped them up a bit, Hattie felt bad about the beating they took, so she give them her apartment. We ended up staying at the Soho Grand. Room service sucked, man."

"The squatters are in Hattie's apartment?" Morris asks. "The one downstairs?"

"They were there for the night, man," N.J. says. "She's calling the cops once we reach the airport, reporting that they broke in. Then she'll collect the insurance for theft, damages."

"What a nice friend," Morris says, now worried about his new downstairs neighbors.

"Hey, man," N.J. says, "why don't you ride with us to the airport. We've got a limo filled with liquor and snacks and stuff, man. And some ice for that shiner," he says, pointing to Morris's eye. "Come on, ride with us."

"Stop it," Morris says to N.J. He's still recovering from his father's conversation. The request that he find his own place. "Stop it with your stories. You're not going anywhere."

"I'm going ranching, man," N.J. says. "Real buffali, real meat, the real West," he says, then, his tone turning somber, he continues,

"Hattie told me the whole thing about you and her, your little tiff Saturday night. I got to tell you, man, not cool on your part."

"Not cool on my part?" Morris asks, piqued. "She and her friends fired roman candles or something at Jetski and me. Did she tell you that she nearly burned us to death?"

"She told me, man, but she's a girl. And that's not cool, attacking a girl like that, even if she did attack you first. She still has welts on her back, man. Anyway," he says, straightening the strings of his bolo tie, "no worries. She's not going to press charges."

"Press charges? You're fucking kidding. I should be the one pressing charges."

"She was defending herself, man."

"She was—" He breaks off, shakes his head. He's got a headache and his eye throbs. "Whatever, N.J.," he says.

From out on the street, a car horn sounds. "Listen, I got to go, man," N.J. says. "Got a limo waiting. Wish me luck."

"Good luck," Morris says, still not believing his friend. "I'll walk you out," he says, grabbing his keys. "I want to see this limo of yours, see it with my own eyes."

"Eye, man," N.J. says. "The singular. You only got the one."

Alternative side parking is in effect. Cars are double parked all down the street, waiting for the street cleaner to roar by before they grab their spaces again.

There in front of the building is a black stretch Mercedes.

"Shit," Morris says, seeing it, "you weren't kidding."

The back window slides down halfway. "We're late," Hattie calls to N.J.

"Come with us," N.J. offers again.

Morris shakes his head. "This is all you," he tells N.J. "This is your trip, not mine."

"All right, man," N.J. says, visibly nervous. He's following through on a plan. He's truly doing what he claims. "Okay, man, take care," he tells his friend of twenty years.

"Let's go," Hattie calls from the limo.

The realization strikes Morris fully, like a blast from a jet engine; N.J.'s leaving. He's losing his closest friend to the wilds of the West.

N.J. gives Morris a quick half hug, with one arm. But before N.J. can escape, Morris takes hold of him in a solid embrace, buries his head to his friend's chest. The leather shirt is warm to his face. "Newton," Morris says, holding his friend the way N.J. held him in the pool that morning so many years ago. He held him for dear life, fearing to let go. "Newton, you're not going."

Arms reach around Morris, take him tight. "I'm going, man," N. J. says. "I've got to go."

The limo driver honks the horn again.

Morris's one eye brims with wetness. The other stings. He fights back tears. "What's happening here?" he asks, letting go. He forces a laugh, trying to sound at ease. He gives N.J. a playful punch in the arm. From a half block away, the workers pound and tear and rip apart the precinct. "What's going on with us?"

"Life, man," N.J. says. He gives a nod, a smile, then slides into the waiting limo.

It pulls away.

Thirty-nine

Morris orders a bacon, egg, and cheese sandwich and a coffee at Marcelo's Hot To-Go-Go.

N.J. gone. It's for real.

After the limo had left, Morris waited a solid five minutes, expecting them to circle the block and come back, expecting the long, black Mercedes to pull up and for N.J. to roll down his window and say, "Gotcha, man. You really thought I was leaving, didn't you?"

It didn't happen.

They didn't return.

Sitting at a sticky table with his coffee and breakfast sandwich, Morris picks up a copy of the *Post* someone left behind. He needs a job, needs to start looking for a place to live. His father wants him out.

The bacon in his sandwich smells rancid. His coffee is bitter. Nothing tastes good. Still, he eats, needing something in his stomach.

Looking at the paper's headline, Morris nearly chokes. Plastered on the front page: ES'SEX' STREET SCANDAL. The photo shows the police raiding the Essex Street Retail Market.

Morris doesn't believe it. "I don't believe it," he says aloud.

He turns to the full story on page four. The market had been raided last night, the police breaking up a large sex ring. "The atrocities, the sin," the mayor's quoted. "We need to ensure it never happens again."

It's just as N.J. claimed.

"My God," Morris says, stunned. His friend's creditability's finally found footing.

As he rereads the article, Morris's eye wanders to the opposite page, which shows the body of a nine-year-old African boy, an AK-47 at his side. COUP ATTEMPT IN CONGO the headline read. A group of fifteen youth, all under the age of twelve, and all dressed in powder pink camouflage, launched a failed attempt to take over the presidential palace. They'd parachuted from purple hot air balloons and showered the palace with bullets and grenades.

All the boy rebels were killed.

One line in the article stood out. It stated that "each of the youthful rebels had a red string around his neck, giving them the look of a slit throat."

The Red Thread.

A new member's initiation into the cartel.

Forty

Sofar knocks on the Blisses' apartment door. No one answers. No one's home. Seymour's at work, Morris is at Marcelo's.

Taking a stuffed envelope addressed to Morris from his suit pocket, he shoves it under the door.

Back at his apartment, Sofar finds everything's as he left it. Nothing's touched. Hatfield will have to deal with all the items. He stole all my things once, Sofar thinks, let him steal them again.

He combs his hair then dials 911, asks for the fire department. "Yes," he calmly tells them, "a fire." They ask if it is big, out of control. "Not yet," he tells them. "But soon." He gives them his address then hangs up.

Carrying everything he needs up the stairs to the tar covered roof, Sofar finds it hot, even this early in the day.

He sweats as he pours the paint thinner over his clothing, his hair. The odor bites his nose. He's thought it through; he isn't ending much. His life has been over for years, or rather, never fully got started.

From the east, the breeze carries the sound of sirens. Fire engines for Sofar. For his fire.

The first match sparks then fizzles. The second does the same. "Come on," Sofar says, listening to the sirens gain strength. He wants to be well immolated by the time they arrive; he doesn't want to be saved.

Striking two matches together, a beautiful tight flame leaps forth. "Yes," Sofar says, pleased, then is surprised when it jumps to his hand.

His skin bursts into flame. The fire runs up his shirt and engulfs him.

At first he doesn't really feel anything, the fire burning the paint thinner and not his skin. Then he feels a pain so painful that it doesn't hurt; it feels cooling and strange.

Then it's immensely painful.

Sofar changes his mind. Killing himself is a mistake. He wants to be saved, wants to live.

The scream of the siren increases, but not quick enough for Sofar. He flops to the roof and rolls and rolls, hoping to kill the flames.

They hold, chewing his skin, clothing, and hair.

Sofar, rolling, sees no flashes of his life, no scenes of childhood. He only sees the immediate: the tar covered roof, his burning limbs, and a few pigeons cutting the sky.

The flames gain.

"Not like this," he yells, flailing about, rolling toward the building's edge. "I don't want to die like this," he pleads.

He gets his wish.

Sofar rolls off the roof. Gravity abides. He blazes out into the morning, down toward the street and the city below.

Forty-one

"To us," May says, lurching about Hattie's apartment like a wounded deer. She raises her glass for a toast. "To the Skunks." The stereo plays the soundtrack from *Dr. Zhivago*. "Lara's Song." May wears a new dress, a burnt orange one with the price tag still dangling from it. Six hundred and fourteen dollars, not including tax.

"Fuck the Skunks," Torc tells her, refilling her wine glass, a third of which spills to the floor. It's their eighth bottle. May's thrown-up twice. They have no plans of stopping. "To you," he says.

"To me," May says, swinging her glass.

"No, to me," Torc tells her, wiping his mouth with the hem of the dress he's wearing. Red and flowing, it's tight in the chest. But he likes the color, thought it went well with his eyes.

"No, no," May says. "No, we should toast Hattie," she says. It's Hattie's wine, her dresses, her apartment.

"Yes, Hattie," he says. "Hattie, Hattie, Hattie." He drinks straight from the bottle even though he has a full glass of wine in his other hand. They've used Hattie's Jacuzzi tub, bubble bath, bath bombs, lotions, and perfumes. They've styled their hair, used her blow dryer, mousse, gel, and holding spritz. They rifled her drawers, tried on her silk nightgowns, thong panties, and socks. They've eaten her cheeses, lox, carpaccio, and lemon grass capers. They've taken over her place.

It's now their place.

Hattie gave it to them. At least for a day.

When they saw her last night with the man in leather, they were overjoyed: it was Hattie, the Skunk leader, the one who held them together, the one they thought missing or dead.

When they saw her last night with the man in leather, they were disappointed: it wasn't Hattie. Not the Hattie they knew and respected and loved. This woman was just another person, another *anybody* who showered and didn't have to defecate in the bushes when all the park toilets where closed.

She was Hattie, but she wasn't.

She wasn't a Skunk. She was clean.

And she nearly walked right past them, walked by like they were nothing, no one. Like she didn't know them.

"Hattie," Torc said. "Hattie," he called when she and the man in leather had come flush with them.

Hattie stopped, reluctantly turned to them. She seemed intimidated, frightened, like she didn't know how to deal with her old comrades.

"What's happened to you?" May asked, repulsed and concerned, like she was seeing a diabetic sister for the first time since she'd had her leg amputated. "Something awful happened to you."

"She smells nice," Torc said, sniffing at her. "Like she's showered, cleaned up. Which is in violation of the Skunk manifesto." Torc looked her over, like he's calculating the best angle to take her by the jugular. " 'When the world stinks,' " he said, " 'we stink back twice as much.' "

"Listen, man, you need to step down," the man in the leather said, moving forward to defend Hattie.

Hattie stopped him, placed her hand to his chest, said no.

"Fellow Skunks," Hattie said, her confidence somehow returned. Hattie Skunk, with all her brashness and self-assurances, returned. She took control. She handled the situation.

She lied, masterfully.

Placing a hand on May and Torc's shoulders, she said, "I've gained retribution against the attackers. I've taken care of those who hurt my fellow Skunks."

"I wasn't really hurt all that much," May said. "A couple bruises on my—"

"No one fucks with a Skunk," Hattie said.

"What'd you do, kill them?" Torc asked. Both he and May laughed.

"Yeah, you cut their balls off?" May asked, grabbing her crotch.

Hattie said nothing, her face a mask of seriousness, eyes shielded by silver sunglasses.

Torc and May's laughter waned, then petered to a stop. A ripe odor of spunk wafted off them. "You didn't kill them, right?" Torc asked.

Still, Hattie stood, unwavering.

"Holy shit," May said, "you killed them, didn't you?"

Hattie held them a moment longer. "When one fucks with a Skunk," she slowly said, but didn't finish. Then she added, "The cops are out for us. All of us. That's why I'm in disguise. Best you both stay off the street." She opened her purse, took out a set of keys, a roll of twenties. She hands both to May. "There's a squat around the corner." She gives them the address to her building. To Morris's building. "I store stolen items there," she said. "Go there, get off the street. Change your clothes, your hair. Make yourself look different. Normal. Then take the money and get out of town."

"What about the others?" May asked, her face showing profound respect. Hattie killed for us, she thought. No one's ever killed for me.

"The others," Hattie said, "have been taken care of."

"You've killed them, too?" May asked. "You killed a fellow Skunk?"

"Disloyalty holds a high price," she said, smiling a smile far from friendly. "Go, and be quick," she said. She and the man in leather strode off.

Torc and May looked at each other, looked at the money and the keys, then looked at each other again. "You heard what she said," Torc said. "Get off the street."

They stopped at Mr. Charlies and bought supplies for the night, four forty-ounce beers and two bags of stale corn chips, paid for it all with a new, crisp twenty, which they got no change for. But they didn't care. They had cash.

When they got to Hattie's apartment, they dumped the cheap beer and snacks. Hattie had a full refrigerator, and bottles and bottles of wine with labels in French and Italian and other languages.

They found a corkscrew and haven't stopped.

"I feel like a dancing queen," Torc says, spinning about to the music. Wine spatters the floor in a circle.

"You look like a drag queen," May replies, feeling ill again. She sits with a thump. Torc reaches out his hand, lifts her back to her feet. "Dance with me," he says, and twirls her about twice. She vomits on the couch.

"Wow, not good," she says between dry heaves.

"But it's vintage," Torc says, not intervening. "The wine's a vintage year."

"Aren't all years vintage years?" she asks, staggering. "Okay, I'm good now," she says, not looking so good. Her hair is mussed and frizzy, like she's been sleeping in a cave, and her eyes are unfocused, glazed. She picks up the CD of the music playing. "Doctor Z-have-a-go," she reads aloud. "What kind of doctor you think he is?" she asks. "What kind of name is that?"

Torc waltzes up to her, runs his fingers down her breasts, places his hands to her groin. "A gynecologist," he says, working her dress up off her hips.

"With a name like that?" she asks, oblivious to his groping. "With a name like that, I'd think…I'd think he'd treat feet."

"Treat feet?" Torc says, his attention not on the conversation.

May laughs. "Treat feet," she says. "That sounds funny. Treat feet, treat feet," she says, then starts chanting it over and again.

"I've got a foot for you to treat," Torc says, lifting his own dress.

Seeing him in an aroused state, May laughs even harder. "That's not a foot," she says, drunkenly swatting at his genitals. "It's not even six inches."

After forty seconds of fumbling foreplay, May's bent over the Mies van der Rohe Pavilion chair with Torc addressing her from behind. "Texas, Torc," she keeps saying, dazed. "I want to move to Texas. Buy some land. Have a family."

"Working on that last part," Torc says, sweating profusely from his labors. "God, it's hot." Wiping his forehead with the palm of his hand, he shakes off the perspiration. "Open that window, would you?"

May leans forward, slides open the window. Torc stays joined, waiting until she's done.

"A beautiful morning," May says, staring out at the tree, the street, the sky.

Torc glances over her, out the window. "Yeah," he says, "it is. It really is."

As they both gaze out at the morning, naked and conjoined, feeling the sweet breeze seep through the open window, feeling their futures changing for the better, the fiery blaze called Sofar shoots directly past them on his way down to the concrete. On his way out of his lease.

~~~

"Texas," May keeps saying through her tears as the bus pulls from Port Authority.

"Yes, yes, Texas," Torc echoes, still drunk and awkward in a pair of Hattie's yellow Capri pants and flip-flops. They'd hastily dressed and bolted from Hattie's place—got out of there immediately after seeing the man on fire scorch past like a faulty firework.

They had to step around the charred body on their way out. Crumpled like a singed blanket, the sight and smell of the dead man knotted Torc's stomach. He instantly vowed to become a vegetarian.

They slipped into a cab just as the fire trucks arrived in front of the building.

At Port Authority, they tipped the driver six dollars on a fourteen-dollar ride, and with the remaining money Hattie had given them, bought bus tickets for Austin, Texas.

Or rather, tickets for Memphis.

They didn't have enough for tickets all the way to Texas so they settled for Tennessee. They'd figure the rest out later.

Torc puts his arm around May, comforting her as she cries. The driver grinds the bus into gear. It yanks forward, exiting Port Authority and heading toward the Midtown tunnel. Heading out of the city.

Out of New York.

Forty-two

The school bell rings, starting the day at St. Benedict's Ukrainian Catholic High School. "Lettuce?" Robby asks, dialing his father's Subway Sandwich shop on his cellphone.

He and Stefani have finished making out for the morning. Stefani smokes a cigarette. "No lettuce," she tells him. "Salami, ham, and cheddar cheese. Extra salami. And make it a twelve-inch. With mayo, but not too much. And onions. And they got chips, right? Tell them to send some chips. And tell them to make the sandwich with that good bread, not that spongy white stuff."

Robby places the order. It's to be delivered to the school in time for their lunch. "You want a Coke to drink?" he asks her, the phone to his ear.

"Yeah, a Coke," she says. She tosses her cigarette, flips her hair. "No, make it a Diet Coke." She pinches her soft belly. "I want to look good for prom. I want to look good for you." she tells him, and gives him a kiss, tongue included.

Forty-three

The police and two fire trucks are out front of the building when Morris returns. The area's roped off, no one allowed in. A crowd's gathered in the street, on the sidewalk, blocking the view. Morris smells a charred, damp odor, like rotten hamburger. "What's happened?" he asks an officer.

"I'd say you caught a bad case of whip-ass," the officer says, pointing to Morris's black eye. "Girlfriend problems?"

"Yeah, kind of," he says, then, "I live here. What's going on?"

"You know this guy?" He nods toward the body bag the paramedics are wrestling onto a stretcher.

"Who is it?"

"That's what I'm asking you, Winky," the officer says. "We're not sure. No I.D."

"Winky?"

The officer motions to the building. "He jumped. From the roof. A flamer."

"A flamer? You mean, what, he was gay?"

"I mean he was on fire."

"Jesus," Morris says, then suddenly worries it might be his father. "What's the guy look like?" Morris asks, his stomach knotting at the realization of what he's smelling.

"Burnt. Dead," the officer says. "Pretty sure he lived on the top floor. His apartment was wide open."

"Mr. Sofar?"

"That his name?" the officer asks, pulling out his notepad. "You know the guy?"

"He used to be a family friend," Morris says, feeling like he's just been operated on, like something's been stripped from him. "He's lived here over thirty-five years."

"What's your name?" he asks, jotting notes.

Morris tells him.

"How long have you live here?"

"All my life," Morris says, staring up at the building. He's never noticed the cornices before. "Thirty-five years."

"Long time," he says, working his pen over his notepad. "When was the last time you saw this Sofar?"

"Yesterday," Morris says. "Or no, maybe twenty years ago."

The officer looks up at Morris, his black eye. "Keep it straight, Winky," he says. "When did you last see him?" he asks again, more forceful.

"I stopped by his place yesterday, but he didn't answer the door." Morris explains the entire relationship, tells the officer about his family, his mother's death, how, just this morning, after living with him thirty-five years, Daddy had told him he'd have to leave.

"Daddy?" the officer asks.

"Danny," Morris lies. "My father's name is Danny."

The officer eyes him warily. "You said Daddy." The ambulance with Sofar's body flips on its sirens then pulls away, in a rush. There's no race. Sofar's status isn't changing.

"No," Morris tells the officer, "I said Danny."

Finally, he's allowed into his building.

The halls are dimmer, clouded with dust. The stairwell has narrowed, appears more worn. Nothing's changed, only now, Morris is noticing. Thirty-five years there and now he's noticing.

Opening the door to his apartment, Morris finds silence and emptiness.

On the floor, he finds a letter addressed to him.

Forty-four

"That's it?" Seymour asks, looking at the items spread on the kitchen table. He took the news of Sofar's death as he takes all bad news, with stoic resignation. There's nothing to be done.

"That's it," Morris says, standing opposite him.

Laid out before them are twelve one-hundred dollar bills and four unused tickets to a 1983 performance of the musical *Cats*. All that was in the envelope for Morris.

"What kind of suicide note is that?" Seymour says, frustrated.

"I don't think it's a suicide note."

"It's a suicide note," Seymour says. "Of some kind." Pausing a moment, he says, "Sofar got the tickets for us, wanted to take us out, his treat."

"Back in August of 1983?" Morris asks, picking up one of the tickets. "Who was the fourth one for?"

"Your mom."

Morris looks to his father to see if he's joking. He's not joking. "But," Morris says, "she was dead by then."

"That's why we didn't go," he says.

Morris doesn't understand.

"Your mom wasn't doing well, was in the hospital," Seymour says. "Sofar bought the tickets a good eleven months in advance, thinking—" He breaks off, swallows hard. "I don't know what he was thinking," he says.

Morris places the ticket next to the other three, aligns them, his fingers lingering. "It was probably his way of giving her something to look forward to," Morris says. "Giving her a reason to hang on."

Seymour keeps his head down, closes his eyes. "And the money?" he asks. "Why leave you the money?"

"I don't know," Morris says. The bills are lined-up like a Sunday morning brunch crowd. "I guess," he says, "it's Sofar's way of giving me something to look forward to."

Forty-five

It takes more than eight phone calls to track her down, but Morris finally gets his Aunt Christina's number. His aunt and her husband and son, who's a few years younger than Morris, have moved back to Greece, to Christina's home island of Kos, the island that holds half of Morris's heritage.

Morris gets the international code wrong twice before the phone finally rings its odd foreign ring. It's after eleven p.m. in New York and Morris hadn't even thought about the time there, if it's morning or evening or dead of night.

A woman answers. "*Malesta*?" she says.

Morris pauses, uncertain what to say, uncertain he's dialed the right number. Uncertain he's even talking to someone in Greece and not someone in Guyana or the Gaza Strip. "Yes, hello," he says.

"*Hallo*?" the woman says. "Yes?"

"Yes, is this Christina?"

It is.

"This is Morris Bliss," he said. "Your sister Stavroula's son."

A cry sounds across the miles of wire. "Stavroula's baby," his Aunt Christina says, overjoyed. "My sister's baby."

They speak for nearly two hours. Christina wants to know all about him, all about his life in New York. She tells him about how they'd returned to Greece, and how her son, Christos, is running a parasailing business for the English and German tourists that visit during the summer months. "You must visit," she tells him.

"I'd like that," Morris says. He would. But he fears her joy is false, fleeting. Where has she been all these years, all his life? He flatly asks her.

Christina makes the sound all Greeks make when something is either too simple or too complicated to explain. "I called many, many times many, many years ago," she tells Morris. There was a crackling on the line, a pause. "Then I called no more," she says. "Did your father not tell you I called? Did he not tell you I called and he hung up each time?"

"No," Morris says, clearly seeing his father doing that. Once he'd cut someone from his life, they no longer existed. Stavroula's family was dead to Seymour. He'd have nothing to do with them.

Christina's tone shifts, turns cheerful again, glad. "You must come," she tells him. "Come now. You'll have a place to live, food, family. Stavroula's baby. You can come and live here with us, work with your cousin Christos."

"I'd like that," he says. "Maybe this summer."

"This summer's good. But now, come now. Come tomorrow," she says.

"Unfortunately, right now is—" He stops. Right now is *what*?

It's nothing.

It's perfect.

"Okay. I'll come," he tells her, already planning. "Tomorrow."

Forty-six

"Ah, Mr. Charlies," Mr. Charlies says, seeing Morris. He frowns. "Your eye, what happened?"

It's late, three in the morning. Mr. Charlies' shop is empty, save for the overwhelming stench of stale spices and floor cleaner.

"I've got a present for you," Morris says, sniffing from allergies. He sets a grocery sack on the counter. It's heavy, double bagged.

"Oh no, Mr. Charlies," Mr. Charlies says, suspiciously eyeing the bag. "No presents, no. Thank you and no."

"I feel I must, Mr. Charlies," Morris says, shaking the bag. It jingles and rattles and sings. Morris emptied his large Mason jar of coins into the bag, dumped all the pennies and nickels and dimes, but not quarters. He kept the quarters.

A look of terror hits Mr. Charlies' face. He knows what it is and wants nothing of it. "Too kind, too kind," he says, waving Morris off. "But no, no, no. No presents, Mr. Charlies."

Morris takes hold of the bottom of the bag, spills the coins over the counter. They spin and dance and pour onto the floor.

"Oh no, oh no, no," Mr. Charlies yells, like he's witnessing the destruction of his home. The sight of the coins, of change, whips him into a rage. "No change, Mr. Charlies. I have no change." He acts as though the coins are vinegar and he's a pearl: any contact will cause corrosion. Grabbing a flyswatter, he frantically flips the coins off the counter, trying to get them away from him, trying not to touch them. They fling across the store. "Take them back, Mr. Charlies."

Morris shakes his head. "No," he says, and turns to leave.

"Take them back or you are outlawed here," Mr. Charlies shouts at him.

"Okay," Morris says, waving goodbye. "I'm outlawed. Good luck," he tells him, leaving.

"Leave my store." He comes from behind the counter, follows Morris.

"I'm leaving." He steps outside. The street is calm, few people out. The traffic's thin.

"Out of my store," Mr. Charlies says, threatening him with the flyswatter.

"I am out," Morris says.

"You no longer Mr. Charlies," Mr. Charlies tells Morris. He swats him. "I take back your name. You have no name. Mr. Charlies is now Mr. Charlies, and Mr. Charlies says stay out of his store," he says. "You are nothing. Mr. Nothing. You come and Mr. Charlies will call the cops."

A bright sense of accomplishment settles over Morris. He's been barred from going where he never wants to go again.

Forty-seven

Lying in bed in his underwear, Morris holds the bundled letters and photos of his mother to his bare chest. He's going to Greece. He reserved a ticket, seven hundred dollars, round-trip. Open ended. He's leaving, has no plan on when he'll come back.

"How do I know I'm doing the right thing?" he asked Seymour after he'd bought the ticket.

"You don't," Seymour said.

"Then what am I supposed to do?"

"Do like the rest of us," Seymour said, turning from his son. "Blunder through as best as you can."

Morris thinks of Andrea. Already, she seems like a distant weekend at the beach, fun but long past. Stefani remains in his mind, but she, too, is fading, like the bruise on his eye.

How can something once so important end up not being important? There are seven defining moments in a person's life, N.J. had once told him. We're born with them, like a tongue and toes. But how do you differentiate between what is defining and what isn't? How do you know when it is real?

Forty-eight

It's only at the airport that it starts to feel real.

He's checked in, has walked through the metal detector, shoeless. The air's filled with the thin odor of spent jet fuel. Security made him hold out his arm, spread his legs. They waved a wand over him, verifying he was not carrying anything he shouldn't, that he's left all things dangerous behind.

He has no right to be here, he knows. The money he used to buy the ticket wasn't his. It was Sofar's. It was N.J.'s. Still, he spent it.

Saying goodbye to his father was awkward, painful. It took all the strength he could gather. He was breaking from something he's always had. It was something he needed to sever himself from, an umbilical cord that no longer provided life. It held him back. "I'll be back," Morris told his father. "To see you. To visit." Seymour nodded, said nothing. His face was blank, his eyes hard. Morris could tell his father didn't want to speak, feared his voice would betray his rigid façade. His son was leaving and he didn't want him to leave; he wanted him to leave. The boy needed to be on his own.

To Morris, his home already didn't seem his home; it was now a part of an older life. On his blank wall, where the world map had hung, Morris placed a single red-headed pin. It stood out, a drop of blood in a field of snow. "I am here," he wrote below it.

"Okay," Morris told his father. "I'm going." Seymour held out his hand.

Morris embraced him.

Not one to display his affection, Seymour didn't fight. He let his son hold him.

"I'll miss you, Seymour," Morris told his father. "I'll miss you."

Forty-nine

The smell of wild sage and sea salt hangs sharp in the morning air. Kos, Greece, with its whitewashed houses and jagged bluffs, all looking out to the sea. The craggy mountains are covered in thorny brush and wild flowers. This is the island of his mother's birth. The home of his ancestors, of Hippocrates, and a resting place for Ulysses on his journey home from the battle at Troy.

Pili, the village his mother's family is from. The narrow streets seem built off a drunkard's design; they turn and rise and dip for reasons Morris can't see. His aunt welcomed him as her son, took him in and made her home his. Christo, his cousin, has him helping with his business.

The light here is different than in New York, Morris has noticed. It's stronger, heavier. Morris can see a difference, sees that it's both tender and more potent, as though it can give birth to and kill a thing with a single beam. It colors everything in a way he's never witnessed.

Morris feels a strength he's never felt before, feels an aspect of himself he never knew. An aspect he likes.

Late morning and he's at the village's main café. It's located near the fountain, a fountain that has flowed for centuries, the water rushing down from the mountain, working its way through the tons of stone. His mother drank from this fountain. Morris drank from it his first morning here; the water was so cold his teeth ached.

The café owner greets him, says hello in his stilted English. Morris orders a coffee, a snack. He has all the letters and pictures his father gave him, spreads them out on the table, studying each. The café's empty save for him. The owner sets a small, thick coffee and a *tyropita*, a cheese pie, before him. The bitterness of the coffee fills his mouth.

From across the square, an old man with a face of weathered ravines slowly works his way toward the café. He takes a seat at Morris's table. He could sit anywhere. He sits with Morris. "*Kalimara*," Morris says to him, practicing his few words of Greek. He gathers his items, stacks them.

The old man greets him with a nod, then summons the café owner over, and speaking to the owner in a voice of creaking timber, points to Morris, then to himself. He reaches over and picks from Morris's stack a photo of Stavroula, Morris's mother.

The owner translates. "Mr. Paleo," he tells Morris, "is related to you, far, far down the line. He knew your mother as a little girl."

The old man taps the picture, then reaches across the table, takes Morris's hand in his. His fingers are long, thin, like Morris's. Morris feels the warmth, the kindness of the man. Feels the years and years of toil, heartbreak, and joy that this man's experienced. His hands offer this all, a record of his life and all he's touched, all that's touched him.

The old man speaks again. The owner translates: "He remembers many things about your family. He wishes to tell you about them, about this island, Kos. It is your island, too, he says. You have its" — he searches for the proper word — "its soil; it's in your skin."

"I'd like to hear his stories," Morris says, leaning toward the old man. He raptly listens. Wanting to know. Wanting to be told.

The old man speaks. The owner translates — the words shift from language to language. "There are two theories," the old man says, his voice sonorous and resounding, like the earth sprung from his throat. Like life itself originated there. He tightly holds Morris's hand, holds it like his search is finally ended. "The first theory," he tells Morris. "After creating a world with water and soil and fish and plants and beasts that stand on two feet, God dipped his finger in the wetness between Athens and Africa and summoned forth the rock called Kos…"